CLIFTON FALLS

A ZOMBIE STORY · PART I

LEE ANDREW TAYLOR

CONTENTS

This novel is dedicated to my cousin, Jason Mckay.

16th July 1973 - 13th October 1984

A cool cousin.
Never forgotten.

Also, a huge dedication goes out to a good friend of mine who helped launch the original version of this novel. But sadly he passed away in 2015. Thank you, Ian Brown, for being a fan of this story.

WARNING

This novel contains strong language & gruesome violence.

ONE

Christmas should be a time of joy and shopping for that perfect turkey, but not this Christmas, not in this small town, and not this year.

Everything was running smoothly at the National Bank for *Vincent Smythe*, the manager, as he mingled with the customers on another festive eve day. He was a larger-than-life character, always chatty and polite, but at sixty-five was ready for retirement.

"Only six months to go," he would tell people.

But he'd been saying that for the past year. Now, customers just smiled and nodded at him.

He stood by the main door, peering outside to see *two*, unknown men wearing long, thick coats, hurriedly walking towards the bank, but his jovial attitude remained firm as he opened the door to let them in. He greeted them with a wave, but quickly lowered his hand after they ignored him to stand in the queue.

"Good morning, gentlemen," he asked. "How are you

today? Have you come to take money out because you've forgotten to buy presents?"

But the men just smiled at him and looked away.

Vincent felt nervous as he looked them up and down, noticing their clothing and footwear dirty. But the customers took no notice as they happily waited to be served.

Vincent assumed someone knew the men so nodded and walked away, but one of them briskly released a metal bar from beneath his coat and violently smacked him across the back of the head. He fell to his knees, cowering as the second stranger rushed to the main door, shouting words, not in English to leave the customers spooked. They backed against a wall as the man holding the metal bar crashed it against the face of a second victim; also yelling out foreign words as Vincent held his head to stem the blood flow. He wanted the cashiers to raise the alarm but they were as freaked out as everyone else, so couldn't do it, their terrified eyes seeing the metal bar point in their direction before crashing down on the unfortunate man again to bust his nose wide open. He shrunk to the floor next to Vincent, screaming in agony.

The crazy-eyed attacker grabbed Vincent by his hair, nastily hauling him off the floor to spit out more threatening words, but Vincent tried fighting back. He grabbed hold of the weapon and attempted to twist it out of the man's hand, but the man was too strong; gaining control in seconds to kick Vincent against a wall. He kept kicking until Vincent begged him to stop.

The second stranger stayed where he was, flicking his attention from the outside to the frightened customers as he sadistically grinned at Vincent's woeful pleas for mercy. He said something to the other robber whilst pointing at the door leading to the cashiers; nodding after seeing the man lift

Vincent again to push him towards it. But the loud thud of Vincent being slammed against it caused the cashiers to weep. They shuddered after the metal bar almost busted a hole through the door; crying louder after the man screamed at them. But neither opened it until Vincent told them to.

He was thrown to the floor beside them, his head still pouring out blood as the man pulled bin bags from his coat before dropping them next to a cashier.

"Do what...he wants," Vincent murmured, staggering to his feet. "Just do it."

The cashier nervously handed bags to other staff members before silently emptying her cash drawer, as the others did the same, fearing they too would taste cold metal.

The customers huddled in a corner like they were sheep being rounded up by a sheepdog. Neither were used to what was happening because the town was normally a ghost town for any serious crime, but a *woman* in her mid-fifties plucked up the courage to reach for her phone.

"Don't do it, Maggie," a close friend whispered, watching the man by the main door stare outside again. "These guys are dangerous."

"I'm not letting them win," Maggie replied. "Just hide me."

The other customers moved in front of her as she rushed fingers over the digits, but they gulped after the man stared at them.

"Maggie, stop, he's looking this way," her friend whispered.

"Just keep him busy..."

But the phone rang out loud.

"...Shit!" Maggie continued, sweating as she turned off the loudspeaker.

The man stormed in her direction, raging as she remained hidden. He shouted to scare the customers until seeing Maggie raise the phone to her ear; pushing her protectors to one side and grabbing her arm as a faint voice came out of the phone.

"Help!" Maggie bellowed as the man yanked her away from the others. "The bank is being robbed."

But the man snatched the phone and threw it across the room.

A few of the customers glared at him, feeling brave to close in, but he panicked; pulling a one-foot sword from beneath his coat to petrify them into submission. He shouted out more words but no one was retreating, their glares making him feel agitated as he whipped his vision from them to Maggie.

He became paranoid, imagining her trying to escape.

His face suddenly poured with sweat as the sword was plunged into her mouth; the force smashing teeth and the neck bone as it appeared out the other end.

Maggie fell motionless to the floor as blood formed a puddle around her head; her expression showing shock as the sword remained embedded. The man stared at her, knowing she was dead. He screamed as he pulled the weapon out, wiping the blood from it down his clothing before swinging it towards the customers; scaring them even more than before.

The other robber raced out of the cashier door holding *three* bags of cash, scowling at his partner as he ran for the main one. He shouted at him to hurry as a faint voice was heard coming out of the phone - "Are you still there?", the person said as the men fled the building.

They ran away from the bank and headed in the direction of the forest, but one of them pushed over a

4

homeless man who got in his way; leaving him sprawled out on the road as the robber followed his partner towards the end of the street. But they panicked as they scouted the area until hearing a car horn beep. They hurried towards it to see *Norman* sitting in the driver's seat, waving his fingers back and forth.

Norman was the brains behind the robbery; a scrawny man with a scar on his left cheek. He'd been hatching a plan with his girlfriend, *Cheyanne*, for a few months which involved using the foreigners to carry out the bank job. Norman was the local gravedigger and someone who dreamed of a better life, so he let his petite, dark-haired and tan-skinned girlfriend manipulate the men.

He heard the alarm from the bank echo in the distance so became nervous as the men entered the car; seeing them grin as they sat in the back.

"You two are nuts!" he yelled, eyeing up the money bags. "But it looks like you did well...Now put your heads down. I don't want the fuzz seeing you..."

But the robbers just smiled at him.

Norman shook his head, pointing to the floor until they understood before turning around to start the engine; pleased to not see their faces in the rear-view mirror. He inspected the area; keeping calm before driving off with a Cheshire-cat grin on his face.

"...Stay low. The police could be close by."

Norman took a detour away from the main road, heading into the forest and down a private dirt track; seeing the farming fields on one side and the forest on the other. He reached an iron gate to see a sign attached, with the words – **No Trespassing** – painted in red before turning off the engine to stare towards the trees; smiling after spotting another car.

He exited as Cheyanne rushed towards him, kissing him softly before glancing at the two men.

"Did we get enough?" she excitedly asked.

"Baby, unless those goons picked up monopoly money, I think we did..."

Norman picked her up and kissed her again.

"...Now do what we planned."

"You got it," Cheyanne said; saluting him as she opened a back door. "Wow! Three bags."

She grabbed them from the robbers; smiling to leave them excited before hauling the bags over her shoulder.

"Are you sure you weren't spotted?" she asked, calmly walking back to Norman.

"Nah...You know me, babe. I sneak in and I sneak out unnoticed."

Norman laughed as Cheyanne winked at him.

"You can sneak in and out of me later," she said, kissing him on the cheek.

Norman blushed as she walked away; opening the boot of her car to throw the bags inside.

"Oh, yeah," she said, looking over at the robbers again. "Did you finally come up with a name for them?"

Norman laughed again. "I sure did...I've named them *Chip* and *Dale*."

"You tell Chip and Dale I said well done." Cheyanne closed in on the driver's side door. "That's if you can speak their language now."

The sound of the robbers bouncing around inside the car received their attention, but it wasn't until one of them did crazy hand gestures indicating someone lunging a knife that Norman and Cheyanne became worried.

"What's going on?!" Cheyanne shouted. "What did they do?"

"I'm not sure," Norman replied; witnessing one of the robbers reeling around in the backseat after the other brought the imaginary knife down on him. "But that looks quite nasty."

Cheyanne's facial expression suddenly dropped.

"Norman...What the *fuck* did they do?!" she screamed.

"I don't know." Norman shrugged his shoulders. "But I'll find out."

He tried talking to the men but they just giggled cruelly; now happy with what happened to the woman inside the bank.

"I can feel this going wrong," Cheyanne nervously said, racing over to nudge Norman in the ribs. "If they've murdered someone, it will come back on us."

"Calm it, yeah," Norman replied; reaching out to hug her. "They may just be acting."

"Then why aren't they acting out the robbery?" Cheyanne pushed him away. "Why act like they've killed someone?... I don't want to go to prison..."

She walked hurriedly in a circle as Norman spat on the ground, both confused by the actions of the men.

"...This doesn't look good, Norman!" Cheyanne cried out; prodding a finger at thin air before rushing back to her car.

She re-entered; not looking at the others as she turned the key; almost crying before driving off as Norman sighed. He did the same, starting up his car to reverse away from the gate before turning it around; heading for the main road to the sound of more giggles.

"Just stay low!" he shouted, becoming more annoyed by the second. "If you get me caught..."

He took a deep breath and calmed down, thinking that maybe the police hadn't arrived at the bank yet. He'd studied the movements of the local constabulary so knew the alarm from the bank would probably take a while to be taken seriously. For a town with so little crime, an alarm going off would be diagnosed as a prank by some kids at first, but eventually, it would sink in. He also knew that the police would look for two, unknown characters, so, if he could drop them off at the destination then he could get back to Cheyanne without being suspected.

———

It took another thirty minutes before he entered the town again. He'd missed the traumatized customers shedding tears during the removal of Maggie's body but saw police cars parked outside the bank, so carefully drove past. But one car pulled out of a side street to scare him. Norman watched it closely follow behind him, trying not to panic as his heart skipped a beat. He slowed down to stop in the hope it would drive past, but it came to a standstill just in front of him leaving sweat dripping off his brow. He saw an officer exit and reach for a firearm. It scared him as he was hauled from his car and thrown onto the road; the gun pressing against the side of his temple until feeling the ice-cold metal against his skin.

"I'm not going to arrest you!" the angry officer screamed. "I'm just going to blow your *fuckin'* brains out"

He laughed.

Norman closed his eyes, waiting for the bullet to kill him. But nothing happened. He opened them again to see that the officer wasn't standing over him and wasn't trying to shoot him. It was just his imagination.

He saw the officer for real this time, exiting his vehicle to walk towards him, so nervously lowered his window.

"What's up, officer?" he said, wiping the sweat from his head.

The officer closed in; placing elbows onto the open window frame, causing Norman to almost wet himself.

"Alright, Norman. Did you know your backlight was broken?"

"No," Norman replied swiftly as the sweat decreased.

"Well, you need to get it fixed." The officer looked thoughtful for a few seconds before adding, "I should be giving you a ticket but I'm busy with a major incident...I don't need more paperwork to deal with so just take this as a reminder."

Norman never asked about the incident. He just wanted out of the situation. "Thanks. I'll get it done today."

The officer removed himself from the car, slowly returning to his own before picking up his radio to speak to someone on the other end; staring at Norman to scare him for real. But he looked away a few seconds later to re-enter his car. Norman watched him drive away, but his hands shook on the wheel to stall him from leaving the scene. He breathed deeply again until calming down before starting up the engine to head back home.

He met up again with Cheyanne minutes later, but she was still fuming about what the robbers had done.

"You said they were just going to scare a few people!" she hollered at him.

"Maybe they didn't understand what I said?" a baffled reply came.

"Maybe? ...Are you stupid? ...Of course, they didn't understand you, you *buffoon*. Sometimes I don't understand you."

Norman did nothing but think about the scenario on his drive home, knowing he needed to soothe Cheyanne's anger. He had a plan brewing inside his drug-fuelled brain, so hoped she would get on board when it was mentioned. But telling her about it wasn't going to be easy to achieve. He hated the way she scowled at him; it made him feel sad. He coughed as he tried to calm her down, but Cheyanne wasn't having it.

"Can you just shut the *fuck* up!" he hollered at her. "Jeez! Cheyanne, you are like the Duracell bunny. You just keep going on and on and on..."

Cheyanne was stunned.

She sat down and poured a glass of vodka before rushing it down her throat, seething at the thought of what Norman was about to say next.

"...I have a great idea," he said, winking. "You work at the morgue, right, so just check to see if a body was brought in."

"Then what?"

"Then you stash the cash inside the coffin."

"And how do you assume I do that?"

"I don't know, Cheyanne, I'm the stupid one, remember, but you'll find a way...I know you will."

Cheyanne thought hard for a moment. "Maybe I could do it when I put the makeup on the body? ...That's if there is one."

"Just don't stash the cash inside if it's going to be cremated."

"Ha, ha, ha, very funny," Cheyanne said, looking at her watch. "Shit. I'd best get to work...I'll phone you later, once I know more."

Norman placed a comforting kiss on her lips before watching her grab her work stuff; breathing easier as she left the house.

————

Cheyanne scurried around at the hospital, trying not to seem too keen on whether or not there was a body recovered from the bank. But she was pleased there was.

"Okay, we have a corpse," she said, sneaking a phone call to Norman from the morgue room.

"Good...We'll wait for the right time...The police will be too busy searching for those clowns to even think about checking a coffin for the cash."

TWO

Three months had drifted by since the brutal bank robbery, but for the people inside the bank, the fire of torturous horror was still there, eating at their nightmares.

Vincent Smythe had spent *two* weeks in hospital; collapsing at home within forty-eight hours after the incident from a blood clot on the brain, or so he'd told people, but his absence from work had been very much noticed. The staff had made a plaque for him; putting it up so every customer would remember his bravery, but, even though Vincent had returned to work, he was still getting headaches when standing near the spot where he thought he would die.

The last three months had also been tough for the Clifton Falls police department, especially for the chief of police, *Mike O'Sullivan*. He was being harassed by the media for not arresting anyone, leaving him stressed to the point of quitting. He stared at the witness statements lying scattered on his desk, sighing because none were useful to him after no one recognised the robbers. He listened to the people outside holler for him to retire, cursing under his breath as he swiped a hand to knock the statements onto the floor. He sighed again, taking a deep breath to hear footsteps closing in; waiting for the knock to arrive on his office door.

"Come in," he said, bending down to pick up the statements.

He looked up to see *Susan Chester*, a slim, brunette officer who worked mostly at the front desk, shaking her head at him.

"He won't give up, chief. He just keeps calling, wanting you to quit."

"Mrs Maudlin's son?"

"Yes, chief. He wants to know why you haven't found her killers yet."

Mike grunted. "Is he on the phone now?"

"He sure is...I don't think he's going to quit calling until you speak to him."

"Oh, fuck..."

9:00 AM SATURDAY - *FIVE DAYS LATER...*

Blake Taylor sat with *three* friends inside *Chino's* restaurant; an old hangout situated in *Westbrook County*. It was a few miles south of the Yorkshire countryside and ten miles from Clifton Falls.

He was nervous, scratched and bruised after escaping a slaughter-filled situation; one where he had to kill or be killed; battling against a zombie outbreak that rocked Clifton Falls to its knees.

He stared at his friends, choking from thoughts of what'd

happened; quivering after remembering how close to death he was. He had smashed his way through one of the living-dead reincarnates whilst protecting an injured person, kicking out to almost feel its teeth; knowing he could easily have been its next victim. He looked down at his palms to see blood, but his friends saw nothing.

They turned to see a newsflash appear on a television situated high up in the corner of the room before noticing Blake's eyes flicker; watching him shrink into his seat after seeing the aftermath of last night. A *reporter* was at the site, appearing frantic after seeing worn-out survivors carry a mutilated corpse towards an ambulance before coughing up spit as they placed it inside. Blake's friends knew something major had happened so waited for him to explain, but Blake was still shell-shocked and wasn't saying anything.

"Let's hear what the reporter has to say," *Dave* said, concentrating on the screen. "Hopefully, we'll be able to understand what Blake went through."

"Can you turn it up a bit?" *Tony* asked a waitress, happy to see her do it. "Thanks."

They saw the reporter point at bodies on the ground to leave them wishing it was over before seeing him reach out to grab a microphone from the person behind the camera.

"There's been a terrible catastrophe here, ending with too many fatalities to even count...The police had been in a battle with an unknown terror, an enemy consisting of the walking dead...A sadistic murdering spree that's left behind torn body parts from victims, that eye-witnesses say, was brutally bitten by vicious, man-eating maniacs who were supposed to be resting in their new homes inside the cemetery."

Dave approached Blake with tears in his eyes, but Blake was too lost inside his mind to notice.

"Blake. Look at me...What do you see?"

"Death everywhere...That's what I see and it won't go away."

Dave knew Blake had been at the centre of what had happened on the news report because he'd told him brief accounts after turning up on his doorstep last night, but Blake had left out the uncut version.

"If you want to talk about it, then we're here to listen."

"I don't think you can stomach what I've seen," Blake cried out, turning away from staring at the screen to glare at Dave. "Or can you?"

"Hey!" Tony said; interrupting the conversation before Blake lost control. "Let's get outta' here...You don't need to see a reminder."

Blake shook himself; agreeing with him before rising from his seat, breathing deeply as he left the table.

"Come back to mine," Dave said, following him. "Away from all this."

"Yeah," *Gary* popped up to say. "You may relax and tell us more."

He rose from his seat to join the others, leaving Tony last to move away from the table; all smothering Blake as they escorted him outside.

———

Blake struggled to fight the demons plaguing his mind during the journey to Dave's house, as the others watched him perform a wrestling match between telling them and not saying anything. Tony sat beside him, smiling as Blake lowered his head.

"It's all down to you. You can tell us all or nothing at all."

"Thanks," Blake replied, lifting his head again.

———

They entered Dave's house to find the atmosphere dropping, the moment becoming more awkward as they reached the living room. Dave, Tony and Gary sat on a three-piece suite, eyeing Blake as if unsure of how to treat him, not knowing if they were ready for what was to unfold before their eyes. They followed his movements, catching him close to crying, waiting for him to speak and hoping it would be soon.

Blake turned to them, wiping a hand across his face.

"Do you still want me to tell you how it all began or shall I not bother now?" he asked sharply.

Gary rose from his seat, placing a hand on Blake's shoulder. "It's your decision," he said, walking towards the kitchen. "I'll put the kettle on."

But Blake cringed as he stared at bruises on his arms; touching one to shudder as a memory of when he got it almost brought him to his knees.

"If I don't get this *fuckin'* nightmare off my chest soon then I'm going to explode!" he hollered. "It's eatin' me up inside."

"Okay, mate, cool it, yeah," Dave said, rushing over to hug him. "If you're ready to talk, then we're ready to listen."

Blake mellowed, but he felt embarrassed as Dave let go.

He knew Blake was still nothing like his usual self, but his appearance was a massive improvement from how he'd looked last night, and first thing this morning. Dave had let into his house a clone-like figure of his friend. Blake's hair colour had changed from golden-red waves to grey as a frightened casing wrapped around his body. Now Dave needed to crack it open before the real Blake could return.

He escorted Blake into a chair before sitting back down, but the only noise heard came from the kettle as they waited for Gary to return.

He arrived a few minutes later, placing a tray with hot drinks onto a small table located between Blake and the others. Everyone grabbed a cup, eager for Blake to begin.

He slowly took a sip from the hot, sweet coffee, glancing at each of his friends in a desperate attempt to produce a smile. But it wasn't to be. He just felt exhausted, fragile, and on edge, but knew he had to focus on the long conversation ahead. He was now ready to relate his awful journey to his friends.

"Let's go back to the beginning."

THREE

MONDAY... *AGAIN*

Blake arrived at an agricultural factory to start his shift. He was the *boss*; a happy man who treated his staff like equals. Everyone enjoyed going to work when he was there, but times were hard now, crops were slow to develop, and maintaining a profitable business was at its lowest. He'd been upset recently after laying off staff, but they understood. They knew it wasn't his fault.

His company had been the main crop supplier for nearby towns, and not so long ago was one of the leading suppliers for companies abroad, but that was until a new insect arrived on the scene. The *toxic beetle*; a deadly plant-eating bug was about to come out of hiding. They had originated from countries with a warmer climate, like Australia and New Zealand, but somehow had sneaked into the UK via a delivery a few years ago. It was a mystery to Blake as to why the climate hadn't killed them off, but the climate in Britain was changing. So, all in all, he wasn't too surprised.

The bugs resurfaced every spring, unleashing devastating diseases onto the crops by eating them and the soil.

And they also attack humans.

Once bitten, a toxic residue called *Cantharidin* is injected, causing a nasty, blistering rash on the unfortunate victim.

Blake entered his office to find a letter on his desk, picking it up to read the words – Head Office - before opening it. He smiled after reading the contents. The chemical-testing company, (Crop-techno Ltd), was about to launch its latest invention of pesticide/fertiliser, and his company was chosen to try it out.

He took the letter and left his office, walking towards the main part of the factory, but news about the fertiliser had spread quickly, so, by the time he'd entered the room, people were already engaged in conversation about it.

"Alright, everyone. Can I have your attention, please?" he said, waving the letter above his head. "I see some of you have already heard the good news about the new chemical fertiliser." He placed the letter in front of him to read out loud. "It's been tested and it works...Not only does it increase the size of the crops but it also eliminates those pesky bugs." He watched everyone gather around him, all silent as they listened. "We're about to put this chemical to use on our fields...It'll be arriving in the morning, so everyone involved with spraying the crops needs to be here bright and early...We must get this done as soon as possible to kill those beetles before they stop us from earning money again this summer." He waited for someone to say something but everyone remained intrigued. "That's all I want to say on the subject at this time, so, if you don't mind, can you please do some work today or I'll be sacking a few more of you by the end of shift."

He winced after seeing a few of the staff panic before

chuckling to relieve their tension; knowing now that his words weren't that funny. Blake usually had a way of making them laugh to brighten up their day, but choosing the 'sack' speech wasn't one of his greatest ideas.

"Okay, that was below the belt," he apologetically said, stuffing the letter into his pocket. "No one's being sacked."

"But what if the fertiliser doesn't work?" a nervous employee shouted out. "You can't guarantee that no one will be sacked then."

Blake puffed out his cheeks as his energy drained from the words echoing around the room. He knew he had to reignite the spark inside the worker.

"It will work," he said, closing in to tap the employee on the arm. "We just need a little faith."

Blake left the worker pondering over what he just said before smiling and leaving the room.

———

He stood by his office window, staring out into the yard as workers left the building; knowing it was now *5:00 pm*. Clocking-off time. He giggled at how quickly they moved when it came to going home, thinking swiftly at how much work could be done if they used this pace in working hours, giggling again as he walked back to his desk to give it a tidy before doing the same and heading home.

———

He opened the front door of his house, smiling wide after listening to movement nearby before shutting the door to walk along the hallway, hearing it again as he closed in on the living room. He smiled wider the nearer he got.

"Honey, I'm back. What's for dinner? I'm starving," he said, opening the door.

He entered to see the curtains were drawn to leave the room in patches of shady darkness, with the only light coming from a small lamp on a table in the far corner. He rubbed his eyes, feeling amazed as a *woman* with long brown hair and soft, silky skin, entered from the shadows, wearing nothing but a see-through negligee. To Blake, she was a magnificently sculptured masterpiece, an angel sent down from heaven.

"You can have me for dinner if you want to, tiger?"

"Tiger" is the nickname Blake's wife, *Karen,* said to him when feeling very sexy.

Blake's jaw dropped as his tongue hung from his mouth.

He trembled with excitement as Karen loosened the negligee; his stare remaining strong as she pulled it down past her breasts.

"If I have you for dinner then what do I get for pudding?"

"You'll not need a pudding after what I've got planned for you," Karen said, close to laughing. "And anyway, you'll be too tired to eat it."

Blake watched her close in, feeling her hard nipples touch his shirt as he leaned over to kiss her. But he suddenly backed away and burst out laughing.

"Sorry, babe," he said, trying to control himself. "You are hilarious."

"Blake!" Karen snapped at him. "I'm trying to be romantic, but you've just ruined the moment for me."

"Believe me, you look incredible." Blake reached out to

hold her, kissing her gently on the lips. "I promise not to laugh again."

Karen smiled and grabbed his arm.

"Good...Now, do you want to fuck me or not?"

Blake nodded.

———

Karen led him to the bedroom.

She pushed him onto the bed and straddled him whilst placing an index finger onto his lips, locking her eyes onto his to leave him paralysed with lust before pressing her vagina hard against his penis, gyrating at speed until feeling his manhood rise.

Blake was curious by her fast approach to them having sex but wasn't going to complain.

"Have you been drinking, girl?" he asked, cheekily grinning.

Karen licked her wet, pulsating lips. She was intoxicated with something but it wasn't alcohol. She had a thirst for some passion and tonight she would get it.

"Do I need to be drunk to want to spend the night with you?" she asked; her eyes glowing bright blue.

She pinned Blake's arms over his head with one hand, slowly kissing his neck before using her other one to stroke the right side of his cheek. She gradually moved it down to rest on the collar of his shirt, but, in the blink of an eye, the buttons were torn off.

"Wooah!! This is new," Blake said smiling.

"Just shush."

Karen slipped off his shirt and threw it onto the floor, revealing his clean-shaven chest before grinning naughtily and kissing him again. Their eyes remained shut as their mouths opened and closed in rhythm to the beat of their hearts, the exciting sensation overcoming them until Karen sucked hard on Blake's top lip.

"Ouch! Be careful, baby...I know you're hungry, but I'm sure you can find something more enticing to suck on besides my lip."

"Really? ...Are you saying your little friend wants to play?"

"My so-called little friend, as you imaginatively put it, isn't so little anymore."

Blake pulled a silly face to leave Karen close to laughing, but she smothered his mouth with a hand until he stopped.

"Okay...I think it's time to let him out, don't you?"

"Anything you say." Blake winked. "You're in control, not me...But please be gentle."

"Ooh, don't you worry, I will."

Karen pushed him further onto the bed until his feet dangled over the side; kissing his chest whilst stroking a finger down his stomach to make him wriggle with pleasure.

"Now, where were we?" she asked, teasing him with glowing eyes.

This woman is like an erotic, filthy-minded nympho tonight and it's not even my birthday, Blake thought, trying hard to concentrate.

"I think you were about to play a musical instrument." He sniggered again.

But Karen stared at him, twitching her nose. "What do you mean, an instrument?"

"I thought you wanted to play the organ?"

They choked, laughing at the joke as Karen got off to lie next to him.

"I love you," she whispered into his ear before planting another soft kiss on his lips.

"I love you back."

TUESDAY

The sun's rays lit up the kitchen as Blake sipped his morning cup of tea. He smiled as thoughts from last night's lovemaking entered his mind before grabbing a mirror to check his body for love bites; cringing after seeing one on his lower neck.

Damn! She almost ate me last night.

He placed the mirror on a table before pulling up his shirt collar to cover the bite; grabbing his work tie off a chair to chuckle as he put it on.

He sure had a spring in his step today.

He felt positive about the chemical fertiliser as he drank the rest of his cup of tea, the thought of it doing its job exciting him to want to get to work.

He smiled again as he crept up the stairs; making sure to avoid the creaking ones in case Karen woke up before entering the bedroom to reach for his shoes off the floor. He put them on while watching her sleep before leaning over the bed to kiss her on the forehead, whispering - 'I love you,' as he exited the room. He sneaked back downstairs again and re-entered the kitchen; grabbing his lunchbox and breathing deeply before leaving the house.

Blake never drove to work unless it was necessary. Like, if he needed his car to drive somewhere else during the day or if the weather was bad. But today the sun didn't look like it was going to fade.

He stared up at it, squinting before removing a pair of

sunglasses from his shirt pocket; putting them on to walk towards his front gate. And, with his lunchbox tucked under his arm began the two-mile walk to the factory. He believed the exercise made him feel great, but today felt he could walk a thousand miles and still feel great.

————

He closed in on a large sign standing by the side of a country road, looking up at it to see the words – Clifton Falls Agriculture Farming Company – with an arrow pointing in the direction of where he was about to walk. He smiled and casually carried on, closing in to see around *ten* staff members waiting to be let inside the factory gates; smiling again after seeing how excited they were.

"Bloody hell! You lot are eager to get some work done."

Todd Kumar, a tall, stocky, West Indian male, turned away from another worker to close in on Blake.

"You told us to be here early. So here we are," he said in a deep husky voice.

"Did I give you a time?"

"No," Todd replied quickly.

"So, what time did you arrive this morning?"

"Four o'clock."

"You're joking...We never come into work that early," Blake said, feeling sad that his staff had been waiting hours. "When I said come in early, I meant about seven."

He felt like apologising but Todd suddenly laughed, followed by outrageous roars from the other nine people.

"Yeah, I'm joking," Todd said, still giggling. "We've only been here for ten minutes..."

The others pointed fingers at Blake to show they had

pranked him, leaving him biting his tongue as he reached for the padlock key.

"...It's about time we got one over on you."

"Todd, yes, you got me," Blake said, tapping him on the arm. "I just hope your victory will inspire you all to get the job done today?"

"Yes, boss," Todd replied. "We're looking forward to seeing what the fertiliser can do."

Blake nodded as he inserted the key. "Right, in we go."

He unlocked the main gate and watched the others walk towards the factory; catching them up to let them in to see them position into groups like they knew what was expected. Blake didn't need to interfere with their daily routines. That task was down to Todd. So, he waved and aimed for his office.

———

Thirty minutes went by before the faint sound of a delivery truck was heard in the distance, gradually increasing until the big machine arrived at the factory gates. Blake saw it from his office window.

"We should be receiving fifty fertiliser sacks," he shouted towards his staff, leaning out of the window. "So you're gonna need at least two wooden pallets."

He shut the window and returned to his desk, reaching for the phone with a huge grin. He dialled a number and sat down, hearing a faint murmur arrive from the other end, the person sounding like they'd just woken up as the word - 'Hello,' was slurred.

"Hey, baby, did I wake you?" Blake asked, close to laughing. "It's gone half seven. You should be up by now."

"Why didn't the alarm clock go off?" Karen asked, sighing sleepily. "Did you forget to reset it again?"

"Yes, I did. That's why I'm calling, to remind you to get up."

"Jeez! Blake! One of these days you'll forget and make me late for work."

"Baby, that will never happen."

"Good...And anyway, how come you sound like you're in a good mood this morning? Did you have a good night?"

"Nope..."

Blake tried his best to worry Karen into thinking he was disappointed by her seduction techniques, but he couldn't keep up the pretence.

"...It was a great night...I didn't know you could do those things with your tongue...Have you been watching porn again?"

"Blake!" Karen shouted, becoming alert. "You know I don't watch that type of stuff."

"I know...I'm kiddin'."

"I should ask you the same thing, considering what your tongue did...I'm surprised you're able to speak today after the exercise it got."

Blake almost choked after hearing the delivery truck come to a standstill in the yard, followed by his workers talking amongst themselves.

"Sorry, love. I've got to go," he quickly said, rising from his seat. "We'll finish this conversation later."

"Blake, not again...You always do this. Talk rudely on the phone to make me hot-and-bothered then hang up."

"Sorry, babe. The delivery has just arrived...Love you. Bye."

"Okay. I'll see you tonight...Love you back."

Blake left the building.

He walked towards the truck; seeing the *driver* standing next to it smoking a cigarette as the staff unloaded the fertiliser.

"Alright, pal," he said, closing in on the man. "Do you know if this stuff's as good as they say it is?"

The scruffy, stubble-faced driver flipped the cigarette from side to side between his lips, staring at Blake before removing it to spit on the ground.

"Yeah, man...I've heard it does what it says on the packet... They've been testing it for months inside some giant greenhouse in the city, but I don't know where...I think you're the first ones to try it out." The driver grinned like an evil henchman before spitting on the ground again. "You're gonna be a fuckin' guinea pig."

"Wow! I feel highly honoured." Blake laughed.

"Too right you are, pal."

Blake turned to see Todd double-checking the number of sacks on the pallets; his smile indicating that the full fifty had been unloaded as he signed the delivery note. He walked past Blake, peeling off a copy to hand back to the driver before seeing him grunt and nod as he returned to the lorry. He slammed the door shut as he sat down.

"I'm off!" he shouted; placing a hand through the open window to produce a thumbs-up sign. "I've got deliveries to finish."

He started the engine and slowly departed out of the yard.

"He was a bit of a *dick*," Todd said, sighing.

"He sure was," Blake replied, looking at the fertiliser.

"Okay, Mr foreman, time for you to organise the workers...I want this stuff on the fields before the end of today."

"You want all fifty spread out?"

"Nah...Start small...I need to see if it works before using all of them."

"Okay...We'll use around twenty or so, get the large field sorted."

Blake smiled as bodies flowed towards the palettes; some to remove bags for the field while others to take the rest to the storage barn.

Now the work would begin to destroy the insects.

FOUR

Karen had been employed at the National Bank for the past *two* years and was one of the cashiers who'd witnessed the awful murder on Christmas Eve when the violent robbery took place. Her nightmares about that day hadn't eased since. Many a night she would wake dripping in sweat; her nose tingling after smelling the unwashed odour the robber with the bags gave off. She had seen the workplace return to as normal as could be but her mind still spurted out memories. Even though the bank had put up new security cameras and sensors, it still wasn't enough to stop her from worrying about her safety. She feared it could happen again.

Karen also had a work-related problem to deal with and it came in the shape of her boss. Vincent's manner had changed dramatically since the robbery. He'd flipped from being a pleasant man to an obnoxious sex pest in the past month but, if anyone complained, he would blame it on the knock on the head. Karen hated the way he used sexual gestures towards her, especially when attempting to persuade her to go out for a drink, but the threat of telling Blake always made him back down.

She looked up from her cashier's desk to see him walk by; fearing he wanted to say something. But he turned and walked away without saying a word. His silence freaked her out.

She returned to doing what she was doing but the sound of his footsteps closing in again annoyed her to stop, causing her to shiver.

"Karen! May I see you in my office for a minute," he creepily asked, as other staff members cringed. "I've got important information to discuss with you."

"Okay. I'll be right there," she nervously replied, slowly exiting her seat.

She smiled at the staff members before walking past to follow Vincent towards his office; mumbling the words – 'Grunting old fool' – as she neared. She was happy he never heard.

"Please, sit down," he said, pulling back a chair. "There's something I need to ask you?"

Karen's heart beat faster as the words floated in the air.

She scanned the room, feeling trapped being alone with him, his gentle, polite approach causing her to worry.

If he's about to say something resembling a sexual act then I will tell Blake this time.

Vincent smiled at her as she sat down.

"I've just heard there's a new type of fertiliser being delivered to your husband's works today..."

Karen squinted at him as he walked towards his desk, feeling stunned that he chose to mention what was going on with Blake rather than throw rude gestures at her. She disliked Vincent for talking about rude things to offer her but for him to change the subject in favour of discussing fertiliser had now lowered her self-esteem.

Maybe he's thinking of harassing another female colleague instead of me? she disgustingly thought, watching him sit down. *I suppose I should be grateful.*

"...Do tell," he said, grinning like someone who'd just won some money.

"Yes, I know of it...He received the delivery this morning," Karen replied, leaning forward in her seat. "Why are you so interested in the stuff?"

"I'm interested because I want to grow vegetables in my garden. However, I can't until those pesky plant bugs are eliminated...They keep spoiling my chances of achieving it." Vincent frowned before adding, "I've heard the fertiliser kills them."

"Does it?... I have no idea what it does. I'm only the wife."

Vincent giggled.

"Would it be possible to have a word with Blake, see if he can be so kind as to spare me a bag? I'll pay whatever it cost...Could you do this for me please, my dear, and tell me what the outcome is? ...Thank you, that'll be all. You can go now."

Karen was left flabbergasted for not being able to get a word in; feeling annoyed with herself for allowing him to answer for her.

She exited her seat and walked towards the door.

"I'll ask him, but I don't know if he'll have any spare to sell you," she said, opening it. "I'll let you know."

Inwardly she was fuming - *Who does he think he is? Demanding I ask my husband to save him a bag of fertiliser...The man's got a cheek.*

"And don't forget to mention the bit about me paying...

I'm sure you could do with some extra pennies," Vincent shouted out as Karen left the room.

What's he going on about this time? Extra pennies?

Karen still couldn't believe that he'd not tried to be obscene in a sexual nature, but he did make up for it by making her feel small.

She walked towards the cashier tills to see no customers inside the bank before doing a U-turn and aiming for another room; glancing through a small window in the door to find it empty. She opened it and entered, reached for her phone and called a number.

"Hey, sex machine. Have you missed me?" she said, as the phone was answered on the other end.

"This is a surprise at ten o'clock in the morning. Anything wrong, love?"

"No, no. Everything's okay...Did you get the delivery sorted?"

"Brilliant. Exactly the fifty sacks they said we were going to get...Now we've some spare for later on in the season."

Karen paused, wondering whether to tell Blake that Vincent was an utter twat.

She listened to him talk some more about feeling excited to have the fertiliser until his tone made her grin. But his happiness was making it harder for her to mention what Vincent asked her to do.

"So, you have some left then," she rushed out.

"Yes...Why?" Blake seemed confused. "This isn't like you, Karen, wanting to talk about a grubby bit of compost instead of mentioning how shiny your new fingernails are." Blake laughed. "What's going on? Do you want some?"

"Very funny..." Karen smirked. "I was just wondering if you could spare a bag for Vincent. That's all...He wants to try the stuff in his garden...I think he wants to grow the world's largest marrow."

Blake sighed.

He was normally a stickler for abiding by the rules but Karen's words got him thinking.

"Is he gonna pay for it?"

"Oh yeah! He said he'd pay whatever it cost to get his hands on the stuff, and I mean, whatever it cost...He's that desperate for it."

"Okay...Tell him to get in touch. I'll see if I can come to some kind of arrangement."

"Will do... I'll speak to you later." Karen paused. "Oh, what do you want for dinner tonight? ...We could eat out?"

"Yeah, eating out sounds like a good idea." Blake smiled. "We can celebrate in advance the success of the fertiliser."

"Sounds good to me."

Karen switched off her phone, smiling as she left the room. She walked back to Vincent's office, accidentally disturbing him as he talked to someone on a video call; seeing him smirk as she mimed – 'Blake said to call him.' – But, as she turned around again to leave, heard Vincent roar with laughter as he returned to his call.

————

Twenty minutes passed before Vincent ended the call, but he suddenly became nervous as he searched for Blake's number. His hand shook with excitement as thoughts of holding a bag of the new wonder growth pumped up his adrenaline; feeling the hairs on his arms rising as the number was found.

He dialled it and grinned, already guessing Blake would

say '*yes*, as his heart slapped against his chest faster than the sound of the ringtone.

"Hello, B-b-blake," he stuttered, as the phone was answered. "It's Vincent Smythe here...Your wife's boss."

"Yeah," Blake replied. "She mentioned you wanted to speak to me."

"Yes, indeed I do." Vincent's eyes lit up like a child's on Christmas morning. "She has informed me that you may be able to offload one of your new fertiliser bags...Is that correct?"

"Yes. Something like that." Blake walked over to the window to see the yard empty of sacks, smiling because everything was running smoothly. "I may have a spare bag, but It'll cost you."

"I did tell her I would gladly pay...How much?"

"A hundred should do it plus letting her leave early this afternoon...If you can manage that then the bag is yours."

"You don't want much," Vincent said sarcastically; sitting back in his seat to scratch his chin. "Okay. It's a deal...Are you able to deliver the product to me?"

"If you want it then you'll have to pick it up...Make it around twelve."

"Sure thing. I can do that...I'll see you then."

———

Blake wiped the sweat from his brow as the morning's sunshine warmed up his office, but gave in to turn on a small *fan* resting on a table nearby. He sat back, letting it flip his hair from side to side as he sipped his coffee; reaching out to click his computer mouse to save the morning's paperwork to a file before rising from his chair. He gazed out of the window again to see Todd in the yard giving out orders, so waved at him and smiled before moving away to finish off his drink. He placed his face in front of the fan again until the wind sparked him into life before taking a deep breath and casually strolling towards the door. He exited the room, walking past staff until reaching the main entrance; stepping outside to feel the sun on his face before shouting out to Todd.

"Hey, boss, is everything okay?"

"Yep. All's good," Blake replied, looking out towards the fields. "How's it comin' along? ...Do you think we'll have it completed by the end of today?"

Todd nodded. "Don't panic, boss. Have I ever let you down?"

"Good point." Blake laughed. "If this stuff is as good as they say it is then we're going to have a fruitful rest of the year."

The thought of the company achieving something huge again brought with it a large smile as Blake reminisced on the farm's previous success. The company meant a lot to him so he needed the fertiliser to work. Maybe then the rumours of a possible closure would stop.

"This stuff they put in the fertiliser," Todd said, reaching for a wheelbarrow. "Do you know what it is?"

"Nah...I don't care what's in it as long as it does what it's supposed to."

"Yeah, you're right." Todd lifted the handles on the barrow, slowly walking it away from Blake. "We should get it done by four o'clock."

"Good...But I won't be here then."

"Why's that?" Todd asked, stopping in his tracks.

"I'm taking Karen out for a meal. She's got the afternoon off."

Todd nodded.

"It's not like you to want time off, especially with what's going on today...Are you celebrating something?"

"Yeah. We're celebrating a better future...Plus, she also needs pampering sometimes."

"Cool...Cool...I take it you want me to lock up?"

"Yep...Use the spare set of keys. I'll leave 'em on my desk."

Todd grinned, lifting the handles again. "No worries." He then headed off towards the fields.

———

Blake sat at his desk twiddling his thumbs as the time reached 11:30 am. He hated being stuck for something to do but knew his office was the right place to be in just in case Vincent popped by to close the deal.

He glanced at the clock at least a dozen times before the handles faced upwards; the sight welcoming as his phone rang. He picked it up; becoming edgy after being told that an elderly gentleman from the bank was waiting to see him; his hands sweating as a feeling of guilt burned his insides.

Blake didn't want anybody finding out what he was up to as the fertiliser wasn't his to sell.

He quickly replaced the phone and raced for the door, attempting to reach Vincent before he gave the game away. But, by the time he'd entered the main part of the building, Vincent was laughing with a female receptionist. His voice was loud and deep. It sent shivers down Blake's spine.

He closed in to pull Vincent away, but the banker pulled back, becoming unimpressed by Blake's attempt to get him on his own.

"Hey, what's the problem?" Vincent rushed from his

mouth. "Can't you see, I'm having a lovely chat with this lady?" He turned to the woman and pointed at her. "...I don't think you discussed your name."

"Vera," she replied smiling.

"Thank you, Vera. It was delightful chatting with you but I must be off, I have some business to attend to."

He followed Blake to a quiet corner, *frowning* as he waited for him to speak, but Blake was still anxious as he wiped sweaty hands down his trousers.

"Did you tell her why you're here?"

"What do you take me for? ...I know you shouldn't be selling the fertiliser to me," Vincent replied, gripping Blake's shoulder. "Don't worry, I'm not going to get you into trouble." He scrunched up his nose and grinned. "You did say seventy-five pounds, didn't you?"

Blake bit his lip. He knew Vincent had him over a barrel and there was nothing he could do about it, so, just nodded quickly in case Vincent decided to lower the amount.

"Okay. You win. But my wife still gets out early...Is that a deal?"

"Deal... I'll let her go at three...I'll get cover for her." Vincent became impatient like he needed to see the fertiliser now. "Well, my friend, it's good doing business with you but where is it?"

"Keep your voice down," Blake snapped at him. "Where's your car parked?"

"It's just outside."

"Good. It's close...Drive up to the main gates and wait for me. I'll fetch you your bag."

They separated, leaving the building, as Blake aimed for the gates whilst Vincent sat rubbing his hands together in his car. He eagerly watched Blake open the storage barn as a vision formed inside his mind of what to grow once the fertiliser did its thing, but Blake suddenly stalled to worry him. He noticed Blake was checking for people, making sure the coast was clear before disappearing out of sight, and, as he did it, Vincent grinned. But the grin became broader after seeing Blake return carrying a sack over his shoulder. He flipped his fingers back and forth until Vincent stuck up a thumb.

He reversed the car slowly to park it next to Blake before unlocking the boot to see him open it, hearing the sack crash down to bring joy to his heart. He waited for Blake to close the boot, knowing he was fidgeting like he expected someone to catch him. But, he finally shut it down to appear at the driver's side window.

"Done...Now pay and go," Blake huffed. "I don't want you talking about this."

Vincent smiled again and turned the key.

"Of course, I won't." He held out the money and Blake snatched it quickly. "You have my word. Karen will leave early today..."

Blake nodded.

"...I'd best be off. I've got some gardening to attend to."

Blake raised a hand as Vincent drove away.

FIVE

Vincent parked outside his house, reaching for his phone as chills of enthusiasm about getting the compost onto his garden still poured through him. He dialled the bank, smiling when the phone was answered; knowing the voice was of the person he wanted to speak to.

"This is your dirty little secret coming back to haunt you."

Karen held the phone away from her after thinking that the call was from a perverted prankster until it suddenly dawned on her that she recognised who it was. She cringed as the phone returned to her ear, feeling unsure about how to respond.

"Excuse me. Who's this?" she asked, pretending it was a customer.

"It's me, Vincent. Who'd you think it was?"

"I thought it was you, but you don't usually phone from outside the bank."

"I know, but this is important...I won't be back in today."

"Why?" Karen asked as confusion struck her. "Are you okay? ...Your head's not hurting again, is it?"

"No, no, nothing like that...Just hold the fort for me until three o'clock."

"Why? What's happening at three?"

"You're going home." Vincent laughed. "My orders...You just need to bring in some cover...You've got two and a half hours."

"Okay. Whatever you say...See you tomorrow then."

"Oh! One more thing before I attend to my garden...If anybody asks to speak to me and it sounds urgent just pass on my mobile number, but don't mention why I'm not there... Be a good girl and you'll be rewarded...Bye."

Karen cringed again after the phone went silent as thoughts of what kind of reward Vincent was thinking of made her feel nauseous.

————

Vincent pulled the compost bag from the boot of his car, puffing and panting as it was placed on the ground. He knew he was out of shape but was determined to get it to his back garden. He took a deep breath before picking up the bag and carrying it; his legs shaking, leaving him staggering as he reached the back gate. He put the bag down, opened the gate and entered his house via the kitchen door, listening out for his *wife* and smiling because she wasn't home. He knew she would've given him a lecture if she'd seen him struggling with the bag.

He walked upstairs to change; finding his gardening dungarees at the bottom of a drawer before throwing them onto the bed. He couldn't remember the last time he'd worn them so hoped they still fit. He stripped off his suit and got into the dungarees; eyeing up a straw hat resting on the top of a wardrobe before reaching for it to place on his head. He then opened the wardrobe and grabbed his gardening boots.

He was ready to tackle the dreaded back garden that he'd not set foot on in the past six months.

Vincent exited the house, reaching for the bag by the gate before dragging it towards the edge of the garden, but stalled after looking at it. He thought back to a year ago when his mother attended it before sighing because the flowers she planted were no longer there; close to shedding a tear after viewing the spot where she collapsed.

Six months later she was dead.

His mother was a keen gardener. She was the one who'd taken great care in keeping it perfect because he'd always make an excuse not to help. It hurt him deeply when he thought about it, knowing he could have aided her more before her stroke last September. So, today he would revitalise the garden in honour of her.

He turned to stare at the house that originally belonged to his mother before awkwardly glancing at the top end of the garden; seeing beyond the overgrown weeds to visualise her grave. That was where she was buried. At the top of the garden. It was written in her *Will* to be laid to rest on the property she was born in, but Vincent didn't welcome the decision with open arms. It had taken him a few months to get his head around it, and now, another few months later was one step closer to touching her headstone again.

Vincent felt his mother was watching him from her new home; her vision digging into him with every step he took to make him feel anxious to want to retreat to the house. But he stayed strong and walked over to the shed.

———

He looked at his watch to find an hour had passed; sighing because only a quarter of the garden was weeded. He shook his head, wiping a handkerchief across his brow; examining a large refuse sack to see it full of weeds, thistles, and litter that had blown onto the garden. But the back gate opening spooked him. He turned to see his wife carrying shopping into the kitchen, smiling at him through the window before heading back outside.

"What are you doing?" *Mary* asked, reaching the garden. "I never thought I'd see the day when you would come out here again."

Vincent wiped more sweat from his brow as he smiled at his wife of thirty years. Mary had retired a few years ago, so never did much apart from housework, cooking, and the weekly or daily shop. She was Vincent's rock and sidekick; always there when he needed her. But she never knew he had changed since the robbery.

"Hello, dear," Vincent said, dropping a rake. "Yeah, I know...I never thought I'd see the day either, but today I decided to attend to it." He folded the handkerchief and wiped his brow again, feeling tired as he puffed out his cheeks. "I know I've been stupid about my mother's grave being on here, but I'm okay now. She wouldn't want me leaving it a mess, so I'm not going to."

"I see you've made a start. I'm glad for you...But don't overdo it."

"Yes, dear. You have my word."

"Good." Mary grinned. "Well, I'd better leave you to it before you change your mind."

Vincent picked up the rake. "Not today. Today is a great day to do some gardening."

Mary turned to walk away. "Do you fancy a glass of your favourite wine? I've just bought a bottle."

"No thanks, love," Vincent said quickly. "I'll be fine...I'll see you inside soon."

———

Vincent moved more swiftly but was tiring again after another thirty minutes.

He stared at the garden, cursing under his breath for only managing to complete weeding on half of it before walking over to the shed, returning quickly holding a bucket and trowel to drop next to the fertiliser bag. He reached into a pocket on his dungarees, retrieving a Stanley knife before slicing the bag open, then scooping out the contents into the bucket.

"This better work," he said, scattering the compost over the weeded part of the garden.

He grabbed the garden fork and mixed it into the dirt before stopping to admire his progress.

"I will finish this off tomorrow," he said, panting as he placed the fork into the wheelbarrow. "This is too tiring to finish today."

He reached for the other tools and did the same before wheeling the barrow over to the fertiliser bag, but scratched his head at how he was going to pick it up. He sighed, checking if Mary was watching; pleased she wasn't as he attempted to bend down. But his back hurt before his hands touched the bag.

"Damn! I can't leave this stuff out in the open."

He breathed in deeply and tried again, grimacing in pain as he reached for the bag; dropping it into the barrow before puffing out his cheeks from exhaustion. He then wheeled it inside the shed, closed the door and locked it.

"Vince, love, could you put your dirty dungarees by the washing machine? I'll wash them later," Mary shouted from the next room after hearing Vincent enter the house.

"I wouldn't bother washing today if I were you. The sky's clouding over. It looks like it'll rain," Vincent replied, removing his dungarees and hat.

"It looked okay earlier. Are you sure it's going to rain?"

"If you don't believe me then take a look outside."

Mary entered the kitchen, laughing after seeing Vincent with just his underwear on.

"Put it away," she cried out.

Vincent laughed back; throwing the hat at her.

"Once upon a time, you would've told me to get it out."

"Vincent!" Mary hollered. "Stop being rude."

She huffed, staring out the window as a huge black cloud formed to darken the sky in seconds. She thought it looked strange, something unfamiliar, but, as she watched on, witnessed smaller clouds join onto it.

"Get ready for some thunder and lightning dear. You're right about the weather."

Vincent closed in as the sound of thunder shook his bones.

"That doesn't look normal," he cried out, gripping Mary.

"I was thinking the same." Mary shrieked as more thunder arrived.

"It's like a freak of nature," Vincent shockingly said, as rain pelted against the windows, splashing them with force. "Jeez! I hope they don't break."

In the space of just five minutes, the garden looked more like a swimming pool than a plot of land ready for seeding.

Vincent shook his head, keeping Mary close as he watched on in amazement. He felt hypnotised by the mixture of darkness and light portrayed in the sky as lightning flashes reminded him of fireworks.

"Don't worry, love," Mary said, smiling awkwardly. "The garden could do with some watering."

"Mary, are you taking the *piss*?" Vincent let go of her. "I've just wasted nearly two hours getting it ready and now my new compost's just been washed away...So please, don't tell me it's fine because the garden could do with some watering."

Vincent never normally swore at Mary, but when he did, she knew he was upset.

"I'm sorry dear. I didn't mean to annoy you."

Vincent mellowed again. He knew it wasn't Mary's fault it was raining like a waterfall.

"It's alright," he said, hugging her tight again. "I'll just have to do it again on another day."

"But right now I need you to put some clothes on."

Vincent laughed. He'd forgotten he was almost naked.

———

Mary entered the kitchen, peering at the clock as the time reached *3:00 pm*. She listened to the rain still pelting down as she opened the fridge, grabbing food to make Vincent's lunch. He was meant to be on a strict diet, but Mary knew he would accidentally on purpose forget if he was in charge of making his food.

Vincent sat in the living room with the TV remote in his hand. He was about to turn the TV on but the *roar* of more thunder spooked him.

I'd better not. Knowing my luck lightning would strike the aerial and blow my TV up, he thought, placing the remote down.

He sat back as Mary brought in his lunch, but his face drooped at what she'd prepared. He wasn't impressed.

"Here you go, love. Get this down ya'," she said, grinning slyly; handing a sandwich on a plate over to him.

Vincent smiled weakly. He knew his life was under threat if he didn't eat properly, so didn't want to let Mary down, but sometimes, the food she gave him tasted disgusting.

"Cheers love. It looks tasty...Yum, yum."

Mary slapped him on the shoulder, huffing as Vincent prodded the sandwich.

"It's not going to jump up and bite you," she said, tutting. "Just eat it..."

Vincent pulled many faces as he lifted the bread he hated so much; appearing sorrowful after not seeing any meat, cheese or butter.

"...Go on, you can do it. Just take a bite."

Vincent grumbled before picking up one of the sandwiches; taking several bites quickly to please Mary.

"Happy now?" he spurted out, as breadcrumbs fell onto the plate.

Mary just winked at him.

Vincent finished off the sandwich and yawned.

"I'm whacked...I think I'll have a lie-down."

"Okay," Mary replied. "I'll wake you when dinner's nearly ready...You're going to love what I've got planned."

Vincent pulled another face before handing her the plate.

SIX

Blake and Karen couldn't avoid the rain on their journey home. It had hit them hard to leave them soaked, making them look like two drenched people who'd just been swimming in their clothing. But now they had dried themselves off and had changed.

They huddled close to peer out of a window, seeing rainwater the size of ping-pong balls viciously splash onto pavements as drainpipes up and down the street gushed out water. There was no sign of a human or animal on the street. Even the birds had flown off in search of somewhere dry. No one was stupid enough to be caught up in this unless, like Karen and Blake, were heading home from somewhere.

"Looks like our celebrational dinner could be put on hold," Blake said with a sigh. "Well, at least until the rain slows down."

Karen shook her head. "It's okay. I'm sure we can celebrate another day."

But Blake knew she was disappointed.

He pulled her closer before walking away from the

window, wracking his brain as he moved into the kitchen to open some cupboards. But Karen felt confused.

"What are you doing?" she worryingly asked. "Are you checking to see if I've hidden the whiskey again?"

"No," Blake replied laughing. "I'm just checking to see where everything is."

"Why?"

"In case I need a plan B for this evening."

Karen smiled, even though she was still confused. She shook her head as Blake continued to search the kitchen cupboards, scrunching her lips when he finally stopped to place his hands on his hips.

"Have you finished?"

"Yes, babe," Blake replied nodding. "If the rain doesn't slow down before six then I'll make us a celebrational meal here...I promise."

"How can I resist such an offer."

"Problem solved then," Blake said with a grin.

Last night had rekindled the flames of desire between the two of them but today, the rain was trying its best to put the flame out.

Blake placed a finger under her chin, lifting it to say, "I know you're upset about the rain dampening our plans, but trust me." He stared into her eyes. "If we can't go to your favourite restaurant then I'll make what you were going to order there...Just wait and see."

Karen burst out laughing. "Stop it, you funny man...You can't even spell Fettuccini, never mind make it."

Blake also laughed.

———

The storm hadn't slowed down as the time reached *6:00 pm.*

Blake rose from his seat to see Karen winking at him; her hands waving him towards the kitchen as she giggled.

"Okay, okay, I'm going," Blake said, pulling a silly face. He looked out of a window as more rain smacked against it. "It doesn't appear too bad outside now if you still want to go out?"

"Are you being serious?" Karen replied still laughing. "It's pelting it down...And anyway, I'm fine staying in now you've decided to go all Gordon Ramsey on me..."

Blake smirked.

"...No more excuses...Get in the kitchen and cook me something."

"Okay, I will. Just give me a moment to compose myself."

Karen knew Blake was a useless cook but was excited to see what he came up with. Even if it wasn't Fettuccini.

She rose from her seat and followed him into the kitchen, watching him approach the fridge.

"Well, open it...It won't hurt you."

Blake smirked again as he opened the fridge door; smiling pleasingly after noticing a couple of juicy beef steaks.

"I take it those were meant for last night's dinner?"

"Yep. But now you can use them for tonight's."

Blake removed the steaks and placed them on the table. He smiled at Karen in the hope it would convince her that he knew how to cook them, but she wasn't convinced.

"You do know what they are?" she asked, close to laughing again.

"Shut up...Of course, I do...I know what lamb is..."

But, before Karen could rectify him, he was roaring with laughter in her face.

"...Just go back inside the living room while I cook the best steak surprise you've ever tasted..."

Blake placed his hands on her shoulders and turned her around.

"...Get your arse in there," he said, pointing at the living room. "And let me impress you with my cooking skills."

Karen giggled over and over again as she stepped back inside the room, but the giggles stopped after concern hit her.

"Just don't burn them!" she shouted. "They weren't cheap you know."

———

Karen remained seated in the living room for the next hour but had come close a few times in getting up to help. All she heard coming from the kitchen was clattering which not only annoyed her but caused her to bite her nails.

"Is everything okay in there?" she asked, hoping Blake would call her in. "You haven't smashed any of my good crockeries have you?"

"Babe, everything's brilliant. It's all under control...And no, I haven't broken anything."

"Just checking." But the aroma of something burning floated into the living room. "Jesus Christ, Blake, what's that smell? Have you burned the steaks?"

Blake stared at the oven door to witness smoke appear. He held his head as thoughts of a fire-breathing dragon inside the oven spraying its deadly flames entered his mind. He knew he had fucked up.

"Don't panic," he calmly said, turning the oven off and opening the door. "It's nothing serious. Just a slight problem...So don't worry." He shook the oven door from side to side, sending smoke in different directions. "Just watch some television. Dinner won't be long now."

"I can't watch it. The picture's fuzzy," Karen replied, holding the TV remote. "Must be the weather...Are you sure you don't need my help?"

"No, no, no, I'm fine...Then do some knitting."

Karen huffed as Blake's words soared over her head. She'd had enough of his excuses and her patience had worn thin.

She walked towards the kitchen door, trying her best not to be heard, hoping to see what he had or hadn't achieved in the last hour. But she almost screamed after witnessing the appalling mess he'd made.

"Blake," she whispered, wafting smoke away from her face. "When have you ever known me to do any knitting?"

"Well, now's a good time to start," Blake said, placing on an oven glove. "You've got no excuses...I might be in here for some time, so knit a jumper for me. Christmas is only nine months away."

Karen tried her best to be angry with him but every time she attempted to shout, she'd stare at him in his apron and smile at how adorable he looked. She knew he was trying so hard to impress her, even if he was the worst chef she'd ever seen.

"You're not as good as Gordon Ramsey," she said, sighing. "I bet Gordon the gopher can cook better than you."

"Come on, babe, that's below the belt...You seriously think that?"

"Right now I am starving so just make something edible." Karen wafted more smoke away. "You've got thirty minutes."

Blake watched her leave. He knew she was angry with him.

He cursed under his breath and opened a window,

fanning the smoke with the oven glove, hoping that the steaks would be okay to eat.

————

At *7:40 pm*, dinner was finally completed. The smoke had cleared and Blake was at last on top of the situation.

"Dinner's ready. Come and get it!" he shouted, taking off the apron. "But close your eyes when you reach the kitchen."

"Why?"

"Because I want you to smell what I've cooked, not see it."

"Now you think you're the 'Rock'." Karen sighed as she reached the door before closing her eyes as requested. "I'm here."

She felt a hand touch hers, gently pulling her towards the table until her leg touched a chair.

"You can open your eyes now."

She slowly did, but her reaction to the sight in front of her wasn't what Blake had hoped for. She felt devastated after seeing what had replaced the delicious steaks she'd bought; shaking her head at the greasy chips, eggs, and beans sitting on a plate.

"What happened to my steak surprise?"

"You've got a steak surprise."

"There's no steak on my plate," Karen replied, still feeling upset.

"Well, that's the surprise." Blake laughed. "There is no steak."

"Very funny...I was looking forward to a nice bit of rump."

"Stop moaning love. You've had enough romp to last you a lifetime."

"I said rump, not romp..."

Blake kept up the laughter until Karen recognised his attempt at trying to be funny. But she still wasn't impressed.

"Okay, you got me...You were referring to the sex we had last night."

Blake winked and hugged her.

"I'm sorry for messing up the steaks and I know this isn't what you expected, but at least the eggs came out okay...I never broke a yolk. Just the way you like it."

Karen calmed down and kissed him on the cheek.

"You're right. It's not what I expected. But hey, at least you tried."

"Maybe I can try again tomorrow? I have Gordon the gopher's recipe book."

Karen glared at him. "No! No! No!," she shouted, trying not to laugh. "I don't want you in the kitchen attempting to cook ever again unless you're cooking eggs. At least they look good enough to eat."

Karen smacked Blake on the back, shaking her head as she sat down.

SEVEN

WEDNESDAY

The crazy storm had ceased by the time it reached *9:00 am*, but it had left *two* female visitors to Clifton Falls stranded during the night. Their vehicle had stalled on the side of a country road, forcing them to take refuge inside as the rain pelted down. They had gotten little sleep because of it but hoped that a few hours hiking through the sodden grass forest would be enough time for the engine to dry out.

Amy, the eldest of the women, stared awkwardly at the car, cringing to see the paintwork had been chipped away.

"I don't think my insurance will pay for a new paint job," she said, touching the bonnet to feel more paint slide off. "How am I going to explain this?"

"How can anyone explain that freak rainstorm," *Paula* replied, yawning into her hand. "We've wasted half a day's travel because of it."

Amy and Paula were cousins looking for a little adventure

in their lives. They were sick of their normal, daily routines, so had packed up to go on a road trip, but neither had carried a mobile phone. It was Amy's idea to have a phone-free zone during their timeout from people they knew but right now she was regretting it.

"Do you want me to call the AA?" Paula asked, smirking. "Oh no, I can't can I because you wanted to live like a friggin' cavewoman for a few days."

"Okay, okay, stop rubbing it in...The car will be fine once we've had a walk." Amy glanced at the sky. "See, the sun's out...Keep the bonnet up and the engine will dry in no time."

"But if we see anyone in the meantime, we ask for their help. Agreed?"

Amy nodded as she opened up the boot; unzipping a small suitcase to fumble inside.

"What are you looking for?" Paula asked, annoyed at having to wait. "I thought we were going for a walk?"

"We are," Amy said, retrieving a pair of trainers from the case. "Did you think I was going to walk across the wet grass in these heels?"

Paula just sighed as she watched Amy place on the trainers, but the sound of the boot slamming shut made her jump nervously.

"Damn!" she said, yawning again. "I could do with a few more hours of sleep."

"No. I need you...You are my sidekick. If I'm going into the forest then so are you."

Paula nodded as Amy reached into the passenger seat; returning with a backpack before placing it on and smiling. She then shut the door and walked off.

"Let's do this."

"But aren't you going to lock it?"

Amy shook her head. "Nah...Who's going to steal something that doesn't start?

———

They walked for fifteen minutes before Paula stopped to rest against a tree. Her stomach was calling out for some food but Amy was too excited now to want to rest.

"Come on. You can't be hungry again," she said, pulling on Paula's arm to get her walking. "You only ate last night."

"Yeah! Exactly!" Paula pulled back. "Last night was ages ago. I need something to eat now."

"I told you to lay off the pot...You always get the munchies after smoking that stuff."

Paula sighed. "I've not taken any recently."

"Sure you haven't." Amy stared at the pockets on Paula's jacket. "So, I won't find any spliffs if I check those then?..."

Paula giggled as Amy placed a hand inside one of her pockets.

"...I bet you have a joint in here." Amy tutted as she retrieved a spliff. "What did I say to you about taking drugs while on meds? ...Paula, you need to listen to me."

"I know, I know, but can we please take a break and have some food now?"

Amy glared at her. "Okay. Let's find a spot where we can sit down, but we're only taking time out for a few minutes...Okay?"

Paula smiled and nodded.

They moved towards a large log spread out across the grass, sitting on it as Paula eagerly watched Amy remove the backpack.

"You did put food and drink inside there?" Paula asked nervously.

Amy smiled and reached inside, pulling out sandwiches and cans of pop before handing them over.

"We've still got these," she said, watching Paula grab them. "They should stop your tummy from rumbling for a while."

Paula ate a sandwich whilst staring at something Amy couldn't see.

What are you gawping at?" Amy asked, feeling freaked out. "Are you high right now?"

Paula choked on her food, coughing to make Amy nervous. But seconds later she stopped and took another bite of her sandwich.

"Don't be daft," she said, spitting out bread. "I think someone's watching us...Just don't stare."

Amy became even more freaked out after Paula pointed towards the trees.

"Stop pointing," she said, slapping Paula's finger. "You'll make it worse."

They listened out for a sign of movement, but whoever Paula saw wasn't coming out into the open. This made the situation worse.

Amy was close to losing her nerve as the silence inside the forest sent a shiver down her spine, but she slowly relaxed after noticing Paula was still eating her sandwich. She shrugged at her, feeling it was just a joke as she watched her swig from the can; becoming annoyed that Paula's game almost caused her to wet herself.

"Very funny," Amy said, rising to grab Paula by her jacket. "You almost had me."

"But it's true. I saw someone. I think."

"Just look around you," Amy said, racing a finger in a circle. "There are loads of animals out here…Maybe you saw a squirrel, or a fox, or one of the other mammals that live here."

"Who are you? You've turned into a presenter of the Animal Planet channel."

"Stop being sarcastic," Amy said, moving away to sit down again. "I'm just making a point."

While they bickered about whether or not a person had been seen, a repugnant-looking figure was closing in, walking as if inebriated.

His living name was *Rodney Wilson*. The homeless man who the robber pushed over. But Rodney had died a few weeks ago. He had collapsed on the edge of the forest, just yards away from the field that was sprayed with the new fertiliser, but no one had known. Maybe it was because most of the people had suddenly stopped noticing Rodney since he'd lived on the street - unlike when he was with his family in the large farmhouse at the edge of town, but the local police chief still did. Or he did until a few weeks ago. He'd often check up on Rodney whilst bringing food and drink to him, but he hadn't told anyone the reason behind why the man had quit his home. He wanted Rodney to do that. But, for the past six months, he'd chosen to keep quiet about his wife taking the children away from him. He said the house never felt the same after that day so couldn't stay there anymore.

The police chief had checked Rodney's home a few weeks ago to find someone had been there, so assumed the man had come to his senses and had either gone home for good or had packed up a few things before moving on.

But the corpse of Rodney Wilson was now glaring at the women through the only eye left because the other had been eaten by a bird.

Tattered clothing revealed decaying flesh as it dragged its left foot along the ground; its top lip missing to reveal insects crawling across infected cigarette-stained teeth.

It snapped at thin air, moaning faintly as it staggered from one tree to the next, not being noticed as it closed in on the women.

"Paula...Did you hear that?"

"Yes, I did...But what kind of animal makes sounds like that?" Paula smirked. "Maybe it's a large bear that wants a good shaggin'?"

"Don't be stupid. I'm being serious...There are no bears out here but what if it's another dangerous animal that's very hungry?"

Paula shrugged her shoulders as she desperately scanned the forest, but nothing was seen.

"Just cool it, yeah...I can't see anything. But, if a hungry animal was coming this way then we can give it some crisps and an apple..."

Amy panicked to the point of sweating, wanting to pack up and go as quickly as possible.

"...Come on. I'm kiddin'." Paula smiled.

"The fun's over...It's time we moved on," Amy said, grabbing the backpack. "We've been here long enough."

"Are you worried that I'll give the animal the crisps you like?"

Amy shook her head frantically, hearing the moaning sounds closing in; turning to see the corpse appear from behind a tree as Paula bit into an apple.

"You were right about seeing someone," Amy said pointing, watching the corpse slobber. "He must be the local farmer."

Paula gawped as the creature staggered from side to side; its moaning drilling through her, making her cringe.

"You did say I can ask someone for help," she said, laughing at how awkwardly it moved. "But that person looks fucked up...I can't see him being much help."

"Just ask him."

"Hey!" Paula shouted as the zombie held out its hands. "Do you live around here?... Do you know anything about cars?..."

She waited for a response but the thing that she thought was still a person was just walking towards her, moaning and snarling.

"...Hey!" she shouted again. "Are you listening to me?"

"Let's just leave him alone," Amy said, not wanting to upset anyone. "We're probably on his land."

She placed the backpack on the grass as the zombie got closer and closer, its disfigured face spooking her to fall back over the log, but Paula burst out laughing. She walked over to help Amy, ignoring the beast, but was soon rubbing her nose once a revolting smell wafted nearby.

"Damn, woman, have you just shit yourself?"

"No, I haven't!" Amy angrily replied, holding out a hand for Paula to pull her up. "That person just scared me."

"Smells like rotting meat."

But, before Paula could help, a hand gripped her shoulder, forcing her to trip over the backpack and crack her head on the log. Amy stared horrified at the skinless, weightless being growling at her until finding her voice to SCREAM. But her shouts only enraged it. She returned to her feet, shaking as drool dripped onto Paula. She was happy to see Paula rise and throw a punch, but her fist was left embedded in the zombie's right cheek. Amy puked as Paula removed her hand to reveal maggots crawling over it. She shook them off and YELLED, but the zombie pounced on her, dragging her to the ground.

Amy froze as the zombie snapped its teeth at Paula, shedding tears because she was too scared to help. She backed away as Paula screamed again before turning to run in the opposite direction; not looking behind as she aimed for the car.

"I will get some help!" she shouted, as her legs kept moving. "You need to fight him off."

Paula gripped the zombie's arms as it pinned her to the ground before lifting a knee into its face, but it shook off the attack, moving at speed to try to bite her.

"Fuck off and leave me alone!" she hollered, trying to kick it.

She became soaked by the wetness on the ground, the grip on the zombie's arms slipping to leave her in tears as she desperately tried to break free. She screamed out again but a torrent of maggots dropped from the hole in the zombie's face to land in her mouth. She tried to spit them out but was forced to swallow some as the zombie wriggled more frantically; getting closer and closer to biting her face as its toxic breath momentarily strangled her.

Paula lashed out with every ounce of energy she had but the zombie remained on top of her, snapping its teeth and snarling. She shook her head as more maggots landed on her face before cringing hysterically when one of her hands let go. She cried after the zombie's nails ripped down her cheek; its nose twitching as it sniffed the blood dripping down her face before its grotesque tongue licked it. Paula was close to fainting as the creature thrashed about in excitement, the taste of the blood driving it crazy to want to taste more. But Paula couldn't keep it at bay any longer and her other hand let go.

She stared at its eye socket, watching it get closer and closer until feeling a sharp pain in her *neck*; listening to the zombie drink the blood that was pouring out of her as it chewed on her flesh. She tried kicking out again, slapping at the zombie's face to get it to back off, but it growled, biting her throat for a second time.

Paula was too weak to move as the zombie bit into her shoulder; her eyes flickering to remain open until releasing her last breath.

The zombie growled like a wild animal before sniffing the air and rising to its feet, licking blood off its face as it glared in the direction of where Amy was last seen.

————

Amy stopped running to catch her breath, as her mind overflowed with the recent trauma. She cried into her hands after a reminder of Paula's echoing pleas for help almost sunk her to her knees; dripping sweat fast as she sadly looked over to where she'd come from.

"Paula! Paula! Are you okay?... Please answer me?"

She shouted for the next few minutes, waiting for a reply she knew she wasn't going to get; fearing the worst as more tears fell. She felt guilty, cowardly, and disgusted with herself for her actions, wanting now to run back, but her feet wouldn't move. She knew she was in deep trouble if she remained inside the forest but was too heartbroken to budge.

She heard the zombie's groans closing in but couldn't pinpoint where it was. She knew it was slow, but, as it appeared from a cluster of trees, its movement increased and it was close to running. The sight petrified her, even more, making her legs heavy, feeling like they were encased in concrete as her heart pumped faster and faster. She could see the bloodstains and chunks of flesh trapped between the zombie's teeth as it howled at her; snapping them to leave her cursing in fear because it reminded her of Frankenstein's monster. But this monster was picking up speed.

Amy shivered as sweat dripped down her brow, but she didn't move until the zombie almost reached her. She screamed at it and ran as fast as she could, not looking back until knowing she had made some distance. She scanned the area to see a fence she recognised, smiling nervously as she followed it back towards the car, but her heart skipped a beat after finding no car keys in her pockets.

"Shit! Fucking shit! Where are they?" she bellowed.

She sobbed some more as she kicked the car until remembering she'd left the keys in the ignition; wiping her eyes dry before reaching for the driver's door. She sighed when it opened, feeling thankful for being stubborn enough to leave the keys behind; leaping into the seat and shutting the door to lock it quickly and turning the key. But the car still wouldn't start. Again and again, she tried, but nothing was happening. She slammed a fist against the steering wheel before making sure all the doors were locked; her heartbeat slowing again after feeling safe. She swiftly looked all around her, hoping and praying that the thing she saw had gone down another path; thinking that maybe someone would pass by soon to save her from the madness.

There must be farmworkers around these parts. Perhaps my knight in shining armour will appear on a tractor and save me from the madman.

She leaned over the passenger seat before opening the glove compartment; rushing a hand inside to flip items out of the way in the hope of finding something she could use as a weapon in case the strange weirdo attacked. But something shuffled outside the car that briefly froze her again. She breathed deeply as she slowly moved towards the passenger side window, lifting her head and smiling to see a *rabbit* run away. She sighed again and moved back into her seat, but, as she returned to an upright position, became freaked out by the sight of the zombie glaring at her, drooling down the window as maggots squirmed around on its face. Amy frantically bounced up and down in the seat as fear for her life overtook other emotions; screaming louder and louder until her voice croaked.

The zombie slobbered some more before sending out a droning moan; slamming a fist against the window to scatter glass particles over Amy's face and body as the fingers from its insect-filled hand clenched her hair tight. But Amy just placed arms over her face, crying until the tears stung her eyes.

The zombie pulled harder on her hair to leave infected scratches on her scalp, close to ripping chunks from her head to make her cringe as she plucked up the courage to slap at its arm. It was a desperate attempt to gain freedom, but it was no use, the thing wouldn't let go.

Amy yelped when her hair finally tore away, but, instead of escaping out of the other door, she bit deep into the zombie's colourless hand, drawing lifeless blood. She stared at the monster as the thick redness trickled from her mouth, hoping her bravery would spook it to back off. But the zombie snarled at her.

She spat out the rotten, maggot-tasting blood as her hair was grabbed again, but this time the zombie retreated its arm to pull her head towards the broken window. Amy yelped over and over again but the zombie wasn't letting go. She tried punching the arm but her head was still closing in, getting nearer and nearer to the jagged edges of glass still embedded in the window frame. She knew there was no escape.

She took a deep breath as her head entered the frame; her right eye puncturing to leave dark juice seeping down her face as a weak scream escaped her mouth. She gritted her teeth as the zombie pulled her out of the car, glass tearing flesh from her body as she was tossed onto the ground.

She lay on her back as the blood drained out of her, too fragile to move as her damaged eye hung over her blackened face, the grass around her slowly turning crimson as the red liquid spluttered from her mouth.

She gulped as the zombie picked up a shattered piece of glass, watching it stand next to her to quiver as the blood in her mouth filled up faster than she could spit it out.

The zombie grinned sadistically as it studied her before slowly kneeling to almost touch her head. It raised the piece of glass and thrust it down, pushing and pushing it through her head until the point sunk into the grass.

EIGHT

The soil covering the new resting home of Vincent's mother slowly shifted, revealing fingers as an arm stripped of skin landed on top of the grave. Seconds later another arm appeared before the head and a frail body followed, showing a grotesque figure wearing a torn dress with a crucifix around its neck lifting out of the ground. It snarled, exposing *gums* as it sniffed the air.

It stared at the high fencing separating the garden from the next one as a whimpering sound was heard behind it before snarling again after a loud scratching loosened one of the wooden fence panels.

Behind it was *Bruno*; the neighbour's Doberman dog. He'd become excited by the zombie's sounds.

The dog growled before chewing the panel until it cracked; tearing a piece away to leave a hole big enough to place its head inside. It saw the zombie move away from the grave but it didn't bark. It just whimpered excitedly even more as it tore away more wood; squeezing its body through the hole to enter the garden.

Bruno wagged his tail as the zombie staggered from side to side; its mouth snapping at thin air as it walked barefoot across the dirt and onto the grass. It stopped to glare at Bruno, twitching its head as loose flesh hung down from its face, but it wasn't snarling anymore. It just looked at the dog closing in, sniffing the insects dropping from its body.

Bruno didn't seem frightened by the zombie's appearance, somehow seeing beyond the mutilation to still vision the old lady who used to give it baked cookies, so ran around the zombie, hoping it would give chase. But it didn't.

The dog stopped running and shuffled closer, almost touching the zombie's dirty feet to shake falling insects off its back. It looked up to see the creature point a finger before a rasping sound escaped its mouth. Then the word – "Brrruuunnnooo" was heard.

It excited the dog.

It wagged its tail at twice the speed after the zombie reached down to touch its fur; feeling the bony hand stroke down its back before sitting upright. But, as both sets of eyes connected, the zombie lunged for Bruno's throat, tightening its grip rapidly. The dog yelped but it didn't react aggressively or try to escape. Even whilst choking, Bruno just stared at the zombie, thinking it to be the frail old lady.

A soundless squeal escaped as Bruno's tongue flapped in the cool breeze, its eyes turning cloudy white as a final breath was released.

The zombie stared at the animal, not letting go as flashbacks cluttered up its mind. It tried to smile but quickly became aggressive again, feeling the desire to feed on the dog. But, as it lifted Bruno to its mouth, was left angry for not being able to take a bite. It snapped gums onto Bruno's neck again before letting go; snarling as the dog dropped to the ground.

The zombie turned to face the house, sniffing the air again to leave a huge grin on its face. It slowly moved away from the dog to spot something glistening at the edge of the garden, the sun's rays bouncing off the item to make it shine as the creature neared. It bent down awkwardly and picked it up, revealing the Stanley knife that Vincent forgot to store away, with the blade still showing.

The zombie turned the knife in its scrawny right hand, glaring at the back door of the house as dribble rolled down its rotting chin. It walked towards the door, touching it to slide a hand up and down before groaning like it had forgotten how to open it; bumping its head against a wall in rage until accidentally flicking the door handle down. It opened it, pushing it wider to enter the kitchen, but it stopped and scowled at the new worktops, cooker, and cupboards. It wasn't impressive.

The zombie growled.

It held the knife out in front, turning it again and again as if wanting to attack an invisible enemy; swinging its hand as it moved along the room. It saw another door, so slowly neared it, but the swinging hand crashed against a saucepan hanging on the wall, sending it smashing to the floor as the door burst open.

Mary stood in the doorway, open-mouthed and struggling to breathe, the sight of the zombie spooking her to collapse to the floor as her heart beat faster and faster until she was close to fainting. But she pushed her bum into the carpet and retreated like someone rowing a boat, moving her legs and hands at speed to get away from the thing in front of her. But the zombie followed, waving the knife in the air.

Mary reached a wall, sweating fast; eyeballing the intruder to see if it would strike. But it stopped and just watched her, giving her time to rise off the ground. She shivered, too scared to shout out for help; watching the zombie stare at her like it was studying her; seeing it lower the knife before rasping out the word – "Mar."

Mary swallowed hard, blinking fast; seeing beneath the flaking, stinking mass of filth that covered the zombie's face and body. She recognised the way it stood. It reminded her of *Margaret*, Vincent's mother, but it wasn't until seeing the crucifix that she believed it.

The zombie tried to say her name again but Mary was freaking out more and more.

She slowly moved to her left to reach another door but the zombie's head turned in the same direction to stop her, frightening her into not knowing what to do next.

She gulped as insects squirmed out of the zombie; seeing them drop to the floor to carry on across the carpet as the creature touched what was left of its hair. Mary winced when some fell out in its hand. She heard the zombie snarl as it raised the knife again; swinging it rapidly towards itself to slice into its left arm as coagulated blood seeped out like thick, dark oil.

Mary wanted to, needed to escape, but she couldn't budge. All she could do was watch the thing in front of her tear at its arm until it was close to hanging off before it stopped to glare at her; making her freak out even more.

She took a deep breath before racing towards the nearest door, gripping the handle to pull it to her, but the zombie picked up speed, closing in to drag her back before skimming the knife blade across her left cheek, leaving a deep cut. Mary yelped as she placed a hand over it, but the stinging, throbbing pain as the blood seeped beneath her fingers brought tears to her eyes. She stood in the middle of the living room in a state of pure shock, not able to think straight as the zombie grinned; licking its decomposing lips as it sniffed the blood.

"Who are you?! What do you want?!" Mary shouted at it as the blood ran down her hand. "You look like my husband's mother, but you can't be, she's dead. So, who the hell are *you*?"

She was now covered in a blanket of fear as crazy thoughts about her mother-in-law overloaded her brain.

What the hell had happened?

She watched the zombie snap its mouth, as what was left of its nostrils twitched before desperately searching the room for something to fend it off with; seeing a walking stick that Vincent used on his long walks standing in a corner. She retreated to more snarls but was able to make some distance to reach an armchair before the creature moved towards her; pushing the chair out in front for protection in the hope of keeping the mad freak at arm's length. But, as the tears suddenly rolled down her cheeks followed by another burst of nerves, she became too petrified to reach for the stick. She stared at the phone, trying to convince herself that she had enough time to make a call, but reality kicked in and she knew it was too risky to try. So, she just waited to see what the zombie would do.

It snarled again, moving towards her, pushing against the chair to force it away from her grasp, but this time Mary screamed, sending a shrill bouncing off the walls to stall the zombie's attack. She took another breath, hoping that her cry for help would cause the zombie to back off, but it refocused to lash out, smashing into the armchair to send it spinning across the room.

Mary pleaded with the human-like creature but knew her words were being wasted. It snarled at her again, raising the knife to scare her into almost shrinking to her knees in submission, but she plucked up the courage to move towards the stick; reaching for it as a *sharp pain* stung her back. She turned awkwardly, seeing the knife blade drip blood, knowing now what had happened as the pain increased. She felt the wetness of liquid slide down her back, turning her cream-coloured long skirt red as the blood dripped onto the carpet. She closed her eyes for a second, hoping it was just a dream, but the zombie grabbed her, pinching fingers into her flesh.

It eyed the recent wound, licking its lips as Mary pulled away to grab the stick. She swung it as hard as she could at the torn arm until it ripped away and dropped to the floor, choking as it slithered along the carpet to try to reach her.

She kicked it against a wall before stupidly barging into the beast to escape into the kitchen, but her trailing arm was gripped tight to stop her. She frantically shouted at the zombie, slapping a hand at its face until popping out an eye to watch it swing from the optic nerve cable, but, as she tried to pull free, was violently launched into the air. She crashed hard against the television set, sending it smashing against a wall, and leaving a painful *shiver* down her back as she silently lay on the floor. She heard the *neighbour* screeching out his disgust at the racket coming from her house, with the last few words being - "*Keep the fucking noise down!*"

Mary tried to move but her body was battered and bruised. She knew she had at least one broken rib. She slowly returned to her feet, feeling dazed as her breathing became harder to achieve; unable to avoid more stinging cuts to her face as the blade swung in her direction to blur her vision. She lifted her hands to protect herself but they too were sliced. She pleaded once again to be left alone, not knowing where the beast would strike next.

She became more frightened as thoughts of being killed by the hands of the thing that reminded her of her mother-in-law smothered her mind, but, even though she wanted to scream again, she couldn't do it. She was too petrified to try.

She swung her wounded hands at thin air, hoping to catch the creature with a lucky strike, but it clamped a hand onto her jaw to slam her head loudly against the wall above the fireplace. Its croaky growl scared her into wetting herself as the cold, bloodied blade rested on the tip of her nose. Then, a second later, the tip was sectioned off. Blood gushed down over her mouth and chin, soaking into her blouse, as the zombie sucked it off her face.

And Mary just let it. She was too weak to move.

NINE

The corpse of Rodney Wilson staggered along the country lane, as the fresh blood slowly mixed in with the crusty mud patches of the worn-away clothing to give it more colour. It didn't seem bothered where it was going. It was just on a journey to anywhere.

———

An engine roared in the distance, increasing as the seconds ticked by; causing the zombie to lift its head as its only eye flicked from side to side. It moaned, pointing out in front as it neared a bend in the road, but the sound got closer and closer to confuse it. It carried on walking as a large, Volvo truck closed in, slobbering and moaning whilst feeling around the hole in its face. But it suddenly stopped, becoming unsettled after the noise increased again. It acted like it wasn't sure of what to do; close to toppling over as it picked up speed to head towards the side of the road, but, after the *driver* of the truck blasted the horn repeatedly, the zombie stopped again to place hands on its head. It heard the horn blast again, becoming more confused as it faced the truck.

"Get out of the fuckin' way!" the driver hollered, slamming on the brakes.

But the zombie acted like a statue.

The truck screeched along the road, leaving black tyre imprints behind as it smashed into the living corpse to sever it on impact, the head landing in the path of the front wheels to be squashed as the truck came to a stop. The driver sat in a state of shock, pure white as he stared at the body parts attached to the blood-spattered windscreen; gulping hard before suddenly puking violently over the passenger seat. He felt lucky not to have lost full control.

He composed himself and exited, breathing deeply to hold back tears as he moved to the front of the truck, seeing chunks of flesh, organs and more blood attached to it before collapsing to his knees after spotting a torso on the edge of the road. He closed his eyes and sobbed loudly as thoughts flashed inside his mind of why the person just stood in his way before opening his eyes and wiping his face. He purposely avoided the carnage before returning to the truck, shaking from thoughts of what to say to the police.

How do I explain this?

He sat in his seat, reaching for a mobile phone to curse under his breath as the number dialled; breathing loud and heavy as he waited for someone to answer.

———

It took over ten minutes before a police car appeared in the distance, flashing its lights as it slowed down to pull up on the opposite side of the road. Its occupants were *Wayne*

Strong, a thirty-five-year-old sergeant who needed to be precise in everything he did, and *Jason Bark*, a twenty-one-year-old rookie constable.

They exited the car to glare at the driver before shaking their heads at the gruesome sight; cautiously walking towards him as he jumped down from the truck.

"Was it you who made the phone call?" Wayne asked, pulling out a pad. "Reporting an accident on the road."

"Yes. It was."

"And you are?"

"*Frank*. My name is Frank," the truck driver said, still shaking at what he'd done. "I can explain."

"No need to explain, sir. I think I know what happened."

Wayne stared the bulky man up and down, hoping he wasn't going to run as Jason aimed for the bloodbath on the road, writing down notes as he tried to make his conclusion on what happened.

"But I need to tell you the truth." Frank was close to crying again after watching Wayne touch his baton. "I know what you're thinking. You think I killed someone. I can see it in your eyes."

"No one thinks that sir, but if you want to explain it then I'm all ears...We can do it at the station."

Frank shook even more as a severed arm flopped down the windscreen to land at Jason's feet.

"I shouted at the person to get off the road, but they wouldn't move."

"So, you thought you'd run them down instead?" Wayne asked, scrunching his lips. "Did you know the person? Did they annoy you?"

"Yeah...Was the person sleeping with your partner?" Jason interrupted, grinning like a hyperactive child.

"No! No! No!" Frank bellowed; worrying the officers to grip their batons. "You have to believe me...I braked hard to avoid the person, but he just stood in the road like he wanted me to hit him."

Wayne and Jason looked at the skid marks left by the truck. They knew Frank was telling the truth about slamming on his brakes, so backed down thinking it was a deliberate hit. But the thought of how the person became dismantled racked their brains.

They remained cautious as Frank's nervous streak almost caused him to faint; watching him sit on the step below the driver's side door before taking their hands off the batons.

"We believe you never meant to harm the person," Wayne said, closing in to grip Frank's shoulder. "But it's still hard to work out why the person was torn to pieces?"

"I honestly don't know the answer," Frank replied, pointing down the road where he'd just come from. "I came around that corner, saw him, and slammed on my brakes. I was only going around ten miles an hour when I hit him, so it doesn't make sense."

"No, it doesn't," Jason interrupted again. "I can see his torso on the side of the road."

"This is fucked up!" Wayne snapped. "Take photos of the carnage and send them back to base...I think it's going to be a long day."

"Will do," Jason replied, jotting down more words before getting out his phone. "Let's hope someone can work out why it happened?"

Wayne grimaced after watching Jason snap photos of the windscreen and the road before seeing him calmly walk over to the torso, acting like it was just a video game rather than a real-life crime scene. He knew he was in charge of Jason but struggled to keep him in the here and now, hating how easily Jason switched from fantasy to reality to drive him up the wall. He shook his head, letting Jason do what he needed to do, hoping it was just his way of coping with the situation.

Jason took photos of the torso but gulped after feeling something squish beneath his boot; looking down to flinch at the sight of a human heart on the road.

"Fuck me...I've ruined my new boots," he said, wiping off congealed blood before returning to the others. "The man's heart was on the ground." He glanced at Frank and shook his head. "The body looks like it's been macheted to death and not run over, as our witness here described."

Jason always thought the worst in other people, especially strangers. According to him, they were all murderers in the making, so it wasn't surprising for him to find another explanation for what happened, but it usually took Wayne longer before following suit.

Wayne bent down to examine the arm that'd fallen off the windscreen, picking at it with his pen before smelling its putrid aroma; holding his nose to choke at how decayed it was. He knew the person was dead long before the truck ran him down, even though his mind tried convincing him otherwise.

No one could have killed this person within the past few hours or even the past week, so what is going on?

He looked at Jason as thoughts of him being right about Frank being a murderer made him angry. He knew it was the only possible reason. Frank had murdered someone and had tried to dispose of them.

"You said the person stood in the road just before you knocked him down," he said to Frank, trying hard to keep calm.

Frank just nodded.

"...So why does the body look like it's been dead for over a week?"

Frank's eyes widened. "I don't know, but it was walking. I swear it."

Wayne pointed at the arm before ordering Jason to near it. "Can you smell anything?"

"Yeah...It smells like it's gone off," Jason replied, returning to his feet. "I could smell it when I was taking photos of the body parts but I didn't want to say anything in case you laughed at me."

"I can see why you'd think that," Wayne said, turning to Frank. "This is your last chance, to tell the truth. What the *fuck* happened here?..."

Frank stared at the body parts, not saying a word as Wayne lost his patience.

"...I'll tell you what I think happened, shall I?!" he screamed at Frank, clenching a fist like he was about to punch him. "I think you murdered the man over a week ago and stored his body in the back of your truck. Then, you drove down this quiet country lane to dispose of it. But you knew it was too risky so you decided to hack it to pieces before running over it. Then you phoned the police with this bullshit story."

Wayne waited for Frank to agree, but he was still silent.

"Shall I fetch the breathalyser?" Jason asked, wanting to be more involved. "He looks drunk."

"Nah...This man isn't drunk," Wayne replied, glaring at Frank. "He's just in shock after realising what he's done..."

Jason nodded before moving towards the truck; opening the driver's door to step inside. But he exited briskly after seeing the puke.

"...Did you find anything useful?"

"No. It's all good," Jason replied cringing.

Frank crumbled to his knees, repeating over and over the words – "I never killed anyone" – before puffing out his cheeks; shaking his head in an attempt to convince Wayne that he may be wrong on his verdict.

But Wayne just looked at Jason and shrugged before helping Frank off the ground.

"Right, listen, Frank. This whole situation is fucked up. Too fucked up for me to know what to do and what to believe."

"So, what are you saying?" Frank nervously asked. "Am I being arrested or not?"

Wayne lashed out, kicking a tyre before biting his bottom lip.

"There's something in what you've told us." Wayne tried to smile but couldn't do it. "On another day I would be hauling you into the station. But we're short-staffed, meaning my partner and I need to stay here to sort this mess out."

"And me?"

"You'll have to go to the station without us." Wayne pointed at Frank like he was telling him off before slowly moving his finger to aim it down the road. "If you fail to arrive then we'll hunt you down...Are you hearing me?"

"Loud and clear."

"Good...Drive down to the junction at the end of this stretch of road and turn right. The station is about two miles from there. You can't miss it...I'll let them know you are arriving."

"But we need the truck for forensics," Jason barked.

"I know that, but he can still drive it as long as he doesn't wipe away the evidence...The truck will be easier to examine if it's parked outside the station."

Jason just smiled and nodded as Wayne turned to Frank.

"Just sit in the driver's seat and drive. Do not turn on your windscreen wipers. Have you got that?"

"I've got it," replied Frank, feeling less anxious as he climbed back inside the truck. "I'm on my way there now."

He started it up again, slowly moving forward to squash the body parts on the road; looking in the side mirror to see Wayne and Jason shake their heads.

Wayne returned to the police car to the sound of Jason choking after glancing at the splattered mess. Now feeling faint as he caught Wayne up.

"I thought we were staying here?" Jason asked, spitting out puke. "That's what you told the driver."

"I just want to give the area a quick swoop and see if anything else appears out of the ordinary first. Then we'll come back."

"Okay."

————

Wayne drove further down the road, concentrating on what was ahead whilst Jason looked out the side window; whizzing his eyes from right to left in search of more clues. But he almost got whiplash after the car suddenly halted.

"Jeez!" he shouted, rubbing the back of his neck. "Did something run out in front?"

Wayne never answered. He just stared to his right.

Jason leaned forward to follow Wayne's vision, spotting another car parked on the side of the road to make him curious.

"Could be connected?" he said. "Let's check it out."

"Phone it in first...I want to know whom that vehicle belongs to."

Wayne pulled over on the opposite side of the road as Jason made a call to the station; passing over the number plate of the empty vehicle before waiting for a reply. But Wayne's patience faded fast. He exited the car, breathing heavily as he stared at the other vehicle, feeling nervous as he waited for Jason to finish the call.

He did within a minute.

"It's registered to a Miss Amy Thompson!" he shouted, opening the door. "But she's not from around here."

Wayne moved closer to the mystery vehicle until spotting the smashed driver's side window; cringing after seeing spots of blood at the bottom. He held up a hand to stall Jason before slowly reaching out to touch the passenger door; feeling more nervous when it opened with ease.

"Jason, I need you to go around to the other side. But be careful. Something doesn't seem right."

Jason puffed out his cheeks and gripped his baton, leaking sweat from his brow as he warily moved to the front of the car to touch the bonnet.

"No one's driven this for a while," he said, sliding the baton across it. "It's stone cold."

"Then where is she?"

"No, i-" Jason fell against the car, his face becoming pale.

Wayne freaked out and reached for his baton. "What's up with you?" he shakily asked, holding the baton tight. "You look like you've seen a ghost."

Jason never replied. He just remained stuck to the spot.

But he flinched when Wayne reached him, close to running away as a vision of the second sickest thing he'd seen today tore at his insides. But Wayne grabbed hold of him before looking at where he'd stared, dropping his baton as a sudden surge of fear brought tears to his eyes.

Below them was a female body covered in blood, with a shard of glass embedded into her head. It was enough for Wayne to topple to the ground.

"Hey! Are you okay?" Jason asked, reaching down to lift him.

"What do you think?!" Wayne snapped back, clinging to the car. "I just felt a bit faint." He stared at the carnage, blinking a few times before standing upright; his nerves becoming hard to handle as he said, "Who fuckin' did this?"

"There's some strange shit goin' on today," Jason replied, holding his neck again. "First, we find a dead body that was presumably walking around, and now this...What's goin' to happen next in Clifton Falls?"

TEN

Frank drove towards the station, still feeling emotional as he reached the junction. He wiped a tear from his eye as another eerie figure staggered onto the road; rubbing his head after seeing the person walking towards his truck.

What's going on around here? Is there some kind of freaky ritual happening? Or are people just fucked up on drugs?

He watched the person closely, slowing down to see it was a woman, but she wasn't waving her hands in the air or even shouting out for help. She was just walking as if drunk.

Frank felt scared as well as sympathy towards her after noticing a bloodline trail along the road, so parked up. He quivered, grabbed his wheel lock and stepped off the truck, closing in slowly as she moved awkwardly with her head down; groaning like she was struggling to speak. Frank felt sad as the woman lifted her head to reveal sticky blood wrapped around her throat like a red necklace, but he jumped back in shock as she growled at him.

"Are you alright?" he softly said, squirming at how much

she'd bled but was still able to walk. "What happened to you? Do you need help?"

He heard more groans as the woman coughed up clotted blood before snapping teeth towards him. But he just thought she was too traumatised by her wounds to speak properly. He stared hard at her throat, spotting the blood was thick and dark. He felt sick to his stomach.

How can she still be walking? She looks dead.

He closed in even more until reaching six feet away, carefully eyeing the woman as the red liquid spilt out of her mouth. But her vision glued onto his, teasing him into lowering his guard as a sadistic grin etched on her face.

"Do you need any assistance?" Frank asked, reaching out a hand to see her eyes follow it. "You've been hurt...I can drive you to the hospital."

He thought her weird behaviour had something to do with drugs and that's why she didn't feel the pain, but, after touching her cold hand, she snapped at him again, coming close to biting his arm. He stepped back, opening his eyes wide, feeling angry and shaken up from the surprise attack; his fingers tightening around the wheel lock. He tried working out if she was frightened because he was a stranger or she was just a mad lunatic, but either way, she was making him feel edgy.

"Hey! What's wrong with you?!" he blasted out. "I'm trying to help."

But his words just freaked the woman out.

She forcefully grabbed onto his denim jacket, attempting to bite him again, but he swiftly pushed an arm against her larynx to stop her from reaching him. Frank wrestled with her but she was strong, getting the upper hand, so he lifted the wheel lock to scare her. But she kept on snapping at him, slowly getting closer and closer.

Frank's endurance faded fast as the woman's strength increased. She spluttered and spat like a rampaging monster, scaring him to lower his weapon. But her teeth clamped onto his upper arm, ripping away the cloth to get to his flesh. He screamed in agony, pushing her off to see her eat it before slamming a hand over the wound; feeling the blood pushing against it to make him queasy.

"Who are you?!" he shouted, as his fast heartbeat pumped more leaking blood against his palm.

He cringed as he removed his soaked hand to grip the wheel lock, prying it from the wounded one to lift again, but a sharp pain shot through him.

"Right," he said, pouring with sweat. "You'd better fuck off before I hit you with this...You're a sick, twisted bitch..."

But the zombified corpse of Paula just walked towards him.

"...I mean it. If you don't move away now I'll smack your head so hard that it'll end up next to your arse."

The zombie snarled, shuffling closer and closer to frighten Frank even more, as the pain from the wound increased, spreading agonizingly through his body. He watched the zombie try to speak, but all it did was spit out blood every time it opened its mouth. But he was hypnotised by it and couldn't move. He closed his eyes, hearing the beast drag its feet as the droning increased. He knew he would be bitten again if he didn't do something fast, so, as the zombie lunged forward, it was stopped in its tracks by the wheel lock crashing down on its head. Frank opened his eyes to see the zombie's skull split open, reminding him of an egg being cracked into a frying pan as brain tissue and bone fragments slid down its face.

He dropped the lock after tearing up from thoughts of killing someone, as the corpse stared at him in shock before suddenly toppling to lay still on the road. He backed off and watched it for a few seconds as his wounded arm became numb; cringing as he slowly returned to the truck. He grabbed a first-aid kit, cringing again as he opened it; sweating fast as he reached for a bandage. He tightened it around the wound and gritted his teeth; sitting in the driver's seat to re-focus, but struggled to press his feet down on the pedals.

"FUCK!!!" he bellowed.

But he breathed deeply, soaked up the pain, and started the engine, driving the truck further along the road. Frank was exhausted, but the thought of reaching the police station before anyone found the body motivated him to carry on.

———

Frank pulled up outside the police station minutes later, struggling to move his left side as he almost fell out of the truck. He staggered from side to side; his vision blurry as he closed in on the main doors, mumbling out loud in the hope of someone hearing him. But no one was coming to help.

He neared the entrance, pleased to see the door slide open on its own to let him in; mustering up the energy to go inside as a receptionist and an officer raced towards him. They helped him to a seat whilst glancing at each other, shaking their heads and feeling confused as to what happened. But Frank was close to falling off the chair.

"Fetch this man some water," the officer said towards the receptionist. "I'll stay with him..."

But it took her a few seconds to move after witnessing the blood seep through the bandage.

"...That appears to be a nasty gash on your arm, mate," the officer said, returning to Frank to hold him upright. "What happened to you?"

But Frank's seventeen-stone frame became a struggle for the officer to keep seated.

"I need to see a doctor," Frank whispered, gritting his teeth. "The pain is too much. My arm feels like it's falling off."

"Okay, my friend," the officer calmly replied, seeing Frank clench his fists like he was being electrocuted. "I will take a look at your wound."

But the receptionist appeared with a glass of water to spook him. She handed it to Frank, but he couldn't grip it because his arms were too weak to lift, so, she placed the glass against his lips, seeing him rush the water down his throat.

"What's your name?" she asked, touching his head to feel it burn against her fingers. "You're safe here."

"Frank," he whispered, squinting each time his heart pumped blood into the wound. "I need help...I'm in agony."

The officer worryingly stared at the receptionist as he gripped Frank, smiling in an attempt to calm him down.

"Susan, I'm going to need the first aid kit."

"I'm on my way," she replied.

The officer watched the small, slim, spectacle-wearing woman race off again but Frank shook fast, scaring the officer into almost letting go. He quivered after seeing a puddle of water on the floor, looking up to notice sweat pour from Frank quicker now; feeling heartbroken for not knowing why?

"My name's Mike," he said, seeing Frank's jacket become drenched in blood. "Do you know what happened to you?"

Mike was the *Chief Inspector*. A kind-hearted, helpful man, who did his utmost to look after his staff and the residents of the town. When others fell apart around him, he would be the one who picked them up again. He'd proved it during the violence of last Christmas. He was recommended for an award for keeping the town together during that awful time.

Frank's breathing became heavy as he placed bloodied hands over his face. Mike heard tiny whimpers seep through the cracks in the fingers to almost make him want to cry.

"Tell me what happened to you," he said, looking around to see where Susan was. "Did someone attack you?"

Frank removed his hands, revealing red fingerprints on his face.

"Yeah," he rushed out of his mouth. "After I phoned - about an accident on the road."

"So, it was you who made that call," Mike replied, happy to be finally filling in the blanks. "My officers told me you'd run over someone, so who was it that attacked you?"

Frank squeezed his wound as more pain shot through him; shaking his head to splash sweat over Mike before coughing up blood.

"I don't know!" he yelled. "But they looked evil."

Mike let go before rising to his feet, turning in a circle to swiftly gaze around the station. He was in a state of panic - *Who did this?*

"Okay, just try to relax," he said, nervously gripping Frank's jacket to reach a hand inside. "This may hurt..."

But Frank screamed after Mike tried to release his good arm from the jacket.

"...Sorry, but I can't get to your wound unless I remove it."

"Forget about my wound!" Frank cried out, bursting into more tears. "You need to arrest me."

"Why?"

"Because I killed someone."

Mike stood back as everyone close by gulped. He knew they were staring at Frank. He could feel them.

"Do you mean the person you ran over?"

"No!" Frank shouted. "The person who attacked me..."

He held out his hands, feeling ashamed as he waited to be handcuffed, but Mike was still processing what Frank just said.

"...It was a woman and I fuckin' killed her."

Susan returned to witness Frank sink into the chair, as Mike took the first-aid kit from her.

"You took your time!" he angrily said, opening the kit. "This guy is in pain."

"Sorry, but I..."

"No excuses," Mike interrupted. "I know you were nattering again..."

Susan blushed.

"...Just speak to Wayne. Let him know the truck driver's here."

"Will do," she said, turning to leave.

"Also, tell him to check the roadside between where he spoke to the driver and up to here. There may be another body."

"And what about you? What will you be doing?"

Mike glared at her, knowing she was retaliating with questions because he'd upset her. But he wasn't going to let it get to him.

"I'm going to sort out Frank's arm, then take him to the hospital."

ELEVEN

Wayne stood with his phone against his ear, smiling as an ambulance and a police van stopped at the death scene. He nodded, listening to Susan on the other end of the phone before walking over to the opposite side of the road; glancing at *two officers* exiting the van. He watched them move towards the boot, lifting it before removing plastic cones and barriers; happy to see Jason help place them along the road.

"Mike wants us to check for more bodies?" Wayne questioned Susan, making sure he heard her properly. "Today is getting freakier and freakier...Tell him I'll be in touch once I've searched."

"Okay. Speak soon," she replied, as the phone went silent.

Wayne and Susan were a couple, but no one from the station knew about it. They had kept it a secret to avoid the negative comments aimed at dating someone from the workplace, but their romance was three months in. It began just after the Christmas tragedy when Wayne questioned her at the bank. She was one of the customers on that dreadful day. She'd seen the woman being killed, but Wayne couldn't take his eyes off her when they spoke. He felt responsible for her safety after that day so got her a job at the station, but his act of kindness nearly backfired when he found out she couldn't work a computer.

He smiled as thoughts of teaching her behind Mike's back floated inside his mind, knowing all those hours together had brought them closer. But, as he looked over at Jason lining up the final barrier, shook his head to concentrate on what Susan just said.

"Hey, J, we got another job. We need to go."

"And what's this one? We need to unravel an ancient Mummy before it strikes."

Wayne walked over to him, almost laughing as he neared.

"You are always the joker."

"Then what is it?"

"We need to look for another body."

Jason shook his head, cringing like he was expecting another trauma to arrive. He always said they would come in *threes*.

Wayne walked towards his car but stopped to check on the *paramedics* struggling to come to terms with the gruesome sight in front of them.

"I know. It took us by surprise also," he said, closing in.

"Who would hack someone to death like this?" one of the medics asked, coughing into his hand. "The poor woman never stood a chance."

"That's what we need to find out," Jason butted in to say. "But first we need to search for another body."

"Yeah, I thought I heard you mention it," the medic said, looking at Wayne. "Do we have a killer on the loose?"

"Nah, mate; the woman just fucked herself up before

sticking the glass in her head," Jason angrily blurted out. "What a dumb question."

"Hey! Hey! Hey!" Wayne shouted, dragging Jason away from the medic. "It's not helping...Let's just do our jobs...Okay?"

"Okay," Jason replied, punching thin air.

"The body has shaken me up," the medic said, watching his colleague retrieve a body bag from the ambulance. "Someone has been murdered near to where I live...What about my family? How do I know they're safe? Who is safe?"

"You need to keep it together," Wayne said, fearing the man was about to phone someone with the awful news. "Let's not panic, not yet...The other body could be a hoax."

"A hoax or not, I'm not happy with keeping this to myself."

"You have to." Wayne stared at the medic until he turned away, watching him grip the end of the body bag to place next to the corpse. "We will check the area. Just hang around in case we find something."

He received no reply, just grunts, as the medic helped his partner lift Amy's body into the bag before carrying her towards the ambulance.

————

A bloodstained figure was seen lying on the road as Wayne and Jason nervously exited the car to slowly walk towards it; gawping at the scarlet painting formed by the blood.

"Wayne, what's going on? This isn't normal."

Wayne puffed out his cheeks and cringed after glancing at the caved-in head of the corpse.

"No, it's not normal, but you need to stay focused…I don't want you losing it to the point of going off the rails again."

Wayne had seen Jason lose it in the past over a trivial thing that almost cost him his job, so knew something like this could send him over the edge. It worried him to think that Jason could lose control again.

"Hey, don't stress. I'm fine…Just everything's getting too bizarre, that's all."

"You'd better stay that way." Wayne smiled at him. "I'm letting the Chief know."

"What about the medics?"

"Them too."

Jason walked closer to the corpse, releasing his baton before bending down to examine the brain matter oozing out of the split skull. He placed his baton into it, watching it cling on to make him feel sick.

What was used to do this?

He looked along the road, spotting the wheel lock a few feet away; shaking his head to see it covered in sticky, dark, dried blood. He moved over to it as Wayne spoke to Mike on the phone before placing on a glove to pick it up, cursing under his breath at the sound of Wayne shouting - "What you got there?!"

"Proof that the truck driver's a fuckin' maniac," Jason replied, walking over to him.

"Do you seriously think he would drive to the station if he was a stone-cold killer?"

"I don't know…But he bashed this poor woman to a pulp with this wheel lock." Jason held it in the air to show Wayne the bloodstains. "I know she looks like something from a freak show, but he didn't need to smash her skull in. I hope he gets life behind bars…Mike better not let him out of his sight."

"I don't think he will. He's taken Frank to casualty. Said something about him being attacked by the person on the ground."

"The woman on the ground attacked him?" Jason questioned, pointing at the body. "The man is a beast compared to her. He's lying."

"That may be, but until we have the facts we can't assume anything."

"The law fuckin' sucks."

The ambulance pulled up to grab Jason's attention, stopping him from spurting out more words aimed at how bad the law was as the medics quietly exited. They seemed exhausted mentally as they opened up the back to retrieve another body bag before walking with their heads down towards the latest crime scene.

"I hope this is the last one," the other medic said, nervously gawping at the body. "This is doin' my head in." He dropped the bag onto the road and gripped the corpse's arms. "Did you know that the first corpse had been dead for over a week?"

"We figured," Wayne replied.

"But how? It couldn't walk if it was dead already."

"See!" Jason cried out. "Even the medics know something isn't right...That truck driver is insane."

"Yes, we all agree with you," Wayne spoke up. "But we weren't there when it happened so can't judge him yet."

"When can we judge him? When he kills more people?"

Wayne sighed as Jason's response shook him. He knew it all made sense, that Frank was somehow involved and his story was bogus. Wayne hoped Mike had seen through Frank's lies.

"Let's just get back to the station and leave these guys to it..."

Wayne saw the other medic grab Paula's legs before helping his partner put her inside the bag.

"...Remember what I told you," Wayne added, as the medics carried the bag towards the ambulance. "Just keep this to yourselves...Until we know more."

He watched them, waiting for a reply, but all he heard were grunts.

TWELVE

Vincent Smythe drove home after taking his dinner break at *1:00 pm*; happily parking his car in the driveway of his house to surprise Mary with some flowers. He exited and opened the front door, holding the flowers behind his back as he entered the house; shutting the door and turning to his right to face one of the entrances that led into the living room. He was close to touching the handle.

"I'd best put these in water first," he said, looking at the flowers. "Mary, I'm home. What have I got for lunch today?"

Vincent walked towards the kitchen, entering to stare at the closed door leading from it to the living room, surprised to not hear the TV or Mary talking to it. He scrunched his lips and walked towards the sink, leaning down to grab a *vase* from a cupboard whilst glancing several times at the door, but still, Mary never spoke. He shook his head and placed the flowers inside the vase, filling it with water, but a sudden feeling of dread washed over him.

She might've gone upstairs for a rest.

He put down the vase and went back the way he came

before walking up the stairs to enter his bedroom. But she wasn't there.

"Mary! Mary! Where are you?" he shouted, picking up speed.

He checked every room until the panic dug into him, now fearing she may have had a fall somewhere, so headed back down and rushed into the kitchen. But he suddenly stopped to glare at the garden.

"What's happened to my mother's grave?!" he shouted, noticing the back door slightly ajar. "I hope that noisy dog from next door isn't to blame."

He stepped outside, moving quickly along the garden, spurred on by a mix of fury and concern. But, as he reached the burial site of his mother was left shell-shocked to find just a coffin full of dirt.

Where is she?

Vincent sunk to his knees to drag the dirt to one side; desperately searching for his mother's body to feel a sharp pain of guilt wash over him.

"Mother, I'm here...You're safe now."

But his heart skipped a beat after finding no trace of her.

He didn't know whether to laugh or cry but did neither as he returned to his feet to brush the mud from his clothing, his face turning pasty white as sadness quickly arrived.

His head slumped as he slowly returned to the house to call out Mary's name again, but, after not receiving an answer, he glared at the wall that separated both houses. Vincent contemplated on whether to go around next door to complain about what their dog may have done but soon changed his mind after remembering what happened the last time he complained about Bruno. He'd received a load of verbal from the dog's owner which almost escalated in him being punched, so, thought it best if he let the police handle it.

He suddenly noticed dirty footprints on the kitchen floor tiles leading to the living room door; shaking his head at not spotting them before.

What's Mary playing at?

He cautiously walked towards the door before catching sight of the fallen saucepan, his mind melting to leave him more confused as he reached for the door handle. He sucked in a deep breath, hoping that Mary was inside the room, but, as he entered, stopped to stare at bloodstains covering the wall above the fireplace.

"Mary," he whispered, noticing the furniture had been rearranged.

He heard a noise coming from behind the sofa, increasing to make his ears twitch, so closed in as a strange sucking sound was heard. But he stalled as thoughts of being in the twilight zone made him nervous. He stared at the sofa, cringing as the sucking annoyed him; his heart pounding fast after a faint moaning arrived. But his anger motivated him to near it. He closed in with caution, kneeling on the piece of furniture before leaning over it, but almost puked after seeing a tiny, deformed figure with an eye dangling down hold a piece of a human brain within the only hand it had. It was biting and sucking on it, not worried that Vincent was hovering above.

He gulped hard; sweating from a sudden dose of fear after seeing the bloodied corpse of Mary with her face unrecognisable by his dead mother's side. He spat out sick after noticing the top of her head was missing, looking away to see the Stanley knife coated in red lying a few feet away. He froze, not able to think or do anything, but the zombie ignored him and sucked up more brain tissue.

Vincent snapped out of the shock and rushed out of the nearest door, slamming the front one behind him as he headed for his car. He opened it and sat inside before grabbing a mobile phone from the glove compartment, shaking at speed as he glared at his house to phone the police.

"I need help! My wife's been murdered," he frighteningly rushed from his mouth before the person on the other end could introduce themself. "Please come now."

"Can you give me your name and address? I'll send someone to you right away," Susan asked, shaking her head.

She was having a shift she wouldn't forget in a hurry.

Vincent's voice trembled, but Susan recognised who he was before he told her his name. She spoke in a soothing tone, hoping it would settle him down as it did with Frank, but she knew she'd have to tread carefully to prevent him from losing it completely.

"Okay, Mr Smythe, there'll be someone with you very shortly."

Vincent poured with sweat as he placed his feet on the newly paved driveway, ending the call to choke as his head spun. He was scared.

———

It took just a few minutes before a police car arrived on the scene, its siren attracting neighbours to emerge from their homes.

Don't they have anything better to do with their time? Wayne wondered as he exited the car.

He placed on his police issue cap, closing in on Vincent to notice him shake rapidly.

"What seems to be the problem?" Wayne asked, kicking himself because he already knew the answer. "You said your wife had been murdered. Is this true?"

But he cringed after hearing the neighbours talk amongst themselves, knowing they'd heard at least part of what he said.

One of them slowly moved closer, but the passenger door of the police car opened, spooking the person to return to the others.

Nash Hopkins was a nineteen-year-old, fresh-faced newbie to the force. He had only graduated a week ago, but here he was, starting his first shift with the Clifton Falls Police Department. He exited the car as a mix of nerves and excitement raced inside him, smiling at the nosey crowd standing nearby.

"How are we all today?" he calmly asked, taking everyone by surprise. "This is my first shift. I'm so excited."

"Hey!" Wayne hollered. "Get your mind on the job and keep those people back."

"No worries," Nash happily replied, shutting the car door.

Vincent rose from the seat but his legs buckled to leave him grabbing onto his car.

"Listen to me very carefully," he said, reaching out to grip Wayne's shoulder. "My wife's dead inside the house. Have you got that?"

"I got it."

Wayne hugged Vincent as Nash arrived, but he didn't know what to make of it all. He imagined it to be a twisted game concocted by Wayne to scare him on his first day, waiting on Vincent to suddenly burst out laughing, but he was crying into Wayne's shoulder to leave Nash freaked out. All he did was stare. He didn't know what else to do.

Vincent pulled away, wiping his face as he took another glance at the house.

"I never told this to the woman on the phone but my dead mother isn't dead anymore...She's inside and she killed my Mary."

His words left Nash in a trance as a flashback of him playing a zombie game raced through his mind.

"It's just fiction, right?" he nervously asked. "Dead people don't wake up again in the real world."

But Vincent scowled at him, making him feel uneasy.

"Go inside and take a look!" he snapped.

Wayne breathed deeply and shook his head. He knew Vincent was scared of something that was inside his house, something that could be similar to the person Frank hit with his truck, so needed Nash to focus.

"Okay," he softly said. "We need to get you out of the limelight before the neighbours start yapping again." He looked at Vincent, passing on a smile before adding, "Can you show us where it is?"

But Vincent gulped.

He looked to the ground in an attempt to avoid eye contact, hoping Wayne would let him stay where he was, but, deep down he knew he had to go back inside to clarify that the figure on the floor was indeed his dead mother and not an illusion.

"I don't want to but I know I need to do this," he said, nervously walking towards the front door.

Wayne turned to usher the neighbours away as Vincent opened it, but he wasn't going to be the first to enter. He stood aside, letting Nash walk by him, knowing he was pumped up with adrenaline to not give a shit about who? or what? was inside.

"My wife's body is in the living room," Vincent shakily said as Wayne entered the hallway. "And the killer was in there as well."

"Okay...Don't enter that room unless I say so," Wayne said, watching Vincent slowly enter the house to shut the door. "Just stay calm. We've got this."

Vincent nodded as he leaned against the door, releasing more sweat as he pointed at the living room entrance. He watched the others reach for their batons, cringing from the thought of them acting like it was just an everyday domestic, his eyes now glued to where they were standing as they prepared to enter the room.

"Nash, are you ready for this?" Wayne said, receiving a smile back. "It could get dangerous..."

But all Nash wanted to do was to get stuck in.

"...Use your taser if you need to."

Wayne touched a *firearm* strapped to his work belt, pleased to have it with him as he moved closer to the door. He knew it was a huge step for Mike to order his trained officers to carry one but, after what Wayne had seen recently going on in town he wasn't taking any chances.

Wayne nodded to Nash as Vincent came close to tears.

He almost sank to the floor as they opened the door. He quickly looked away as it closed to listen out for any noises; feeling angry that his walking stick wasn't resting against a nearby wall to use if the thing he saw attacked.

———

Wayne and Nash cautiously moved around the living room.

They saw the bloodstains on the wall as they neared the sofa, both were nervous as they reached it, but there was no sighting of Vincent's so-called dead mother. They gulped at the sight of Mary's body, almost vomiting to see her brain was missing, as a fetid aroma lingered beneath their nostrils to make them drowsy.

"What the F-," Wayne spat out, choking into his hand. "His wife stinks."

"I don't think it's coming from her," Nash replied, leaning down to smell the corpse. "I think something else is here."

———

Vincent knew he should stay by the front door but the silence coming from the living room caused his patience to fade fast. He moved towards the wall that split the two rooms and placed an ear against it, pulling faces as he listened out for anything before getting annoyed at how silent the officers still were.

He was close to barging into the room but the same foul stench wafted up his nose to stall him. He shivered after feeling stale breath on his neck, close to crying after the smell reminded him of his mother. He knew she was standing behind him but he couldn't speak or move. He hoped her reincarnated corpse would leave him alone but a sharp pain penetrated his left leg, causing him to fall to his knees. He saw her hideous body holding the blood-dripping Stanley knife, her dangling eye swinging to hypnotise him, stopping him from trying to escape. But, as he finally snapped out of it, the knife plunged to pop his orbs.

Vincent yelled out in pain as the zombie slobbered, its decayed gums showing as it licked the blade. But, as it was about to strike again, the officers rushed out of the kitchen entrance to grab its attention. They were gobsmacked to see it whine like a baby; the noise putting them off from making the first move.

"Help me!" Vincent hollered, as he struggled to breathe while spitting out the dark juice running down his cheeks and into his mouth. "It's blinded me."

Wayne noticed blood leaking out of Vincent's leg to form a puddle on the floor, but he wasn't given time to help because the zombie sliced the blade across Vincent's throat. He fell on his face as blood splashed over Nash, leaving him shaken up.

"Move away from him!" Wayne shouted, not sure if the knife-waving creature would obey. "Do it NOW!..."

But the zombie just stared at him whilst drooling over Vincent's head.

"...Release your taser," Wayne whispered, noticing Nash wasn't as cocky now. "You need to put it down..."

Nash breathed in deeply before taking it from his belt, sweating as he aimed it at the zombie. But it moved quickly towards him, swinging the blade close to his face to scare him into almost dropping the taser. Wayne quickly pushed the creature against a wall but backed away once it swung the blade again.

"...Let's move!" he shouted, pushing Nash towards the centre of the hallway. "What is that thing?"

"I have no idea."

The zombie growled, frightening them, causing them to stumble back and stand in the blood. It soaked into the soles of their boots, making them slip to almost topple over Vincent's body.

"We will put you down. Do you understand me?" Wayne's

stomach churned at the sight of the one-armed, one-eyed freak. "Drop the knife..."

But the zombie just glared at him.

"...Put it down," Wayne said, nudging Nash. "And do it now..."

Nash quickly fired the gun to leave the zombie doing a crazy dance, but it wasn't falling to the ground. It was just smiling at him.

"...Is that on full power?" Wayne asked anxiously.

"I don't know. I've not used these new models before."

Wayne checked the gun and noticed it wasn't.

"Press that button," he nervously said, pointing at it as the zombie overcame the blast. "It will increase the voltage."

So Nash did.

He laughed as smoke escaped out of the beast. Its body shook faster and suddenly lifted, flying into the kitchen to crash hard against a cupboard before dropping to the floor.

"What the fuck!" Nash yelled, turning the taser off. "That was insane."

"It sure was," Wayne replied, scrunching his face as he watched the creature. "But let's make sure it's dead before we jump for joy."

"You mean dead again..."

Wayne smiled.

He held up a hand before slowly entering the kitchen, nearing the corpse as Nash replaced his taser and followed.

"...I'm gonna check to see if the fucker's fully dead this time." Nash cautiously approached the deformed figure and kicked it, grinning at how lifeless it looked. "It's not breathing," he happily said, spreading his legs over the corpse before bending over to listen. "It's a-gonna for sure this time."

But, as he turned to look at Wayne again, the zombie's eye

reopened to glare at him. It gripped his testicles and squeezed hard, crunching them to the sound of him yelping like a kicked dog; its gums slapping together to freak him out as it hid behind him.

"Shoot it, Wayne, I'm begging you. Please shoot it," he pleaded, pulling and pulling to release the grip.

But it remained tight.

Wayne released his gun and aimed it, but the zombie made it difficult for him to shoot. It was like it knew what the weapon was used for so stayed hidden behind the shivering Nash, crunching harder on his manhood each time he tried to escape. Wayne cringed when Nash yelped again. He saw Nash desperately try to pull away to leave an angle for him to shoot the beast, but it was using Nash's body as a human shield.

"Use your spray!" Wayne shouted. "Spray the fucker in the face."

Nash tried reaching for the *CS spray* on his belt, shuddering and in tears after the zombie's face almost touched his. He could smell its foul breath stinging his skin.

"Don't kill me," he whispered, hoping to find some energy to escape.

But even though the tiny skeletal figure looked easy to push off, Nash still couldn't do it.

"Just move to one side so I can shoot it," Wayne said, shakily moving his gun. "I still can't see it."

Nash shook vigorously.

The zombie whined and ripped off his testicles, leaving blood gushing out to stain his trousers as his face turned pale. Wayne could only watch as Nash was thrown into the air to land on his back; his shocked eyes slowly hiding behind lids as his final breath arrived. Wayne almost collapsed after staring at the pool of life fluid surrounding Nash, knowing he would never forget it.

He leaned against the doorframe, not noticing the zombie rise off the ground until its dull moans were heard; turning to see it stagger towards him, hungry for his flesh. He wiped his head to feel sweat cling to him, shaking uncontrollably as he raised the gun, but the creature from the grave wasn't scared of it anymore. It picked up speed and snarled but Wayne fired his gun to send it crashing back to the floor; a bullet tearing a leg clean off. It looked stunned at not being able to rise again, but it kept on trying, snarling and snapping gums until Wayne fired a bullet into its head. He saw it collapse, slumping against the kitchen units; his vision zoning on it for the next minute while he took everything in.

He cried into his hands and walked back into the hallway, desperately trying to block the images of Nash's final moments as he opened the front door.

THIRTEEN

Hazel Knutts was a no-nonsense, straight-talking woman who was the head of the nursing department at Clifton Falls hospital. Respected by the staff for her experience and loyalty she was like a textbook when it came to patching up the injured, but right now she was struggling to work out what was wrong with her latest patient.

Frank was extremely weak and his legs were unable to take his weight as Hazel watched him being helped into a chair. She cringed at the amount of sweat dripping off his brow, stunned at how much pain he was in. She had many theories floating inside her brain of what may be the problem but knew she needed to remove the makeshift wrapping that Mike had put on before having a clearer picture. She smiled at Frank while unwrapping the blood-soaked bandage, but he didn't flinch. He just stared into nothingness. Hazel choked from the smell of the wound as the bandage fell to the floor, staring deeply at it as she shook her head.

"This doesn't look very pleasant," she said, smiling at Frank again. "It looks like you've been bitten..."

But Frank ignored her.

She placed a finger and thumb over the bite mark, feeling the area of discomfort; squeezing them together until a gooey liquid seeped out. It surprised her because she didn't recognise it. But, like the professional she was, she remained calm and reached for a test tube from a medical trolley.

"...This bite isn't from an animal," she continued, swabbing the liquid with a cotton bud. "I'm pretty certain it was caused by another human being but I've never seen anyone bite so deep into someone before." She shook her head as if disagreeing with her words, but the proof was right there. "This can't be right. It's not normal."

"It was a human," Frank raspily said, looking up to see her baffled expression. "A crazy person."

Hazel dropped the bud inside the tube and placed it onto the trolley, happy that Frank was at least focused as she moved away. But her smile faded to be replaced by sadness.

"Hold on," she softly said, pulling back the curtain surrounding the cubicle. "I'll be right back."

She left and walked over to where Mike was seated, seeing him sip coffee from a coffee-machine cup before pulling a horrid face.

"Don't drink that," she said, closing in. "I think it's gone off."

Mike grunted as he threw the drink down a nearby sink.

"Thanks for that," he said, looking over Hazel's shoulder. "How's he doing?"

"Not good, I'm afraid...Someone bit him..."

Hazel sat next to Mike to fiddle with her name badge. She often did it when something worried her.

"...And they bit him very deeply...The wound has become infected."

"Is that the reason behind his constant feverish appearance and lack of energy?"

"It surely has something to do with it." Hazel glanced at the floor, pressing the badge hard. "I found some form of puss inside the wound but I won't know more about it until I've had it analysed."

"Is there something you're not telling me?"

Hazel rose to her feet. She slowly stared into Mike's eyes, leaving him feeling a cold chill as she backed away.

"...What?" he said, exiting his seat to panic. "What's wrong with him?"

"I can't rule out rabies. Not yet anyway."

"Damn! ...He mentioned he was bitten by someone but he was in such a state. I couldn't tell if he was lying."

"He wasn't lying...Whoever bit him was either completely insane or had possibly contracted the rabies virus from another source...Frank will have to remain here for further tests."

"And what if he's got it?"

"Let's hope he hasn't...If he has then he'll have to be isolated." Hazel walked back towards the cubicle. "Just be ready. You may have your hands full trying to sort this problem out."

She pulled back the curtain again but was left shocked after seeing Frank's body become soaked. He was convulsing rapidly like he was having some type of a fit; his legs kicking out at the trolley to almost topple it over. But Hazel was quick to move it to one side before the sample dropped to the floor. She reached out to hold him, wincing at not being able to help.

"*Gary, Julie!*" she yelled. "I need your help!..."

A tall, thin, experienced male nurse and a petite, dark-haired, teenage female trainee raced from the next cubicle to see Hazel struggling to keep Frank still.

"...Julie, grab a wheelchair. Gary, you help me with Frank."

Julie shook as she darted off to find one, as Gary quickly bear-hugged Frank to stop him from falling out of his chair.

"...I need you to take him to the isolation testing room, but be gentle. He's extremely poorly," Hazel said, feeling Frank's sweat on her.

Gary nodded as Julie returned with a wheelchair.

She helped him escort Frank into it, shaking her head because she had no idea what was happening. Hazel watched them wheel Frank out of the cubicle, but his sad face made her heart feel like it was being ripped apart to bring tears to her eyes. She mostly got this way because she cared for the patients. She'd always urged her staff to treat them in a considerate manner when wheeling them around, so hoped Gary would be considerate enough not to race Frank through the hospital like a driver at a Grand Prix.

She wiped her eyes as Mike closed in.

"What's happening to him?"

Hazel's head spun as she attempted to speak, but all she could vision was poor Frank becoming weaker and weaker. She heard Mike ask again so knew he cared just as much.

"He desperately needs those tests done. I'm worried about him." Hazel gathered herself before adding, "If he hasn't contracted the rabies virus then I need to know what he has contracted from that bite...In the meantime, anyone who has been in close contact with him needs to take a blood test. And that includes both of us."

She shuddered after screams echoed down the corridor to

frighten patients inside other cubicles before shrugging to see a frantic Julie race in her direction shouting words that made no sense.

"Come quickly! We need help with the patient. He's in a lot of pain."

"All right, calm down. I will give him some pain relief."

Hazel nodded towards Mike as she disappeared down the corridor with Julie, leaving him lost as another scream penetrated his eardrums.

————

Gary tried restraining Frank as the nurses entered the testing room, but Frank was consistently twitching violently, his hands swinging, slapping Gary in the face. He jumped back, holding his mouth to see Frank break down in tears, the pain now too much for him. He needed some form of sedative and he needed it now.

Julie raced over to him holding a wet sponge. She placed it on his brow in an attempt to cool him down, but Frank was yelling angrily, scaring her. Hazel rushed to a medical trolley to reach for a needle, but Frank let out a final scream before she had time to inject him. He grimaced as a tear slid down his face before keeling over to flump on the floor; his breathing gone to leave the others in shock. Hazel kneeled next to him in a frantic attempt to restart his heart. But it wasn't to be, it'd shut down for good. She puffed out her cheeks, breathing fast after feeling emotional, slowly returning to her feet to stare at Frank's body. She was normally used to this kind of trauma but sometimes sorrow crept up on her, affecting her as it did the first time she saw death.

She turned to comfort Julie after hearing her sob into her palms whilst Gary stood over the body.

"Hey love, these things happen in hospitals."

"I've never witnessed anyone die before," Julie sadly replied, sniffing. "It's shocking...It was very sudden and it freaked me out."

"I know, but you have to be ready for the unexplainable in this job." Hazel watched Julie dry her eyes. "I need you and Gary to take Frank to the morgue. Do you feel okay to do this?..."

Julie nodded.

"...Good...I need to talk to the officer now so please stay strong."

———

Hazel sluggishly walked back to Mike, leaving him sensing something wasn't right.

"What's happened?"

"He didn't make it," she raced out of her mouth. "We never stood a chance to save him...His heart just caved in." Hazel gulped as she fought back tears. "His body will need to be examined. Hopefully, we will find an answer."

"Where's the body now?"

"On its way to the morgue."

"I'm sure you did your best for him," Mike softly said, reaching out to hold her.

But she backed off swiftly before shouting, "My best! My best wasn't good enough!"

Mike realised she wasn't looking for a shoulder to cry on. She was just letting off some steam.

"You're not to blame for this. You do know that?"

Hazel glanced at him and calmed down. She apologized for her outburst but Mike just smiled at her.

"Hey, it's okay. I would've probably done the same thing, lashed out at someone."

"But it's not very professional."

"What's professional after seeing someone die?"

Hazel smiled.

"...I need to track down Frank's next of kin," Mike said, hoping his words didn't upset her. "Someone needs to check his clothing for anything useful, like pictures, addresses, phone numbers."

"I'll do it for you."

Hazel was off again before Mike could reply; her head back in the game to find an answer as to why Frank died.

FOURTEEN

Mike walked around the hospital as he waited for Hazel to return with Frank's details, checking the time on his watch to see it was now *2:30 pm*. He entered the public *cafeteria* to see a drained-in appearance Wayne sitting at a table with his hands wrapped around a hot drink, wondering why he never said he was on his way to the hospital.

"Hey," Mike said, approaching him. "You look like shit... What happened at the house?"

Wayne took a sip from the cup and shook his head, shivering as he attempted to speak.

"Sorry for not letting you know what was going on."

"It's okay." Mike sat next to him. "But something did happen. I can tell...What was it?..."

Wayne gulped as he looked around him.

"...Where's Nash?" Mike asked, feeling his heart beat faster.

"He's here."

"Thank fuck for that." Mike's breathing slowed down again. "He's not chatting up the nurses is he?"

Wayne gulped again as a tear dripped down his face.

"He's dead, Mike," he whispered, shivering more constantly as he held back more tears.

"How? Why? And how come you didn't call it in?"

"I wanted to, really I did, but I just couldn't do it." Wayne puffed out his cheeks and took another sip. "It all happened so fast...There was something in that house. It looked partly human but had the strength of ten men...It killed Nash and the Smythes."

Mike cringed as a sick feeling grew inside of him.

"When did this happen?"

"About thirty minutes ago. I've been here ever since the bodies were brought in...I feel ashamed for letting it happen."

"Don't blame yourself."

"I was in charge!" Wayne yelled. "Everything that went on in that house was down to me, but I fucked up big time...I had a gun. I should've put that thing down sooner but I wasn't courageous enough...I am responsible for two deaths."

Mike's heart melted from the words. He wasn't prepared for it, to hear such a terrible account, but he needed his second-in-command to stop torturing himself and to re-focus.

"Take a break to get yourself together," Mike said, glancing at an employee inside the cafeteria. "I know you need one."

But Wayne was losing his nerve and the employee noticed.

"I've taken a break but the horror from that house is still inside my head, eating at my brain." Wayne stared into emptiness as though he could see something only he knew was there. "I keep seeing the beast with the evil eye. It was like some sort of Cyclops...It slaughtered them both and then tried to kill me."

"You need to calm down before someone passes by and hears you. I can't have news getting out that the people of this town are coming under attack by something we don't know about...There'll be chaos everywhere."

"But chief...If we don't warn the people about the danger then we may have a massacre on our hands. We just can't risk keeping it quiet."

Mike rose from his seat. He smiled at the employee before placing a hand on Wayne's shoulder, leaning over to whisper, "I know you're upset but we don't know for sure if any more of those weird people or whatever you call them are still around. You may have killed the last one."

"I'm not too sure about that," Wayne replied, feeling angry inside. "You've seen the truck driver. Something freaked him out and it wasn't what was inside that house."

"Just trust me on this...We don't need a full-scale riot of frightened people on our hands when we don't know for sure what's causing this, so please, let's keep this hush-hush until we're certain that this town is in critical danger."

"You're in charge," Wayne replied, still feeling reluctant to agree. "Let's hope for everyone's sake that you're right."

Mike knew he was alone on the recent choice he'd made but knew Wayne would keep his mouth shut. He moved away from the table, ushering Wayne to follow him as he slowly left the cafeteria.

"Come with me. I need to speak to the head nurse who treated Frank."

"And how's he doing?"

"He's also dead," Mike bluntly replied, picking up speed along a corridor. "I think he was poisoned."

"How?"

"The bite...Whoever bit him may have had it in their saliva."

"That's a little far-fetched don't you think." Wayne caught him up as they turned a corner. "The person who bit him was some type of snake?"

"I don't know, but today is throwing us some fucked up curveballs, that's for sure."

They arrived at an elevator and went inside before Mike pressed a button with the word *'morgue'* written on it.

"Oh, before I forget," he said, watching the door close before buttons lit up on the wall. "You're gonna need a blood test."

"Why? ...I hate those things."

"I know, but the nurse wants to be sure that the people who came into contact with Frank haven't caught anything from him."

"Makes sense." Wayne breathed deeply as the elevator came to a stop. "I'll get one done."

"And Susan needs to get one. She was with me when Frank came into the station."

Wayne raised his eyebrows as he stepped out of the lift.

FIFTEEN

Karen stood inside Vincent's office as a police officer exited, feeling shocked as she wiped her teary eyes with a tissue. She couldn't believe the news about Vincent, that he was dead. She gathered herself and reached for her phone, scrolling down to find Blake's number as another tear fell; shaking after hearing him say – "*Hello.*"

He knew something was wrong as soon as she spoke because her words raced out of her mouth faster than a machine gun firing bullets. She always spoke fast when upset over something but Blake struggled to make head or tail of what she said.

"Calm down and say that again," he said shaking his head. "What's happened to the Smythes?"

"Something awful has happened," Karen replied, blowing her nose. "I've just had a policeman here telling me they're dead...But that can't be true. Can it?"

Blake scratched his head before waving to Todd as he was about to leave his office.

"Tell me again what the officer told you."

"He said they were dead and I was down as a contact in case of an emergency."

"Dead...How?"

"I don't know, Blake, I'm too shaken up to think about it... But he mentioned an accident at their home."

"An accident? Those two? Doesn't make sense."

" I keep telling myself that. They were so precise. They never did anything dangerous...I can't get my head around it."

"It's okay, babe," Blake softly said, glancing at a pile of paperwork on his desk. "So, did the officer tell you to identify the bodies?"

"Yes," Karen replied, sniffing down the phone. "But I don't think I'm ready to do it."

"I'll come now and pick you up...We'll get to the bottom of it."

Karen shivered again as she ended the call.

She left the office to be hugged by staff members, feeling thankful that the officer had spoken loud enough for them to hear.

———

Blake knew Karen would be staring out of a window, eagerly waiting for him to arrive, so parked up and honked the car horn, checking his watch to see ten minutes had passed since the phone call. He saw her rush out of the bank, approaching the car to sadly whine as the passenger side door opened. But, as she sat in the seat her whining stopped to be replaced by a sudden urge to check out the car's interior.

"This isn't your car," she said, holding a set of furry dice attached to the windscreen. "Whose car is it?"

"I've borrowed it from Todd." Blake sensed she was

distracting herself so as not to think about the hospital. "He took my advice and bought a car just like mine."

"I forgot you didn't like to drive to work." Karen let go of the dice and attached the seatbelt. "I could've picked you up."

"You sounded very low when you called me so I didn't think you'd be up for it," Blake said, frowning as he started the engine. "Are you ready to do this?"

Karen shrugged.

———

They entered the hospital to see it had just turned *3:00 pm*, feeling on edge as they neared the reception desk. The *receptionist* smiled at them, looking to Blake, then to Karen as she waited for one of them to speak, but neither could do it. It was as if they'd forgotten why they were there.

"Excuse me. Can I help you?"

Blake and Karen sadly glanced at each other, shrugging their shoulders like one was expecting the other to talk, but, as the receptionist spoke again, Karen quickly turned to her.

"Yes, sorry," she said, placing her hands on the desk. "I was told to come here to identify the bodies of my boss and his wife."

"Okay," the receptionist calmly replied, glancing over at Blake. "Can you tell me their names? And I'll find out if someone can speak to you."

Karen trembled as she gave out the information. She felt unsure about going through with it until Blake placed an arm around her shoulders.

"You've got this," he said, looking deep into her eyes. "I'm here for you."

He kept Karen close as the receptionist checked the names

on the computer, but her face glowed red within seconds. She checked the names, again and again, feeling uneasy as Blake watched her. But, after the fourth attempt, she stopped.

"The computer says 'no'," she said, chuckling nervously.

But Blake didn't find it funny.

"My wife is traumatised," he said, slamming a fist onto the desk. "So why are you performing a gag from a comedy sketch?"

The receptionist gulped and looked to the floor, feeling stupid for her childish humour.

"I'm so sorry," she pleaded. "I've had a long shift...It's been hectic here."

"It's okay," Karen said, smiling. "We just want to know if we can see them."

"Are you sure they were taken to this hospital?" the receptionist asked, checking the computer again. "I can't find them on the system."

Blake stood back as anger brewed inside him.

"Look! My wife was told they were in an accident and the nearest hospital is here, so maybe your computer is wrong?..."

The receptionist wasn't coping as Blake glared at her. She looked from left to right, hoping to see someone of authority, feeling shell-shocked by Blake's sudden outburst.

"...Can you get someone for us?" he asked, cooling down. "Preferably someone who knows what the *fuck* is goin' on."

"Come on Blake," Karen said, shaking her head at him. "There's no need to swear. She's only doing her job."

"A blind monkey can do it better," Blake replied, glaring again.

The receptionist breathed a sigh of relief after spotting Wayne close in but she grimaced when he headed for the main door.

"Hello!" she shouted, hoping to grab his attention. "Are you free?"

Wayne stopped after hearing her shout again, turning to see her wave at him like a crazy fan before sighing at being so close to reaching the outside.

"What seems to be the problem?" he asked her, slowly walking towards the reception desk. "I was just popping outside for some fresh air."

He noticed the circles of crimson on her cheeks, so guessed she'd been put on the spot over something. He smiled at the married couple, even though he didn't have a clue why he was there.

"Do you know anything about a Mr and Mrs Smythe? They were brought in earlier."

"Why? Who wants to know?" Wayne asked, figuring it to be the couple standing beside him.

The receptionist pointed at them.

"Is there a private room we can use?"

"Yeah, sure," she said, feeling confused. "You can use the one to the left of you."

Wayne nodded and walked off, leaving Blake and Karen to awkwardly follow.

"What's goin' on?" Blake asked, catching him up. "We need answers."

"I'll answer all your questions but let's move away from prying eyes first."

Blake turned, seeing the receptionist closely watching on before the sound of a door opening grabbed his attention. He saw Wayne enter the room to usher him inside but, as he did, noticed Karen had stopped in the doorway. She was shivering again.

"It's okay, love. We need to do this," Blake said, knowing she was worried at the thought of being told the awful news.

She breathed deeply and entered the room before shutting the door to stare at Wayne, noticing beads of sweat form on his brow.

"You were there, weren't you," she softly said, reaching out for Blake to hold her. "Inside their house."

Wayne shuddered after the words took him back to the nightmare; his mind exploding as images resurfaced.

"Take a seat," he said, pointing to some chairs. "What I'm about to tell you isn't pretty."

"I don't want to take a seat. I just want to know what happened to them and to identify their bodies. As I was told to do."

Wayne knew he couldn't say too much, especially something resembling the truth. He had to stick with what Mike asked him to do, but Karen's sad face was making it hard for him. He knew she worked at the bank with one of the deceased because he was one of the officers assigned to that murder case a few months ago, so didn't want to upset her by keeping something from her. But he knew Mike was right. It was too risky.

"I take it you were down as a next of kin."

"We're not related...I was just told to come here to identify them."

"Look, officer," Blake interrupted, gripping Karen tight. "My wife was told that her name was on a list of contacts. That's all. But I still don't believe it's real. That something happened to them."

"If I could give you a positive answer I would," Wayne said, hopelessly trying to smile. "But I can't."

"So, what happened to them?" Blake asked, hoping

Wayne wasn't going to go into too much detail. "It just sounds a bit odd to me."

"There was nothing odd about it...They were involved in an accident at home...That's all I know."

Karen shook her head after seeing Wayne look to the floor. She knew he was keeping something back.

"Why does it look like you're holding information from us," she said, removing herself from Blake. "I know you were there. I can feel it."

Wayne closed his eyes for a second and gulped. He had one major flaw and that was convincing people he was telling the truth when he was lying. He knew it was a problem but he still needed to stick with his story. He'd come too far to crack up and blurt out the facts.

"I'm sorry," he sadly said, shrugging his shoulders. "It was just a terrible accident."

"Did they feel any pain?"

Wayne shook as Karen watched him closely.

"No...It was quick."

Karen's eyes welled up but she didn't cry. She just breathed loudly and slumped into a chair.

"What kind of accident?" Blake asked, sitting next to her. "I can't think of anything going wrong for them inside their home, never mind killing them."

"Look, I know you have a million questions to ask me but I don't know how they died."

"Are we able to see them now?"

"I will need to check first but it shouldn't be a problem..."

Wayne silently hoped that Blake had run out of questions because any more could leave him on the brink of slipping up.

"...Just stay here until then," he said, walking towards the door. "I will ask my chief to have a word with you. Maybe he can explain how they died?"

Wayne opened the door and left the room, walking back to the receptionist as she put down the phone.

"I've got a job for you," he said, pointing towards where he'd just come from. "Can you keep an eye on the couple?"

"Yeah, sure," the receptionist eagerly replied. "Anything you say, officer."

"Oh, and take them some food and drink."

"Anything else?" she asked, smiling.

"Just one more thing. If any reporters come sniffing around, don't tell them where the couple are. You got that?"

"Sure. I got it."

Wayne knew the press could show up to pester the husband and wife very soon so needed them to stay hidden. It was only a matter of time before the deaths of the people inside the house and the ones on the road got reporters sniffing for clues. They were probably already gaining stories from the people who were outside the house of horror at the time of the killings. They may not have seen anything but they sure as hell would've heard something.

"I'll leave it with you," Wayne said, walking away.

———

He entered the morgue room to find Mike talking to *Colin*, a short, bald, middle-aged man who was the head of the department. He stood back, listening to the men discuss the identities of the corpses like it was a game of 'Guess Who?' before spotting Mike holding a driver's license. He assumed it belonged to Frank but neither man discussed how he died.

He looked beyond the chatting pair to see bodies

sprawled out on tables, feeling sick to his stomach by how gruesome most of them looked. He stared at Frank's corpse, shaking his head in disbelief at how the man suddenly died not long after he'd spoken to him, rubbing his chin and feeling lost from thoughts of the man running down a body before being attacked by another.

"Did you know you had a patch of blood on your head," Wayne said, staring at Colin. "Looks like a friggin' tattoo."

Colin looked at his blood-spattered hospital coat, sighing at how much whiteness was left.

"Do I?" he replied, not caring about it. "I get so carried away in my work that I fail to notice most of the time..."

He took a handkerchief from his top pocket, spitting on it before dabbing it across his head, smirking as he walked over to the tables.

"...I am baffled by these," he said, touching a limb belonging to the torn-apart body of Rodney Wilson. "Looks like someone went through the person with a chainsaw."

"Yes, the poor sod," Mike replied, closing in. "If you have any questions then talk to Wayne. He was involved in most of the events involving those corpses today."

Colin nodded.

"Sure...I'll tell you what I know," Wayne said, fidgeting as Colin picked up a piece of Rodney's skull.

"I can't wait to hear this," Colin replied, noticing Wayne refocus on Mike.

"The woman from the bank, the one who was told to come here to identify her boss' body wants to have a few words with you."

"Don't tell me you felt guilty about lying to her," Mike said, shaking his head. "You won't go to hell you know."

Wayne shrugged. "You know it's not my thing, chief."

"I know...So, what did you tell her?"

"That his wife and he were involved in an accident at their home."

"Damn! And you need me to elaborate on that?"

"Yes." Wayne patted him on the back. "You did say not to mention the truth...So, let's see you come up with something believable."

Mike sighed before slowly walking away to leave the room.

"Go on, do tell," Colin excitedly said, pointing at the tables. "What did happen to make the corpses look like this?"

"You probably won't believe me but one of them attacked two of the others."

"So what...People attack people all the time. That's nothing new."

"Even if the person had been dead for six months?"

"Fuck! No way! You mean the stinking corpse that got run down by the truck was responsible?"

"Not that one," Wayne said, pointing at the half-blown-away skull of Vincent's mother. "That one did it."

"If that's true," Colin happily replied, wiping a bloodied hand across his face. "Then we may be dealing with the living dead...You know, walking zombies." He held out his hands and groaned. "That'll explain the bitemark on the truck driver."

"You think he was bit by a zombie?"

"You tell me? What did you think when you saw the thing on the table attack someone?"

"I don't know," Wayne awkwardly replied. "It all happened so fast. There wasn't time to think."

"You have plenty of time to think now...You know I'm

right...If we don't get to the bottom of this soon then the whole town could become infected." Colin grabbed onto Wayne, snapping his teeth together. "Who else knows the truth?"

"No one because zombies don't exist...It's just made-up nonsense... You've been reading too many horror comics."

"Is it? How'd you know? What other answers have you come up with?"

The questions flew from Colin's mouth quickly to leave Wayne puzzled. He couldn't believe what he was hearing, that Colin was so easily taken in by the story, but his words sounded so convincing that Wayne began to consider them.

"Damn! You may be right...I'd best let the chief know."

Colin burst out laughing. "I'm playing with you...If you tell Mike zombies are real he will have a heart attack."

Wayne scratched his head and stared at the corpses.

———

Mike watched Karen and Blake closely as he waited for one of them to speak. But they seemed to have gone all shy.

He sat down and poured a glass of water, gulping it down quickly before placing the glass on the table; bracing himself for what was to come.

"I was told you had questions for me."

"What happened to them?" Karen asked, squinting. "What seriously happened to them?"

Mike nodded. He knew she was on the verge of collapsing from not knowing the truth.

"Well, when Mr Smythe returned home on his lunch break, he noticed his wife was sprawled out on the kitchen floor. She'd been electrocuted by an appliance in the room.

But, unknown to him, the electric charge was still running through her body."

"Damn!" Blake hollered after being taken by surprise. "I would never have guessed it to be that."

"And he was also electrocuted?" Karen sadly asked.

"I'm afraid so...He bent down to touch her but the charge ran through his body, causing him to have a coronary."

"Wow! It was one hell of a freak accident," Blake said, pouring himself a glass of water. "I'm going to need more than this to drink when I go home."

Karen shook Mike's hand, thanking him for his honesty.

SIXTEEN

All was silent again inside the house next door to the Smythes' as *Sid Gilbert* stood inside his kitchen, feeling guilty for his angry outburst when Mary was being murdered. He wished he hadn't slammed on the wall to tell her to be quiet.

He stared out the window and smiled at Bruno in the backyard lying face down in the kennel, waiting for his loyal dog to look up at him. But Bruno wasn't moving, so he tapped on the glass.

"Betty, do you know what's up with the dog? He's not touched his food."

Betty Gilbert entered the room with annoyance plastered on her face, glaring at Sid to make him frown. He knew she was about to kick off with him again. There wasn't a day that went by when they didn't argue over something, and Sid was convinced she did it on purpose. It was like some love-hate thing with her, something she preferred over an actual conversation.

She closed in to stare at Bruno as curiosity took over, but within seconds she was back to glaring at Sid.

"How the hell should I know what's up with him? Do I look like a bloody vet?!" she shouted, as Sid backed away. "Did you give him that cheap food again?"

"No," Sid replied, whimpering. "I gave him the good stuff."

"I know you feed him shit so you can use the extra cash for your gambling habit...I watch you, Sid. I'm always fuckin' watching you."

Sid backed away some more as he imagined her blasting out flames like a dragon; almost laughing to make Betty furious.

"What's so fuckin' funny?"

"Nothing...I was just wondering when you would give me grief today...I was only asking about the dog."

"Whatever!" she yelled, walking back towards the door she came through. "The next time you want to ask a question, ask one I can answer. You thick twat..."

Betty had a way of manipulating Sid and knew which buttons to press, but it was her swearing that upset him the most. He'd told her many times to not do it, especially in front of the children, but Betty sometimes slipped up when they were around before punishing Sid for making her do it.

"...I get more sense out of the kids than from you...Why do you always try to make me look stupid?"

"I don't need to try," Sid said with a grin, hearing the children coming down the stairs. "You are stupid."

He waited for Betty to blow a fuse, knowing she was ready to, but the sight of the children racing into the room stopped her. She shook her head at Sid and scowled before breathing in deeply to compose herself; smiling at the kids closing in to hug her.

"Look," she said, grabbing Sid's attention. "If Bruno's off his food then he's probably just tired or something...Just phone the vet if he's still the same later."

Sid nodded as he glanced outside again, but he frowned when Bruno still wasn't raising his head.

———

Betty stood by the kitchen sink peeling potatoes, glancing at the clock to cringe because it was now *4:00 pm*. She hated not having dinner prepared by a certain time. She had a ritual and that was eating dinner by *4:30 pm*, so was now peeling potatoes at speed whilst cursing under her breath because Sid had made her angry again.

He watched her, knowing she was losing her cool, but he didn't say a word as he looked out of the window again. He saw Bruno slowly lift his head but his bloodshot eyes and frothy mouth caused Sid to gulp hard.

"What's wrong with you now?" Betty asked, peeling another potato. "The dog will be fine."

"I don't know about that," Sid sadly replied, pointing at Bruno. "He looks ill...Take a look."

Betty brushed his attempt at grabbing her attention away, thinking he was going over the top. She knew Sid exaggerated over mostly everything just to annoy her so wasn't falling for his frantic behaviour.

"I'm doing the bloody dinner!" she snapped, dropping the peeler into a bowl. "I haven't got time to check on him. I'm already behind on my schedule."

"You and your goddamn schedules...Just take a look."

Betty grimaced and nibbled her lip before snatching a tea towel to wipe her hands.

"I told you already. If he's ill then fetch the vet in...It's that simple."

"Where's the number for the surgery?"

"It's on your phone, under V for vets."

"Stop being sarcastic, you mad cow. This is an emergency."

Sid sweated as he stared at the dog again, seeing the froth form into a liquid beard to scare him. He moved away from the window and aimed for the back door, shivering as he reached for the handle.

"Where are you going? Aren't you calling the vet?"

Sid stopped and nodded before opening the door. "Yes, but Bruno needs me first."

He left the house and walked towards the kennel, closely watching Bruno in the hope he would get up. But the dog just lay with its head on the ground, staring at Sid like he was a stranger.

"Hey, boy. I'm gonna get you some help..."

Sid closed in to hear a faint moan, fearing Bruno was struggling to breathe. But the dog slowly rose to stop Sid in his tracks.

"...Bruno, what's wrong, boy?..."

The dog snarled, showing fangs before barking loudly; frightening Sid to almost trip over as he retreated towards the door.

"...Bruno. It's me...What's wrong with you?"

But the dog wasn't recognising his voice.

It growled again and again until Sid reached the house. He raced inside, slamming the door shut behind him before turning to see Betty stare at Bruno.

"Jeez! Sid. What did you do to him?"

"I did nothing to him," he nervously replied, breathing heavily. "He's just gone mental."

Sid placed sweaty hands onto her face but she freaked out, pushing him away before choking violently into her hand.

"You filthy animal. Your hands stink!" she yelled, pushing him again until he quivered by the sink. "You're starting to worry me, Sid. Why is Bruno making weird noises?"

The low drone from Bruno's growls sent shivers down Betty's spine as she plucked up the courage to look out of the window again. But, after seeing Bruno cough up congealed blood she quickly looked away.

"Sort out your dog!" she snapped, feeling her stomach churn over. "And do it now before the kids see."

"But he doesn't seem to recognise me anymore." Sid grabbed his phone, squirming after more drones drilled into him. "This isn't right...I'm phoning the vet."

"You do that...I'll tell the kids to stay upstairs."

Sid watched Betty race out of the room as Bruno sniffed and scratched the bottom of the back door; the noises now panicking Sid until more sweat poured out of him.

"It's okay, boy," he whispered, dialling a number as he walked towards the door. "I'll make you better."

He held the phone away from his ear as he listened out for more noises, but it was now too silent, leaving him guessing where his dog was. He sighed as he returned to the window, feeling sad to find Bruno wasn't to be seen.

"Damn!" Sid shouted, hearing a voice on the phone.

He placed it to his ear, calming down to describe the condition of the dog, but, as he leaned over a worktop to get closer to the window, his heart pumped hard against his chest. He listened to what the *vet* had to say but the words – *stay inside* - worried him.

"Okay, got it," Sid responded, gulping after glancing outside again.

"I'll let my family know."

But Betty raced back into the room to startle him.

"Where's your dog!" she screamed, close to crying. "I can't see him outside."

She opened a drawer and reached for a knife, releasing tears as she held it like she was about to attack; her eyes sore as Sid swiftly ended the call.

"Wooh! Love!," he hollered, taking the knife from her. "Keep calm...The vet's on his way with the police."

"But what about the people outside?" Betty shivered. "Bruno has to be out front. Someone will see him..."

Sid raised his hands as if not sure of what to say, muttering under his breath as he dazedly walked in a circle. And it freaked Betty out.

"...Come on Sid...What are you going to do?"

He stared at her and puffed out his cheeks, panicking to the point of hiding. But Betty's glare stopped him.

"...Sid, you need to do something...Be a man for once..."

She watched him race into the next room, curious to know more; smiling after seeing him flip open the staircase closet to remove a putter from a golf bag. But Sid was close to putting it back again.

"...What?" Betty nervously asked. "Are you worried because you may have to use it?..."

But Sid wasn't talking. He was just staring at the putter in his hand.

"...I know you don't use it for golf so you may as well use it for something else...You're always at the casino...I know, Sid...I know what you get up to. You pretend to play golf."

Sid closed the closet door, raising the putter like some macho man defending his family from an intruder as Betty's moanful words washed over him. But he knew she was right. He did need to do something.

"But what if Bruno goes for me?" he asked, frowning. "I don't think I can strike him."

"Not even if he goes for the kids?"

Sid slowly shook his head. He glanced up the stairs, close to tears as he gripped the putter tight.

"I'll go look for the dog...You stay here and watch the kids."

Betty smiled, touching his arm as he aimed for the front door.

———

Betty placed the potatoes on the stove, feeling anxious after not hearing back from Sid. She turned quickly to the sound of a police siren blasting outside her house, slowly relaxing to control her breathing as thoughts of Bruno being found made her smile. But something scraping against the window spooked her. She looked outside to see Bruno standing on his hind legs scratching nails against the glass; his bloodshot eyes scaring her to fall back into a table before looking away. But, after finding the courage to look again, saw that the dog was gone.

She felt nauseous as she clutched a chair, her knees trembling after a reminder of seeing Bruno shook her, but, as she slowly moved away from the table she saw him race towards the window, crashing through it to shower broken glass over her. Betty swiftly raised her arms to protect her face but cringed after a sharp pain shot through her, her eyes opening wide from intense fear at seeing glass sticking out of her arms. She quivered at the sight of Bruno vomiting up blood, close to fainting as he licked it up again.

Sid raced into the kitchen, followed by the *vet* and *two officers*, but they stopped after shrilling growls scared them. They saw Bruno move from side to side, shaking his head at everyone as if deciding on who to attack; showing teeth before sniffing the floor.

"Are you okay?" Sid nervously whispered, seeing blood drip off Betty's arms. "Just don't move."

She nodded, but Sid knew she wasn't okay.

The officers reached for *tasers* while Sid stupidly raised the putter; sweating fast again as he shouted at Bruno. He hoped his voice would make the dog back off, but it growled more fiercely.

"Betty, I love you," Sid rushed from his mouth, swinging the putter until it broke a ceiling light. "I won't let you come to harm."

"You silly fool. I love you too," Betty shyly replied, backing into a corner. "Now sort your dog out."

The officers pointed the tasers at Bruno as the vet stayed behind them, but his face turned pale once the dog glared at him. He pushed the officers to do something but they were shaking from fear, their movement slow as they watched the dog. They waited for it to move but it just growled at everyone, not once making an effort to attack. The vet pushed the officers again to annoy them until they slowly walked towards the dog, surrounding it in an attempt to force it back against a wall. But Bruno still wasn't budging.

"You need to talk to it!" the vet snapped towards Sid. "Keep it occupied while I inject it."

"Why me?" Sid asked, still worried because he knew Bruno didn't recognise him. "Those guys have tasers. Get them to do it…"

He kept an eye on Bruno as he slowly edged over to Betty, hugging her to tremble when the dog's fangs extended in length. He glanced at the vet, knowing he'd seen it also.

"…Come on, man, my dog's turning into a walrus. Do something."

"Hey! The dog knows you," the vet replied, placing a medical bag on a nearby shelf before opening it. "Get its attention and I will inject it to make it go to sleep."

"But Bruno doesn't like needles."

Betty quickly released the hug and sighed at Sid, close to laughing nervously at what he just said as the officers moved closer. But Bruno swung paws at them, stopping them in their tracks.

"Don't let it scratch you!" the vet yelled, reaching into a small box to retrieve the needle. "It may spread what it has if it draws blood."

Sid cautiously moved away from Betty, closing in on Bruno to stare into the dog's eyes, but blood dripped from them, leaving Sid feeling sick to the stomach.

"Bruno, mate," he said, pleased to see the dog lower its paws and look at him. "Do you not recognise me?"

The vet watched on, smiling to see Sid's voice was being noticed. He watched the dog whimper and roll around on the floor, acting like it was playing with its master instead of being fierce; confusing him to stall on making a move. He nodded towards Sid and sighed before slowly creeping to the side of the dog to raise the needle, but Bruno stopped rolling and stared at him. He froze as carnivorous jaws clamped down on the hand holding the needle; his fingers snapping off to leave him sobbing in pain as they plummeted to the floor. He frighteningly fell to his knees as the dog licked the blood from its lips; his body weak as he stared at his fingerless hand. He was close to fainting from the stinging pain shooting through him, cringing each time his heart pumped out more blood, but the sound of tasers firing came to his rescue. He watched Bruno crash against a wall, shaking fast before flopping to the floor; not moving as the officers turned the tasers off.

"Betty!" Sid shouted, rushing over to help the vet. "Get something to tie around his hand – quickly!"

"I'll get some bandages from the cupboard," she replied, close to crying herself after seeing Bruno sprawled out as if dead.

As everyone suddenly stared at the fingers sitting in a pool of blood, Bruno was moving slightly; his eyes opening to see Sid help the vet up off the floor as the officers walked towards Betty. No one noticed the dog; the frantic moment had left it invisible.

It sniffed the aroma of blood before springing back to life, barging into Sid and the vet to knock them over like skittles at a bowling alley, Sid colliding with the table whilst the vet fell on his stomach. He shivered like he was taking an ice bath, feeling the dog's breath on him as it closed in, wanting to get up and run but being too scared to try. He closed his eyes and winced as the dog bit into his wounded hand, hearing it growl with pleasure as it tugged on it to dislocate his shoulder.

Betty dropped to the floor to crawl under the table, placing her hands against her ears to drown out the heartbreaking squeals coming from the vet as Bruno crunched into the bone before wrenching his hand away.

The officers nervously fumbled with their tasers, but Bruno howled to scare them before calmly climbing on top of the crying vet's back to sink teeth into his skull; ripping off the top and spitting it out.

The dog had no fear.

It glanced at the officers as they aimed tasers at it again, growling as it sunk teeth into the vet's brain to suck into its mouth like it was eating jelly from a spoon. But it was tasered before taking another bite. It shook rapidly and fell off the dead man, howling like it was injured before rolling around on the floor until the probes fell off.

"Do something!" Sid shouted, cowering under the table beside Betty. "We have kids upstairs."

A loud deafening 'BANG' scared him into whacking his head on the table, the noise echoing around the room as an officer reholstered a handgun. Betty burst into tears and pushed Sid before screaming in his face, close to collapsing as she crawled from underneath the table to see Bruno dead on the floor. Sid slowly followed her; his legs wobbly after seeing his pet with a collapsed eye socket.

SEVENTEEN

News spread quickly amongst the residents of the street as a large crowd of worried people watched the Gilbert family sadly leave their house; their heads bowed to hide the tears. One of the officers smiled as he led them to the police car but suddenly cringed as a reminder of what he did to the family dog sent shivers down his spine. He watched the family slowly enter before sitting in the driver's seat, glancing at the restless neighbours as he quickly shut the door. He turned the key as the family huddled in the backseat before nodding to his partner standing on the side of the road, seeing him sadly back away to be engulfed by the crowd.

The neighbours stared at the police car as it made some distance. They felt angry for being left in the dark and the remaining officer sensed it. He turned to walk back to the house, sweating as glaring eyes made him nervous.

"Hey!" one of the residents shouted, feeling courageous. "Did one of you fire a gun inside there?"

Just the mention of a gun was enough to get the others talking amongst themselves.

Doug Carlton turned to stare at the neighbours, revealing lines around his ageing eyes. He had been an officer for over twenty years but today had been the worst, so was struggling to speak as another resident shouted at him. He didn't know what to say so hoped his silence would work, allowing him to carry out his duty of placing '*no entry*' police tape around the house. But the crowd wasn't giving up as more people came forward to holler at him.

"Come on officer, you must know if a gun was fired?" someone said, as another cried out - "Who did you shoot?!"

Everyone who had witnessed the medics carrying corpses from the Smythes' house earlier had seen something disturbing again in the street where they lived, so none were going anywhere without finding out answers. But Doug ignored them and re-entered the house, slamming the door shut behind him to more outbursts of words. He shivered as he stared at the kitchen, gulping hard after realising the struggle to cope on his own; reaching for his phone as he stumbled towards the staircase. He sat down and held it against an ear, releasing a tear as he made a call; feeling exhausted as a voice was heard on the other end. But the sound of banging against the front door made him jump.

"Doug!" Susan yelled. "What's going on down there? It sounds pretty noisy."

"I wouldn't say it was pretty," he replied, cringing from the racket. "Is Jason still there?"

"He's just finishing off the paperwork from earlier. Why?"

"Can I speak to him?"

Doug glared at the door as a loud THUD echoed around him. He knew someone had kicked it.

He heard Susan mention his name before seconds later hearing Jason take the phone from her; listening to the man breathe as if he'd just been running.

"Doug...What's up?" Jason asked, puffing out his cheeks. "Who's shouting?"

"I'm inside the house of the crazy dog, but I need to be cordoning it off." Doug heard more shouts rip through his ears. "But the people outside won't go home."

"Are you having another panic attack?"

"Yes...I thought I was over them, seeing as I'd not had one for years, but I'm losing control of the situation...I need your help."

Jason shook his head at Susan and mimed – 'He's not coping' – before focusing again on the call.

"Where's Craig?" Jason asked, even though he knew where he was. "Do you need me to find him?"

"He took the family to the hospital...They were so traumatised."

"No problem," Jason calmly replied. "I'll give him a call. Get him to meet me outside the hospital before coming to you."

He replaced the phone and raced back to his desk, grabbing his jacket before leaving the building.

———

Jason parked the car outside the hospital's main entrance before beeping the horn after spotting *Craig Bennett* standing inside the doorway, wiping sweat from his balding head. Craig nodded as the sliding doors opened to let him out, but he soon stopped walking after someone called out his name.

"Slow down," Mike said, catching him up. "I'm coming with you."

"Did Jason call you?"

"Nah...Susan filled me in on what was going on."

They reached the car and entered, bowing their heads as a cold shiver raced through them. There was only one person on their minds now and that was Nash. They closed their eyes as Jason quietly sobbed; his heart pounding after realising it could've been him lying in the morgue.

"Hey, don't blame yourself," Mike softly said, touching Jason's shoulder. "Nash knew the risks when he became a copper."

"Knew the risks?!" Jason snapped at him. "Where does it say in the police force manual that dead people will rise again to kill?"

Mike didn't have an answer.

He sat back in his seat, staring at Jason whilst nudging Craig for support; hoping the man would say something soon before the situation strangled him.

"Where's Wayne?" Craig asked, snapping Mike from staring. "I didn't see him inside the hospital."

"I've sent him home...He's no good to us right now."

"What do you mean?" Jason popped up to say, feeling sick for even thinking about what Wayne had recently seen. "Does it have anything to do with Nash?"

Mike nodded. "Wayne needs some rest. We need him fully focused."

"If you're sure." Jason gulped as he started the engine, saying nothing else as the car was driven away.

———

Doug slowly opened the front door, pushing his way through the crowd of people to reach the street. He breathed fast as everyone followed him, close to hyperventilating as a police car closed in. He raised a smile as it stopped outside the house, but the bystanders smothered the car before anyone could get out.

"Hey!" Doug screamed, pushing through them again. "Let us do our jobs and go home."

"And what is your job exactly?" an irate *man* asked. "Hiding inside the house instead of telling us what's going on?"

Doug grimaced, close to losing it as the car doors opened, but he calmed down when the others got out to stand beside him.

Jason was the first to approach the crowd, close to giggling after seeing them surround the car like they were at a car boot sale. It reminded him of his car boot selling days, feeling a rush after persuading a stranger to buy some piece of tat he would otherwise throw out. He nodded to Mike, not waiting for an order as he raced to the back of the car, whistling to get the attention of the crowd as he lifted the boot.

"Roll up! Roll up!" he hollered as the crowd closed in. "Have I got some goodies for you people..."

Mike opened his mouth to speak but shut it quickly after seeing the crowd become sucked in by Jason; each ignoring the other officers as they tried to see what was inside the boot.

"...Does anyone fancy a wicked bargain?" Jason asked, putting on his best sales voice. "Only available for today... These crazy creature comforts will explode your brain."

His words became baffling for everyone but at least now they were calm. Even the irate man was intrigued. He pushed to the front of the crowd as Jason pointed inside the boot, but all he saw was a spare tyre, a car jack, and a few police-issue jackets.

"Where's the brain-exploding creature comforts?"

"Please move away from the vehicle," Mike politely said, standing next to the man. "And go home."

But the man pulled out cash from his pocket and waved it in Mike's face.

"I'm not going anywhere until I get one of those creature comfort thingies."

"Sorry pal, they're all sold out," Jason said, sniggering loud to annoy Mike.

The man lost his cool again, but this time his anger washed over the rest of the crowd as voices suddenly echoed the same words – "What the hell is going on?" –

Mike knew they would become impatient, especially now Jason had acted like a little shit, but he was overrun before he could move. He tried shifting people out of his way as Jason slammed down the boot but his ears rung from the constant shouts of – "Are we in danger?" And – "We need protection." -

"Okay! Everybody back off and calm down," Mike ordered, pleased to see the crowd give him some room. "I'll answer your questions but you need to settle down."

"You want us to be calm after what we've witnessed?!" cried out an elderly woman with a rolling pin. "You're havin' a laugh." She raised the pin to worry Mike. "I haven't put this down since the commotion started."

"Yeah!" shouted another woman. "We're all worried sick about our families. What's going on, eh?"

Craig and Doug raced over to Mike, giving him a hand as more yells arrived from the seriously scared people. But, as they ushered most of them away from the car, the irate man kicked it.

"Stop that!" Mike snapped, taking a deep breath. "I understand you are angry but whatever went on here today won't be affecting you."

"How do you know?"

The man was close to kicking the car again but Jason sneaked up to him, surprising him into backing away.

"Just tell us something that'll help us understand?" the man asked, pointing at the crowd. "But don't even think about bullshittin' us..."

Mike was scrambling to think of something to say to appease the man, feeling extreme pressure to come up with one of his 'get out of jail card' speeches, but his mind went blank after seeing everyone glare at him. He knew it was too risky to mention the same story he told Blake at the hospital because the man could flip and give him a fat lip, so he said nothing. But the silence made the man angrier.

"...Come on, we want answers!" he shouted.

Mike felt sweat seep through his shirt as the pressure increased, but still, nothing was coming to mind and it bothered him. He knew he should be used to a group of troubled people demanding answers, but he had nothing to say to make them feel better about going home. And, to make matters worse, a television crew van had just arrived, with the most hated reporter, according to the police getting out of the vehicle. This guy would sell his mother to get a story. It didn't matter what the investigation was, he'd find a way to get what he wanted.

Mike glared at him.

He saw the man close in with the confidence of a champion boxer, holding a microphone like he was hosting a talent show; his swagger annoying to make Mike forget about the irate man.

"...Are you going to tell us what's going on, officer?" the irate man asked, smiling at the TV crew.

The reporter winked at Mike as his crew gathered around the police car, setting up a video camera on a tripod.

"Your audience awaits, Mike," the reporter sarcastically said, pushing the microphone into his face. "I do believe these people want some answers...In fact, I think the whole town needs to know what's going on." The reporter was loving every moment of this and Mike knew it. "Don't forget to comb your hair before we record you."

The reporter's name was *Chris Maudlin*. A man of only five feet six inches but whose voice was feared by most, including Mike. No one wanted to be interviewed by him because he had no filter with the questions he asked.

He had become an enemy of Mike's ever since almost costing Mike his job a few months ago. He'd written a story about Mike for the local newspaper that included information not relevant to the interview, like Mike's younger years when he'd dabbled in drugs and alcohol. Mike was furious when he read it. There was no need for Chris to add that but he wanted the locals to know what type of law enforcement they had protecting them. But Mike knew the real reason behind why Chris wrote it. It was because the bank robbers were still at large. Chris still blamed him for their escape after murdering his mother.

"I might've known you'd be sniffin' for a story," Mike said, glaring at him. "But, as you can see, we're very busy dealing with a crisis...We don't need you stickin' your nose in."

"On the contrary," Chris replied, waving the microphone from side to side. "I believe, if anything is going on, then the public should have the right to know about it. Don't you?"

Mike wasn't impressed that someone, maybe from the street, had leaked information to the television station. He wanted to smack Chris in the face but the camera was pointing right at him.

He shuddered as the crowd became restless again, hearing more shouts of – "We need to know the truth" – and – "Don't mess us around" – to almost make him want to leave. He knew he needed a different approach to not only gain the respect of the crowd again but to also quieten Chris, needing to find one now before the TV crew started filming. He smiled as he tried his best to ignore Chris, hoping the plan he'd just thought of would get the bystanders off his back and put the reporter under pressure.

"I agree," he softly said, confusing Chris. "But may I have a word with you in private first?"

"Are you being serious?"

"Yes, I am...Away from the camera."

Mike was aware of the crowd following his every move as thoughts of the plan not working made him quiver. He wanted to put the ball in Chris' court by letting him in on some information, knowing the crowd would wonder what it was and then turn on him for answers instead.

But how much information would be enough?

He slowly walked away from the car before heading towards the side of the Smythes' house, smirking as Chris handed the microphone over to a crew member and followed.

"What's going on now?" muttered one of the neighbours, as the men disappeared from view.

"I have no idea but it's doin' my head in!" cried out the irate man.

But no one moved. They just observed, hoping to see a sight of the two men.

———

Mike waited for Chris to reach the back garden, but he gulped and panicked after a dubious expression spread across Chris' face. He felt sad as he choked on the memories relating to the robbery, leaving him desperately trying to find something to say before losing his nerve. But Chris just looked him up and down.

"Come on!" Chris snapped, turning to walk away. "I've not got all day...I need to get my report done."

Mike stuttered.

He couldn't help it after Chris' ability to crush people without touching them had gotten to him.

"Come on, Chr-is," he spilt from his mouth. "I don't want another fi-ght with you."

"Another fight?" Chris scowled. "We're still having the same fight from three months ago...Do you remember my mother?"

Mike moved closer, reaching out a hand, but Chris backed away.

"How many times do I have to say that I'm sorry for her loss?... Hey?"

"As many times as it takes until you catch the bastards who killed her."

Mike glanced down the side of the house, sweating from

thoughts of the crowd approaching, but, after seeing no one there breathed a sigh of relief.

"I'm still working on that. You need to trust me...I'll find them and bring them to justice." He reached out and touched Chris' arm. "I just wish you'd stop blaming me...If I could turn back time and capture the robbers before they entered the bank I would."

Chris sensed Mike was being genuine. He'd known it all along but needed someone to hate for a while until he'd grieved.

"I'm not blaming you, not anymore," he sadly said, smiling weakly. "I'm just pissed off that you haven't found them yet."

Mike frowned.

He felt sick to his stomach after pouring cold water over the plan to get the crowd to dislike Chris. He knew he couldn't do it. Not now.

"This is what I'll do...I'll let you in on all leads regarding your mother's case if you help me with the restless people out front?"

Chris smiled. He was glad to have let some of the sadness off his chest. He nodded as Mike nervously peered down the side of the house again.

"What's got you spooked?"

"It's hard to explain," Mike replied, shuddering from the thought of talking about what was on his mind.

"Just tell me."

Mike passed on the information given to him by Wayne when they were at the hospital but the words left Chris feeling puzzled and lost. He waited for Mike to laugh but he was close to crying instead.

"Mike, I'm confused...How can the dead get up and attack the living?"

"I have no idea." Mike bowed his head before twisting his neck to crack the bone. "But it's over now...Whatever it was it's been put down again."

"So, what do you need from me?"

"I need you to come up with a story to keep the townsfolk at bay. But don't mention what I told you." Mike studied Chris' reaction, sensing he wasn't up for the challenge. "You owe me, Chris...If you do this then I'll forgive you for writing that shit about me in the paper."

"Sure. Why not...But I also want in on further investigations into this case." Chris stared at the garden and the hole in the fence. "Even though it sounds too weird to be true."

"I told you, the case is over. The thing that took the lives of the Smythes' has been put down."

"Even so," Chris replied, grinning. "It would still be cool to tag along with the great chief of police for a while."

Mike sighed.

"Okay, but you need to say something quick to the feisty mob in the street."

"I'm sure I can think of something to keep them happy."

————

They returned from the house expecting to be swamped by people demanding answers, but everyone was silent. Even the other officers were quiet. Mike had a feeling he was being studied. He could sense it and it freaked him out. He stayed close to Chris, hoping he was about to keep his word, but some of the crowd drifted away to leave him surprised. He watched on as the people suddenly became more interested in the camera, doing poses and acting silly in their efforts to get on TV; close to laughing after the cameraman told them the equipment wasn't switched on.

Mike nodded to Chris as the reporter approached the crowd, acting like he was about to faint after being given bad news. But Mike assumed it was part of his act to gain sympathy from the people in the street. If it was, it was working, as the people suddenly gave Chris their full attention. Mike squirmed when Chris started to speak. He expected him to spill the beans on the truth, but his version of events sounded way off from what happened. Mike smiled as he listened to Chris explain a false truth about a domestic incident involving the residents of both houses; knowing he'd met his match when it came to talking believable bullshit.

He heard someone cry out – "Yeah! I knew Sid and Vincent never got on. It was only a matter of time before something happened." – Before someone said – "But did you expect this?" – to leave the other person speechless.

"Get inside the car," Mike ushered the officers. "I just need to speak to the reporter before we leave."

He waited for Chris to wrap up his speech before waving him over; happy to see the people dawdle off back to their homes.

"Do you think they believed you?" he asked as Chris neared.

"What do you think?... I had them eating out of the palm of my hand."

Mike wasn't sure if Chris was having a dig at the dead person rising chat they had but he didn't want to bring it up again.

"I'm off back to the station," he said, gripping the car door handle. "What are you up to?"

Chris grinned to creep him out. He had already planned his next journey but wasn't going to let Mike in on it. Not yet anyway. If the chief was letting him off the leash to help search for answers then he would do it his way.

"I'll just finish off here before heading back to edit the report."

Everything seemed to be one giant jigsaw puzzle to Chris, but he was excited to try and put the pieces together.

EIGHTEEN

Chris arrived at the hospital to hear the bells from a nearby church ring six times; checking his watch and smiling as it showed *6:00 pm*. He looked around as he sat inside his car, feeling nervous and excited as he placed on a wig. He looked into the rearview mirror and giggled at his attempt at a disguise before adjusting his fake nose and glasses; stepping out of the car in the hope of not being noticed once entering the building. He knew he was recognised by most people in the area and that made him more arrogant, but right now he needed not to be. Especially if he required some information.

He entered the main doors holding a large flower, smelling it to almost puke before checking to see if his phone was recording. It was. He placed it inside a pocket and calmly walked past reception, but a few nurses stared at him. They never spoke, but Chris did get a cheeky giggle and a smile as they passed. It pleased him because he knew his silly disguise had worked.

He walked down a corridor, acting like he didn't know

where he was going; almost bumping into Hazel to see her glare at him to make him feel uneasy. He stopped swiftly in his tracks, glancing into her eyes to stiffen like she'd turned him to stone. But she suddenly smiled.

"Can I help you?" she said, checking him up and down. "Are you lost?"

"I think so." Chris relaxed and smiled back. "I'm looking for my uncle...I was told he was here."

Hazel was close to laughing at the weird outfit Chris was wearing but thought better of it after thinking he may be part of a religious cult she'd never encountered before.

"Tell me his name and I'll help you find him?"

"His name's Vincent Smythe."

Hazel *frowned* and scrunched her lips. "I'm sorry. Who are you?"

"My name's John...I'm Vincent's nephew."

"I was told he never had any living family members?"

Chris gulped, thinking he had been caught out.

"We haven't seen eye to eye for many years," he rushed from his mouth, cringing from the thought of Hazel shouting out for a security guard. "So, maybe he'd forgotten I existed?..."

He raised the flower to grab her attention, hoping that the smell would hypnotise her into letting him go. But Hazel just watched him.

"...The police contacted me. Told me to come here...I've got Vincent a flower. It's his favourite."

Hazel leaned over to smell it but quickly held her nose; choking into her hand as Chris lowered the flower.

"That's Vincent's favourite?" she asked, choking again. "It smells like death."

"It is strange you should say that...It's called an

Amorphophallus Titanium. Otherwise known as a Corpse Flower."

"I've never seen one in the UK before."

"That's because I got it whilst travelling in Indonesia... Vincent used to order them when I was a child."

Hazel had no idea if he was making it up but felt it was her duty to tell him the truth. She reached out to hold Chris' hand, passing on a sorrowful smile before pointing down the corridor.

"He died today...I'm so sorry..."

Chris quivered before shedding tears.

"...Didn't anyone let you know?... His wife was also involved in the accident."

"No...They never." Chris sniffed into his jacket sleeve before saying, "Can I see them?"

"No," Hazel sharply said, shocking him. "They've been taken to the morgue...You can give him his flower at the funeral."

Chris guessed she was weighing him up, seeing if he would falter and admit to his lies, but, as he was about to respond, felt his false nose slowly peeling away.

"Sorry, but I need to use the restroom," he swiftly said, hoping Hazel hadn't noticed. "I had too much kebab earlier and I think it wants to come out and say hello."

Before Hazel could work out the reason why Chris was behaving oddly he was off running towards the nearest toilet sign. She sighed as he pushed open the door before shaking her head in disbelief, not sure if she should wait for him or not.

Chris raced to a sink and laughed out loud, congratulating himself on a fine-acting performance. He did doubt himself whether he could cry on demand but was pleased with how easy it was. But he knew he was given a lucky escape. He put the flower down and restored his nose before checking his phone to make sure it hadn't accidentally stopped recording; smiling to see it was still on as he got back into character.

He returned from the restroom to see Hazel was still in the same spot, but she shrieked at him when he neared. Chris panicked, thinking his nose was falling off; unaware that the glue he'd used to restore it was showing around his nose and cheeks.

Hazel backed away, feeling disgusted after assuming he'd been jerking off.

"You've got something on your face," she awkwardly said, pointing. "I hope you're fully relieved now."

But Chris wasn't catching on as he wiped the sticky solution away.

"Sorry about that," he said, getting emotional again. "I've travelled a long way...Can I see them, please?"

Hazel shook her head again, desperately wanting to give him the same answer as before, but somehow Chris was convincing her he was legit.

"Okay, but only for a few minutes," she snapped, feeling shocked for giving in. "They're disfigured...So, if you haven't got a strong stomach then don't go there."

Chris would swim through a pool full of horseshit to get a story so was up for this big time, but he needed to keep his emotions in check and stick with the heartbroken relative routine.

"I'll be okay...Just lead the way."

"As you wish," Hazel replied, leading him to an elevator.

———

She watched him closely as she escorted him towards the room of death, waiting to see if he exploded from the realisation that his family members were dead, but Chris seemed to cope with it all. His actions worried Hazel, making her think she may be doing the wrong thing.

"You seem fine now," she softly said as Chris took in his surroundings like he was an excited boy off to the beach. "You do know we're off to the morgue to see your dead relatives, right?"

Chris stopped and stared at her before becoming the long-lost nephew again, picking up where he'd left off.

"I know," he replied, snivelling. "I was just trying to focus on something else."

"Oh," Hazel said, feeling embarrassed. "We're nearly there now."

They reached a set of double doors with the word – Morgue – written above before stopping to let a hospital worker walk through them.

"Stay here," Hazel ordered, peering through a small window in one of the doors. "I need to make sure the bodies are ready before you can view them."

"Sure...I'll wait."

Chris watched her open the doors before sitting in a nearby chair; looking around to see if anyone was watching as he checked his phone again.

"Come on," he whispered, noticing the battery was low. "I need to get inside soon."

He knew it was too risky to stop the recording and restart it again once inside the room as someone could catch him, so hoped he had enough time. He was pleased when the doors opened a few seconds later.

Hazel smiled at him as he left the seat to follow her, but

his nose twitched from a smell similar to the flower he was carrying. He prepared himself for what was about to hit him hard in the face as Hazel led him through another door; entering a small room with dark closed curtains. Chris knew the bodies would be on show once they opened, but, as he stared at them, the fake emotions were replaced with real ones. He was sweating, wishing he wasn't there now as Hazel reached out to grip a cord.

"Are you ready?" she asked, smiling sadly.

Chris nodded as his heart thumped loud against his chest; seeing the curtains open like the *DEAD SEA* to reveal two tables in the next room with sheets covering bodies. And standing between them was *Ted* (a member of the Pathology Department).

Hazel pressed a button on a wall-mounted Intercom device.

"Ted...Can you remove the sheets from the heads, please?"

Chris composed himself.

He took probably his deepest breath ever as Ted slowly revealed Vincent's and Mary's faces; both being made to look more respectable with Vincent's eyelids being stuck down and Mary's face being mostly bandaged. Chris wouldn't be able to identify her even if he was a real relative, but he stared at her all the same.

Hazel knew it was the best Ted could do on short notice so was pleased to see Chris hadn't puked.

"Are you okay?" she asked him, seeing him touch his head like he was about to faint. "Are they the Smythes?"

Chris nodded.

"Do you have any questions?" Hazel asked, closing the curtains.

But the faint sound of Chris' phone turning off almost made him cry.

"Nope," he replied, feeling angry for missing out on vital information. "I'm all good."

"Okay then...Shall we head off? I'm sure you have things to do."

Hazel escorted Chris out of the room, leading him back to the main part of the building; watching him as he exited before choking again from the smell coming from the flower.

"What a strange man," she said, turning to aim for the reception desk.

NINETEEN

Chris was still high on adrenaline after leaving the hospital, feeling relaxed after experiencing many draining emotions. He knew he shouldn't have seen the bodies. He regretted it but his reporter instinct to go above and beyond had taken over.

He drove towards the edge of town, smirking from thoughts of what was going to happen once he parked his car. He knew the person he was about to visit wouldn't be impressed to see him again so soon and would probably not let him in, but he wasn't going to clock off from work just yet. He needed more information.

He turned down a quiet street, looking ahead to see the living room light was on inside the chosen house; checking the time on his dashboard to see it was *7:00 pm*. He sighed as he wondered what response the latest news update was having as it was read out on TV; knowing people would be tuning in to find out more information about the deaths of the locals. He knew it could lead to a mass hysteria outbreak so hoped the person doing his job was being professional enough to not let that happen.

He parked up outside Mike's house, laughing to himself for still wearing his disguise; ripping away the fake nose before quickly changing into his usual attire.

Maybe I would have a better chance of being let in if I kept it on? he thought, exiting the car to walk towards the house.

He entered the front garden, breathing in deeply as he neared the door; still holding the flower as he pressed the doorbell. But he cringed from the thought of Mike bellowing out for him to – FUCK OFF –

He pressed the bell again, thinking this was the time when he would get his marching orders, but it was way too quiet for his liking. He stood back and looked at the bedroom windows, seeing if a curtain would move, but sighed again after thinking Mike was either doing a great job at not being noticed or wasn't home.

Chris was on the verge of giving up before a sudden urge to sneak up to the front window crossed his mind. He walked towards it, peering through a gap in the curtains to spot the television was still on; viewing the rest of the room to stop after seeing a pair of legs hanging over the sofa. He smiled after knowing Mike was home, but his smile became sadistic when he banged on the window.

"Come on! Let me in!"

He banged again until the legs moved, watching them closely as the rest of Mike's body appeared, but Chris wasn't feeling guilty for waking him up. Mike stood up and yawned before staring at Chris like he thought he was dreaming, but another bang on the window snapped him out of it. He shrugged his shoulders and frowned before rubbing his eyes after seeing the flower, shaking his head in disbelief as Chris waved it at him.

I'd rather have a visit from one of those dead freaks than him, Mike thought, slowly walking towards the window.

"What do you want?!" he shouted.

"Open the door...I need to speak to you about something."

"I'm very tired...Can't it wait until tomorrow?"

Chris knew he had Mike rattled.

"No...I need to talk to you now..."

Chris pointed towards the front door, smiling as Mike slowly moved towards it, but he rattled the window again to annoy Mike into quickening up the pace.

"...Did you see the news report? What did you think?" Chris asked, pushing the flower into Mike's face as the door was opened. "It's just been on."

"Shit, I missed it...What did you say?" Mike replied, holding his nose.

"I wasn't at the studio to read it because I've been busy with my investigations."

Chris took a step inside the house but Mike stopped him in his tracks.

"You're not coming inside with that thing," he said, wincing. "It smells like it's been dead a long time."

"Funny you should say that," Chris replied, smirking. "Someone else said it smelled of death today."

"Just get rid of it..."

Chris smirked again.

He knew Mike wasn't happy after seeing him frown worse than if he'd just lost the winning lotto ticket, but still hoped he would let him inside. He waited for Mike to change his mind but it wasn't to be, so grunted as he placed the flower on the ground.

"...Not there...Throw it in the wheelie bin."

Chris grunted again as he searched for the bin, acting like a child being told off as he lifted the lid.

"Are you sure?" he said, hovering the flower over the bin. "The smell eventually grows on you."

"Fuck that! Just chuck it in."

Chris did before attempting to enter the house again. And this time Mike let him.

"Why did you let someone else read the report? I trusted you and now you've gone and fucked it up."

"Calm down," Chris jokingly said, entering the living room to sit in a chair. "There's no need to worry. Nothing vital was leaked out...It was the same story I told the people in the street."

"How do you know if you were off galavanting somewhere else?"

"You need to trust me, Mike," Chris replied, holding up his hands as Mike's face turned an angry red. "It was the same story."

Mike glared at him for being so calm, close to punching him for his - 'hey, we got away with it and don't you worry about a thing,' – speech.

"Were you born stupid?" Mike shut the door and entered the room as thoughts of him losing his job made him want to scream. "If you want to work with me then you need to cut the crap and listen...You got that?"

"I got it," Chris softly replied, sitting back in his seat. "I will be obedient from now on. Just like a loyal dog."

"I know you crave a good story over-emotional feelings towards other people but you need to change your attitude and fast."

"Yes, boss."

Mike shook his head and entered the kitchen, returning moments later with a full bottle of whiskey and two glasses; handing a glass to Chris before sitting opposite.

"So, where were you that was more important than reading the news?" Mike said, pouring whiskey into the glass.

"Just at the hospital." Chris took a sip but almost spat it out. "Some head nurse spooked me."

"Why? What were you up to?"

Chris explained that he wore a disguise to not be noticed but wasn't convinced she brought his story.

"At least your disguise worked," Mike said, taking a sip of whiskey. "Just be more careful next time."

"Are you allowing me to continue with my investigations?"

Mike shook his head. "I'll probably regret it...Just don't sniff for more clues until you get the nod from me. Is that understood?"

Chris nodded and took another sip from his glass.

They sat in silence, drinking whiskey whilst watching television for the next thirty minutes; both eager to see a repeated news report. But nothing was coming on.

"Are you sure your chums at the studio did a report?"

"Mike," Chris replied, sinking into his seat. "They must have...It should be on soon."

"It better be." Mike reached down, grabbing the bottle from the floor. "I don't want to fall asleep before it comes on." He then poured more whiskey into his glass.

They drank for another half an hour, close to shutting their eyes from a mix of tiredness and intoxication as the news returned to the screen. Chris smiled after hearing the newsreader repeat the words he wanted him to say but his eyes closed seconds later and he fell asleep.

Mike watched the rest of the report aimed at what went on in Clifton Falls, happy to see Chris had stuck to his word. He turned off the TV and rose from his seat, nudging Chris to notice he was too far gone to respond before sighing and reaching for a blanket spread out across the top of the sofa. He placed it over Chris as he slumped further into the seat, giggling at the man sucking his thumb and talking to himself before letting out a loud fart.

That was Mike's cue to go to bed.

TWENTY

Blake looked upset as Karen watched him from across the room. They'd seen the recent news report, but what seemed to be a reasonable and understanding account of what happened to the chief of police was somehow seen as a shockingly confusing and heartbreaking moment for them. Karen tried hard to hide it beneath the rocks inside her mind but Blake couldn't let it rest. He was angry that the newsreader had said something different to what he'd been told.

"What's goin' on?!" he shouted, leaving his seat. "Why did he say there was a domestic incident between the Smythes and their neighbour?"

"I don't know," Karen softly replied, closing in on him. "But there has to be a reason for it. Right?"

Blake reached for his jacket resting on the arm of the sofa and placed it on.

"The reason had better be a good one," he said, grabbing his car keys.

"Where are you going?"

"I'm off to the police station to get some answers... Something isn't right here..."

Blake hugged Karen after seeing a tear roll down her face. He knew the conversation was getting to her.

"...I think there's more to it."

"Like what?"

"I don't know." Blake let go. "Why weren't we able to see the bodies? We were at the hospital for hours but no one came for us...Why?"

Karen almost broke into a crying fit after thinking back, now feeling sick to her stomach for believing what Mike said as she watched Blake close in on the door.

I should've known something was off...An electrical fault? ... Can't be true.

"Don't leave me on my own," she sadly said, hoping Blake would do a U-turn. "You can phone the police station."

Blake smiled to leave Karen thinking positively towards his next move. She was happy, but it only lasted a few seconds as Blake gripped the door handle.

"Hey, don't be upset with me," he said, opening the door. "I need to go there and look them in the eyes. See if they try to wriggle out of it..."

He was mad but he wasn't mad for himself. He was mad because Karen wasn't told the truth.

"...I'll phone you soon."

———

Blake parked his car outside the police station, shaking in anger as his heart raced from thoughts of being arrested.

I'm here now so I may as well get it over with.

He checked to see if any officers were lingering

outside the main doors before cautiously leaving the car; gulping as he waited for his heartbeat to slow down. And when it did he walked towards the building. He looked through a small window in one of the doors to see an elderly officer behind the receptionist's desk, but the sight of his uniform caused Blake's blood to boil again.

"He's havin' it."

Blake flung the door open, but the closer he got to the officer, the more his anger turned to nerves. He couldn't speak after reaching the part-time, semi-retired, sixty-five-year-old man who was typing slowly on a laptop keyboard. He wanted to let rip and shout at him but the man reminded him of his father.

"Hello, Sir," the constable said, squinting at the keyboard. "I always forget where the letter J is..."

Blake smiled even though he didn't want to before pointing at the letter.

"...Thanks." The constable pressed it before saying, "So, what can I do for you then?"

Blake stared at a shiny badge attached to the man's shirt with the name *George Price* on it before lifting his head to look at him.

"I want to speak to the main man, you know, the officer in charge?"

But George shrugged his shoulders, annoying Blake to repeat the words more aggressively.

"Either lower your tone or leave the premises!" George snapped before calmly returning to the message he was writing. "I haven't got time for anyone's aggravation." He glared at Blake. "You got that?"

Blake puffed out his cheeks but he wasn't backing down.

He'd come this far with the courage to lash out so needed to keep it up to hopefully find some answers.

"I'll calm down when I see the boss." Blake glared back to leave them having a stare-off; his teeth showing as he furiously stretched his lips. But inside he was panicking. "Where is he?"

"I don't think you heard me properly, young man," George replied, moving away from the laptop. "I told you to sort your temper out or risk being shown the door...Now, what's it gonna be?"

Blake backed away once George pointed at him. He knew he was stepping over the line.

"Okay, I'm calm," he softly said, glancing around at what seemed to be an empty station. "Where are the other officers?"

"You're being nosey."

"It's just a question."

Blake received a short version of their whereabouts but George never mentioned why they were where they were. He just said they would be back if needed. But his words brought a curiosity upon Blake and he needed to know more.

"I've heard there have been some unexplainable things going on recently...Do you know anything about em'?"

George studied Blake to see where he was going with the question, becoming defensive once being asked it again.

"Are you a reporter or just a nosey bastard?" he asked swiftly, reaching for a pen. "I'll write down the chief's phone number for you so you can ask him."

"That would be great."

"I'm not giving you the chief's number, you moron." George tutted at Blake before returning the pen to his shirt pocket. "He's a busy man...You'll have to leave a message with me."

"But I need a word with him...It's important...Do you know where I can find him?"

"Yeah, I do know, but I'm not going to tell ya'."

Blake lowered his head and sighed before whispering, "I know about the deaths."

"Speak up," George replied after failing to catch any of what Blake said. "I'm not a young whippersnapper now you know. You'll have to speak louder."

Blake lifted his head. "I know about the deaths."

This time George panicked. He backed away as thoughts of Blake talking about all the deaths from that day spooked him.

Maybe he was one of the murderers and had come in to give himself up?

Sweat suddenly appeared on George's brow.

He concentrated on Blake to see if he would make an aggressive move, not taking any chances as he withdrew a gun from his hip holster to aim at the puzzled-looking man.

"Don't move scumbag...Place your hands on the desk and keep still."

Blake couldn't take his eyes off the gun. It made him nervous.

"I can't place my...hands on the desk," he stumbled from his mouth. "And not move."

"Don't piss me off!" George roared. "Just do it..."

Blake quivered as he slowly approached the desk, placing his hands on it as George kept the gun on him. But both were as jumpy as each other.

"...Just keep them where I can see them," George ordered,

moving from behind the desk to pat Blake's body. "Are you concealing a weapon?"

"No!"

Blake closed his eyes for a second as he waited to be arrested, but George stopped touching him and moved away.

"I had to check," George said, still holding the gun. "Now explain about the deaths before I lose it."

"Look man, you're scaring me...Please put it away."

"Not until I'm certain that you're not a killer."

Blake was close to laughing after being labelled a criminal but the sight of the gun stopped him.

"Me, a killer, you've got to be kiddin'."

"I'm not kidding, fuck face...What do you know about the deaths?"

Blake began to fear for his life.

He shook his head, feeling stupid from thoughts of his plan to storm the station to have it out with the chief backfiring into him being accused of murder.

"The deaths? The deaths were mentioned on the television."

George gulped hard and lowered the gun; his face beaming a bright red after realising he was close to shooting the wrong person.

"So, it's appeared on the news now," he politely said, reholstering his weapon. "I'm sorry...I didn't know."

"It's okay," Blake replied, still on edge. "I probably would've thought the same thing if I was in your shoes."

George's eyes lit up like he was happy and excited all of a sudden.

"Did that sexy woman read it? She makes me horny," he said, acting like a sex-starved tongue-wagging dog.

"You must be thinking about the woman on sky sports

news...The only female you get on the main one is that overweight, dragon-faced, mud wrestler type."

"Yes, that's her...Isn't she a stunner?"

Blake didn't answer back because he couldn't think of anything to say about George's taste in women. But, at least now the tension had lifted between them.

"What's with the gun?" Blake asked, staring at it inside the holster. "The news report only mentioned some kind of a domestic, so why are you waving a gun about?"

George became shy now. He hoped Blake would forget what he'd said but Blake was still staring.

"I was just being careful," George nervously said, touching the holster. "I'm just edgy sometimes. Especially since what happened at the Christmas robbery..."

Blake nodded, accepting the answer. He knew how hard it'd been for Karen seeing as she was still having flashbacks, so thought it to be natural. *But still, it was unusual for an officer to carry a gun.*

"...So, you already knew about the deaths but you still wanted to come here to let the chief know," George said acting curious. "That's weird."

"I came here to have it out with him because he lied to me...He said Mr and Mrs Smythe died from an electrical current passing through them and not a domestic."

George sucked his bottom lip as Blake's words washed over him. To him, it was all new.

"Look, mate. I wish I could help you but I've only been on duty for a short while. I'm still getting to grips with what's been going on today." George patted Blake on the shoulder and returned to the other side of the desk. "Look, I'll tell you what I'll do...I'll ring the chief right now, get to the bottom of it for you."

———

A disturbing sound echoed inside Mike's home as five rings sounded, but he wasn't answering the phone. Seconds later, the sequence was repeated but still, there was nothing. Mike was too smashed from alcohol to wake up.

George smiled at Blake as he pointed at the phone, shaking his head to confirm nothing was happening. He tried for a third time but gave up after two rings, shrugging his shoulders and replacing the handset.

"He's probably just busy."

"But this can't wait...The couple who died were like family to my wife so I need to find out what happened. There can't be two versions of events."

George felt sorry for Blake now. He was desperate.

He'd shown that by coming here without a plan, George thought before holding up a hand to say, "Don't worry, I'm not finished yet...I'll call someone else."

He dialled another number as Blake watched him closely; both smiling as it was answered within three rings.

"Hey, Wayne, it's George...You sound tired."

Wayne rubbed his eyes and swallowed hard. He was surprised to hear from George but he soon panicked, thinking Mike was behind the call.

"You tell the chief I'll be there as quick as I can," he said, frantically reaching for his trousers.

"Mike's not here."

Wayne slowed down, rubbing his eyes again before catching his breath as he sat on the edge of the bed.

"Right...So why are you phoning me at this time of night?"

George peered down at his watch and scrunched his cheeks.

"It's only a quarter to *nine*...Were you asleep?"

"Yeah, man," Wayne replied, lying on the bed. "It's been a hectic day...I came home and crashed out."

"Damn!"

George glanced at Blake, noticing he was intrigued with the conversation before explaining to Wayne his reason behind the call. But, after Blake's name was mentioned, Wayne's mood changed. He knew why the man was at the station long before George finally filled him in. He'd dreamt it would happen.

FUCK! Mike's story has been rumbled.

"I missed the news report," Wayne said, rubbing a hand across his face. "So, what did the newsreader say exactly? It was just a domestic between two households?"

"Yep...and Blake is raging over it..."

Wayne cursed under his breath before looking for his shirt; finding it to put it on as shaking fingers did up the buttons.

"...Wayne! Wayne! Are you still there?"

"Yeah, I'm still here," the reply came as Wayne reached for his shoes. "Just keep him there. I'm on my way...Do you know if he's blabbed to anyone else?"

George smiled at Blake to make him feel more at ease before quickly finishing off the conversation with Wayne.

"Only his wife, I think."

"Let's hope you're right."

Then the line went dead.

TWENTY-ONE

Colin had ploughed through the hideous corpses to leave him shattered. He'd taken Blood and DNA samples before writing notes on what he thought had happened; feeling excited to be in line for employee of the month due to all the overtime. But, of all the years doing this kind of work he'd never had a day as stressful as this.

He stared at a blood-soaked table, sighing from thoughts of what was recently lying on it, as a reminder of what Wayne told him earlier crept inside his mind. He knew it was farfetched and outrageous but it was also the most realistic theory of them all.

Did someone come to life again?

He glanced over at the refrigeration unit to see the written names of the identified people, but the torn-apart corpse of the person rundown by the truck and the woman killed by the driver were still unidentified. He turned away to scrub the table clean but jumped out of his skin when a 'THUD', 'THUD' echoed around the room. He panicked, thinking someone was trying to enter, but, as he opened the door, saw no one there. He returned to the table but another loud 'THUD' almost crushed his heart.

"Who's out there?!" he shouted, tripping over a bucket of red-coloured water to see it splash over the floor. "Come out."

He watched the door to see if it would open but more bangs frit him into almost hiding inside a storeroom. He breathed deeply as he listened out, but, as more thuds gave him a clue of its whereabouts, fought with his mind over whether to believe it. He stared at one of the units, sweating as the sound happened again; knowing now that was where it was coming from.

"No! I don't need this right now...I'm meant to be going home."

He thought about leaving it as he was too tired to check and just sort it out in the morning, but he felt guilty now. He knew he needed to check the unit to make sure it wasn't faulty, but cringed at the thought of having to remove the body.

He pulled the handle to see the coffin-like shape slide out like an upright filing cabinet; surprised that the noise had stopped. He shook his head and reached for the body bag, sucking in a deep breath as he struggled to lift the corpse.

"Where's Ted when I need him?" he asked himself, attempting to lift it again.

He flung the body over a shoulder and walked towards a table, making sure to avoid the wet patch of water as he reached it. But, as he slowly placed the body down, gripped his now aching shoulder. He cringed from the pain as he walked towards the storeroom, entering to grab a toolbox before quickly walking past the table to aim for the unit; not noticing that the body was moving inside the bag. A lump appeared, working its way to the top in a frantic motion until the two-way zipper slowly moved a few inches before two decaying fingers slipped through to rest on the outside.

Colin grabbed a screwdriver from the box as he peered inside the unit. He banged the sides to listen out for the sound again, but nothing happened.

"Maybe I'm just overtired?"

He was so concentrated on the task that he didn't notice the fingers gripping the other side of the zipper, pulling it down another foot until both hands were free. The corpse sat up as the zipper raced down to the end; its evil eyes glaring at Colin as it got down off the table to knock the bag onto the floor. The noise alerted Colin instantly, but, before he had time to turn around, the banging noises started again to make him shudder. And this time they were coming from other units.

'BANG! BANG! BANG!'

Colin dropped the screwdriver as a fourth bang drilled into him.

He was unaware that a slobbering, naked, dead version of Frank was standing behind him, watching him closely. It twitched its head from side to side as it grunted towards the other units, its tone being used to communicate with other corpses to leave Colin momentarily frozen on the spot. But fear had left him now and curiosity had taken its place.

He concentrated hard, lifting his head to follow the sounds until locating two more units, but the ferocity of the noises stopped him from hearing the dead person close in. He flinched, feeling faint as he fell against the units, holding the back of his neck to feel the warm blood stick to his fingers. He screamed in a disturbingly high-pitched squeal, close to collapsing to his knees, turning agonisingly to face the reason behind why he was bleeding; choking at the sight of a man who was supposed to be as dead as a dodo chewing on his flesh.

Colin tried to scream again but the sound was muted.

He teared up as the now alive again man with the *tag* attached to his toe closed in, licking his lips as if satisfied with the taste from the first morsel of fresh meat. The corpse lashed out to bite Colin again but he was quick to push it away before running past; his heart pounding from the fear he now felt as he aimed for the exit door. But he lacked concentration and slipped on the wet floor, hitting his head on the corner of a table with extreme force to leave him dazed and bleeding again. He sat on the floor staring at the attacker with blood dripping from its chin, wishing he was dreaming as it staggered towards him.

Colin shook his head, feeling it pound like a bad migraine as the corpse dropped to the floor in front of him, snapping teeth to scare him.

"Get the fuck away from me, please...I beg you," Colin pleaded, trying desperately to get to his feet. "I just want to go home."

The latest addition to the zombie race sniffed the air, grinning after the sweet aroma of Colin's blood wafted beneath its nose before dripping onto the floor tiles. But Colin couldn't get up. He tried and tried but was sliding on his life fluid, becoming covered by it as terror took over. He waited for the corpse to attack again, imagining the excruciating pain in advance before almost admitting defeat, but the zombie just watched him, giving him time to try to lift again.

He was almost back to his feet after sliding a few more times, but the monster grabbed his trailing foot, pulling him down again. He shook his leg in a desperate attempt to escape but the zombie bit deep into his calf, ripping away flesh mixed with the cloth from his trousers. Colin gritted his teeth, wincing as tears streamed down his face. He lashed out and swung an arm, connecting a hand against the side of the creature's head to knock it across the floor, now able to have another chance to escape, but he found it more difficult to rise, so dragged himself towards the door.

He turned to see lines of blood escaping out of three wounds, choking in pain as the creature walked away to respond to more ferocious BANGS coming from the two units. Colin watched in shocked amazement as the zombie reached them, pulling them open to unzip the body bags, revealing more hideous, newborn creatures. He couldn't believe what was happening. The corpses were rising just like the one that attacked him.

He rubbed his eyes, watching them roll out of the units to plummet hard against the floor before getting up like nothing happened; leaving the bags on the ground as they glared at him. Colin knew time was not on his side but he still didn't move. He stared at the naked trio of flesh-hungry corpses sniffing the air, their mouths open as they followed the smell of blood towards him.

"Go away!" Colin bellowed, hoping that someone would hear him. "Help! Help! Please, can anybody help me?!"

But the light from the room slowly faded as the beasts hovered over him to block out the brightness.

Colin slapped at thin air in an attempt to fend the zombies off before covering his arms over his face to cry beneath them, not wanting to see what was to happen next.

Nash and Fank's corpse leaned over him as Vincent followed the sound of his heavy breathing; gripping violently onto his arm to scare him into wetting himself. He shrieked as Vincent dug fingers into his flesh, tearing at it like a crazed psycho as the new Nash sunk teeth into the same arm. Colin hollered even louder than before as he removed his arms from his face; the pain becoming too much to take as he tried to back away. But Vincent tracked his voice and snapped teeth at him, ripping away a mouthful of his right cheek.

Colin was tearful and bleeding to death, but was desperate to let out a final YELL, hoping it would smash through walls and doors on its quest to find help. And this time his screams echoed out of the room to travel along the corridor.

––––––––

Gary was mopping the floor in the lower region of the hospital, but, as he closed in on the morgue room thought he'd heard a scream over the music playing through his earphones. He stopped and turned off his I-phone, gripping the mop handle tightly as he listened out for it again.

It was unusual for him to be doing what he was doing as nursing was his main job role, but the hospital was low on staff so he'd been given the short straw to mop. But he didn't like being so close to the morgue. It freaked him out. That was why he was listening to music. It was a distraction for him.

He was about to turn it on again but felt the urge to stare at the morgue room door, squinting after hearing something fall to the floor.

"Hello!" he shouted, closing in. "Anyone in there?"

He placed an ear against the door but heard nothing else, so returned to mopping the floor as the three walking corpses savagely fed on Colin. One had used the screwdriver to open up his stomach before pulling out his intestines, liver, and heart, sitting on the floor to smile sadistically as it bit into them. It had no remorse, just the crazed hunger for food of a human.

Nash and Vincent fought over the dead man's arm. They bit into it like hungry piranhas before wrenching it from the body, leaving Colin's corpse looking like a jigsaw soaked in blood.

Gary thought hard as he tried to remember if he'd witnessed Colin leaving the room, knowing he couldn't have without being seen. He placed an ear against the door again but backed away quickly, feeling confused after hearing a strange sucking sound.

"Colin! Are you in there?" he asked, shivering from not knowing. "Did a body fall from the table? Is that why you shouted?"

He waited impatiently for a few more seconds, sweating from the fear of realising where he was; wanting desperately to turn on the music again. But another noise came from the room to stop him. He reached for the door and turned the knob, but it wasn't moving. Something was blocking it.

"What the hell is up with this door?!" he shouted, leaning a shoulder into it.

He puffed and puffed as it slowly moved forward, smiling to see it open halfway, but he suddenly puked after spotting footprint shapes nestled in a pool of blood.

"COLIN!" he screamed, turning red with exhaustion after using up all his strength to fully open the door.

But, whatever had been blocking it was now jammed between the wall and the wooden object.

Gary saw more bloody footprints lead away from the spillage.

He thought at first that Colin had stepped into it with bare feet but knew that couldn't be right unless Colin had grown extra pairs. It was obvious that more than one person had stepped into the blood.

What's he playing at?

Gary cautiously entered the room before slowly peering behind the door, but instantly puked again after seeing the mutilated corpse. He shook his head vigorously until calming down to think, sensing the body may be one of the corpses brought in earlier, but was puzzled to see it so close to the door. He gulped as he prodded it with the mop before shuddering from an eerie sound closing in; turning to face the unclothed creatures appearing from the open stockroom door. He choked after seeing fresh stitches cover the area where a penis and testicles should be, feeling like he needed to puke again after staring at the blind zombie with stitches around its neck. He shuddered as they moaned at him, feeling too creeped out to move, but none were moving towards him. They were just watching him like naughty schoolboys.

But Gary's mind didn't register them to be dead. He just thought Colin had some fetish that involved naked people and blood.

"Shit me, guys, you startled me," he nervously said, hoping they weren't going to ask him to join in.

But his heart pumped faster within seconds.

He now knew something wasn't right after glaring hard at one of the monsters, hearing it growl at him like a rabid dog.

"You're the guy who was brought in earlier," he said, whimpering. "But I saw you die..."

He attempted to locate Colin again but couldn't see him anywhere. Then it clicked.

"...Colin!" he bellowed, releasing more sweat after facing the partly dismembered corpse by the door.

He noticed a nametag spattered in blood on the red-covered lab coat. He shook fast as he kept one eye on the still-staring freaks, reaching for the tag to pull it away before wiping the blood off to reveal Colin's name. He dropped it and cried before suddenly facing the creatures, laughing out loud as they remained side-by-side, covered in blood and drooling onto the floor.

Gary fought with his nerves as thoughts of the zombies being nothing more than comical entered his mind. He laughed at them again to receive the same docile response before placing his earphones back into his ears, pressing play on his phone to listen to another song from Michael Jackson, as the events he now faced reminded him of the tracks - 'Blood on the Dance Floor & Thriller'.

Oh, yeah, they surely resemble the dancers from that song.

Gary imagined them doing the same dance if he put the song on, so scrolled down the music list on his phone to find it. But he was still wary of them, sensing they were studying his every move.

He noticed the corpse of Frank slowly walk in front of the others, stopping a few feet ahead to scare him into acting with more caution as he searched for the track, but his sweaty fingers pressed play on the wrong song, leaving him listening to the nice one about the rat.

Gary giggled again but this time it wasn't because he thought the situation was funny. This time it was because deep down he was shitting himself after realising the things in front of him were frightening.

He eyed them closely as they sluggishly moved towards him, fumbling quickly to find the right song before they picked up the pace. He knew he needed to shift his arse soon or risk being their second course, but the closer they were to him, the harder it was to locate the right track.

"Come on! Come on! Where are you?!" he belted out.

Sweat now dripped into his eyes, stinging them to blur his vision as the sounds of shuffling feet got closer and closer. He could smell the toxic breath lingering beneath his nostrils, causing him to crumble inside, but, as the zombies got to touching distance, a glorious sound was heard.

Gary smiled as the words - 'Well this is thriller, thriller' - came through the earphones. It sent his mind into another weird fantasy as the zombies stopped their vicious-like approach to move in time to the beat of the music. He couldn't believe that it worked. That the song was making them dance. He clapped out loud, laughing at the hysterical sight as the walking dead shook and swayed their bodies just like the dancers did in the original video.

But his fantasy faded and he was sent back to the here and now.

He rubbed his eyes to see clearly before narrowly avoiding a set of snapping teeth; pushing the zombie away to turn and run. But he slipped on the puddle of thick blood and crashed to the floor. He tried desperately to get up but his body was soaked in the slippery liquid, leaving him shivering as he slid on the floor. He lashed out to keep the zombies at bay, crying like he'd just woken from a bad dream.

"Help me, someone, anyone!" he cried out as the zombies lowered towards him. "Get the *fuck* away from me."

He pushed back to give him some room before attempting to remove his sticky trainers, but the monsters scared him into just fumbling with the blood-soaked laces. He yelled again as he reversed out the door on his backside before eyeing the creatures to curse under his breath at not being able to untie them, seething after seeing the fifty-foot gap he'd made slowly decrease.

He bit his lip as the zombies closed in another ten feet, feeling his heart burning hotter by the second as he nervously slipped a trainer heel away from his foot. He was thankful to see the footwear fall to the floor, but the creatures were almost on top of him again, leaving him choking from their dead stench.

He sweated even more as they gained another ten feet, the sight of their naked bodies drooling and groaning making him want to crawl up in a ball and admit defeat. But, he breathed in deeply and pulled on the other trainer. He shook and screamed at the zombies until the blood-drenched piece of footwear flew through the air to bounce off Vincent's head, sending his zombified corpse off track to walk into a wall before falling over.

Gary reversed on his arse some more before quickly lifting off the floor, but, as he ran towards the nearest exit, his I-phone disconnected from the earphones and fell to the ground, still blasting out music to distract the zombies. But Gary didn't look back. He was running for his life.

Vincent slapped colour-fading hands onto the floor in an attempt to reach the phone, twitching his ears as the sound bounced off the walls. The ex-banker grinned as it touched it before scrolling down the playlist like it was reading Braille, changing the song as it rose off the floor.

The last thing Gary heard was the 'Thriller' song playing for real.

He raced around a corner to gain some distance as the zombies danced like they were in a dance-off; returning to looking like scary monsters once the track ended.

They sniffed the air, searching for Gary's scent; locating it before moving down the corridor, but, within a few minutes, they were stuck at the exit. There were only two ways to go if they wanted to reach the main hospital grounds; one was the elevator and the other was the stairs. But none of the zombies seemed capable of working out how to achieve either.

TWENTY-TWO

J ulie was still upset after witnessing the awful death of Frank, but she kept on working and kept on producing the smile she wore for the patients. She couldn't let them down.

She walked past the doorway that led down to the morgue, almost jumping out of her skin after seeing Gary frantically open the door, staggering towards her whilst muttering to himself. He was soaked in sweat and it frightened her.

"Why do you not have anything on your feet?" she asked, gripping him as she listened to what he was trying to say. But nothing made sense. "And why are you sweating like you've been chased by a pack of lions?"

"They are worse than lions," Gary whispered, as Julie escorted him away. "Much worse."

She looked around for assistance but saw no one, so aimed for the waiting room and entered; helping Gary's nervous frame to a seat.

"Stay here," she said, panicking because she didn't know what was wrong with him. "I'm gonna look for Hazel."

She smiled at him as he collapsed in the seat, his eyes flickering like he was having a nightmare before slowly leaving him and exiting the room. She found Hazel within seconds, walking past after doing her rounds, but Julie now became breathless and couldn't speak.

"Hey, are you okay?" Hazel calmly asked, walking up to her. "Are you still traumatised? Do you want to go home?"

"I need you to come with me now." Julie tugged on Hazel's arm. "Gary's not well."

"Hey, calm down and take a deep breath," Hazel replied, releasing Julie's grip. "What do you mean not well?"

Julie broke down, becoming teary-eyed as she explained what'd just taken place with Gary before rushing back towards the waiting room.

"Quickly...He's in here."

Hazel raced after her to enter the room, feeling surprised to see Gary in a traumatised state because he was fine when she'd spoken to him half an hour ago. But Gary wasn't acknowledging her. He was lost inside a real-life nightmare, seeing those evil beings up close leaving him petrified like a lost boy. He wanted to shut his eyes and sink deeply into another daydream but had no chance of achieving it.

Hazel sat next to him, holding his hand to feel the sticky sweat pouring out of it.

"Talk to me, Gary. Tell me what's wrong...Are you in pain?" She glanced down at his feet and sighed. "Where are your trainers? Where'd you leave them?"

Gary stared at her distraughtly.

He pointed towards the door before suddenly bursting into tears, leaving Hazel confused.

"...Look, I can't help you unless you talk to me," she soothingly said, removing her hand to wipe the sweat onto her uniform. "What happened?"

"Don't let anybody go down to the MORGUE room!" Gary hollered; his words knocking Hazel back in her seat. "The dead have come back to life again...They've killed Colin and will kill us all if they escape."

The impact of his speech frightened Julie but Hazel wasn't as convinced. She knew Gary had a drug problem, or he did have not so long ago, and he'd taken some time off work because of it. So, Hazel studied him. She watched Gary shake rapidly as more sweat dripped onto the floor, his actions making her feel convinced that he'd taken something recently.

"What have you put inside yourself?" she asked him sternly, leaving her seat to stand next to Julie. "I can't help you unless you tell me."

"Do you seriously think he's on drugs right now?" Julie asked, feeling more worried than before. "I've never seen him take any."

"I'm afraid he's had us all convinced...This looks like a classic case of drug abuse to me."

They saw Gary quiver in his seat, waving his arms in the air like he was fighting imaginary enemies; his eyes sore from constantly glaring at the door.

"Come on, Gary, what have you taken?" Hazel asked again, hoping her words snapped him out of it.

"Don't go near the MORGUE!!"

Julie puffed out her cheeks, feeling sad that she couldn't help him as Hazel moved closer; checking Gary's eyes to see they weren't dilated as he kept his glare strong.

"What are you trying to tell me?" she asked, shaking him. "Colin's dead...Is that what you're saying?"

"He's probably having a bad trip?"

"A minute ago I would agree, Julie, but I don't think he's high anymore." Hazel turned to stare at the door. "I think he may be right...Something's happened to Colin."

She rubbed Gary's shoulder, hoping he would calm down and explain what happened, but her words messed with his head and he struggled to speak. He tried to get up but turned pale quickly and collapsed to the floor.

"No, Gary, wake up!" Julie rushed from her mouth, sinking to her knees to help him. "He has to be lying about Colin, surely?"

"I hope you're right, but it's a strange accusation to even think of saying, so we need to take it seriously." Hazel grabbed a cushion from one of the chairs and gave it to Julie. "Place this under his head. It's best not to move him right now."

"And the morgue?" Julie asked, squirming from the thought that Colin may be dead. "Do we keep clear of it?"

"For now, yes." Hazel shook herself to release negative thoughts before slowly walking towards the door. "I need to keep this hospital safe...I have a job to do." She opened it and smiled at the unconscious man before turning back to Julie. "This may backfire, leaving me looking as stupid as a penguin wearing a dress but we need to get the police involved...Can you call them? And be discreet."

Julie nodded as she stroked Gary's hair.

Hazel soaked everything in and exited the room, leaving Julie now feeling alone. She waited a few more seconds to see if Hazel would do a U-turn, frowning because she hadn't before rising off the floor. She then shakily walked over to the phone.

———

George was still on duty back at the station when the ringing of the phone disrupted his flow. He felt pleased with himself for increasing his typing speed but was now moaning at having to stop. He answered the call but wasn't given time to speak, as a timid voice on the other end exploded into words.

"One of our workers reckons there are dead people come to life in the morgue and they have murdered someone."

George burst out laughing. The information was too silly for him to take seriously.

He shouted over to Wayne, repeating what he heard, but Wayne didn't react in the same way. Instead, he was stunned by the news and at how easily George gave out the information. Blake was still at the station and he'd heard it, meaning George's stupidity had probably blown any chances of Blake believing Wayne's latest bunch of lies aimed at how the Smythes died. But luckily for George, Blake was laughing also.

"That's a good one," he said, trying to keep a straight face. "Someone's been watching too many Romero movies."

Wayne glared at George like he was imitating *Medusa* with the snakes in her hair, but, even though his glare was a worrying sight, George wasn't turned to stone. But he did sheepishly hand over the receiver before scurrying off to stand next to Blake.

Wayne apologised to the worried caller on George's behalf before adding, "Explain again what happened?"

"Gary told Hazel that dead people were walking around in

the morgue," Julie rushed from her mouth whilst glancing at the still unconscious man. "But we don't know if it's true because he's fainted...What do we do? We're worried."

Wayne gulped as thoughts of the splattered corpse mysteriously walking on the road dug at his brain. He now feared that person could well be linked to what Julie was saying. He knew he had to be professional and take control of the situation. There was no time to inform Mike.

"Just stay calm and block off all entrances to the morgue... Make sure nobody goes down there. I'm coming over now."

Blake stopped laughing as Wayne finished the call, but he never said anything. He just watched Wayne swear at himself.

————

Another member of staff headed for the same door that led to the gruesome and twisted figures before Julie was able to pass on the information. He opened it and slipped past, whistling like he didn't have a care in the world.

His name was *Clive*; an eighteen-year-old college student with long, greasy, dark hair. He'd been working part-time in the Pathology Department for a few weeks, doing shifts to help gain experience towards his exams; mostly doing the night shift because he loved how quiet the hospital was then. It was less stressful and he was able to concentrate.

He walked along the corridor, entering the lift before closing the large, metal shutters, but the screeching noise was heard by the recently immobile creatures on the lower floor. They moved towards the sound, sniffing the tray of blood samples in Clive's hand as he aimed towards the morgue to drop them off.

The lift came to a stop and Clive exited, but his eyes suddenly opened to their full capacity after a sense of shock hit him. He couldn't believe what he was seeing. The floor was covered in bloody footprints.

He cautiously continued to walk towards the morgue room, thinking someone was playing a trick on him; smiling cheekily after remembering the prank he'd played on Gary a few weeks ago.

Nice one, Gary, he thought, moving down a corridor. *Pranking me back.*

He kept up the smile as he neared the corner leading to the morgue room entrance, gripping the sample tray tight as he followed the footprints; ready to surprise the mystery practical joker. He looked ahead as excitement raced through him; his mind spinning as he quivered from thoughts of not knowing where the prank would lead. But, as he closed to twenty feet away saw no more signs. He sighed and lowered his head but soon lifted it after hearing a groan.

If you want to play then bring it, he thought, tiptoeing his way to the corner before sucking up a huge gulp of air.

"YEEEAAAAAAHHHH," he roared, turning it to cough.

But his plan to frighten the noisemaker backfired, leaving him shaking from fear. He stared at the three, un-dead humans growling at him, feeling uneasy until not sure of what to do next. He sweated fast as his knees wobbled; his hand trembling to move the tray like a ship on a stormy sea as he eyeballed the incoming Vincent still holding the phone. But the zombie didn't attack. It just tilted its head and roared back at him.

Clive dropped the tray to see the test tubes crash to the floor.

He quivered on the spot as the creatures acted like

starving animals, dropping to the floor to rub fingers into the red juice before thrusting them inside their mouths; growling at Clive as the sweet taste reignited their desire to feast on flesh.

They moved closer to him, swinging arms like drunks on a dancefloor, but none were able to grab him. Clive may have been numb to speak but was still able to think. He pushed Vincent into the others and headed for the morgue room, racing inside and slamming the door to hear his heartbeat thud against his chest. He sunk to the floor, choking on tears as the groans from outside shattered his confidence.

"Go AWAY!" he bellowed, ramming his back against the door. "Who the FUCK are you?"

He pushed hard until his spine hurt, hoping his weight would prevent the trio of filth from entering, but the zombies slammed hard against the door, leaving him bruised within seconds. He squealed until the pain became numb before wincing as more sadistic groans slipped underneath the door. He reached into his pocket to pull out an inhaler, quickly puffing on it as another THUD brought more tears to his eyes, puffing on it again after spotting the amputated corpse on the floor beside him. He couldn't believe he missed it.

He blamed the lack of seeing it on the terrifying situation he found himself in; the constant groaning and slamming on the door being the reasons to not notice. But, as the reality of what was with him inside the room slowly sunk in, felt his trousers become wet with sticky blood and puke.

He stared at the stockroom, noticing the door was open; itching to move fast to reach it so he could hide. But, the sound of the phone ringing inside the room startled him, leaving him frozen. He stared at it as it rang out a few more times, feeling heavy thuds against his back as the zombies pounded on the door before squirming in agony from thoughts of needing to move to reach the phone. But the chewed-up body twitched, moving its head from side to side as if sensing someone was there. It snapped teeth in Clive's direction, frightening him into almost giving in, as its only hand gripped the floor to pull itself towards him.

The other zombies increased their violent efforts to enter the room, kicking and punching the door to make Clive angry. He lashed out at the thing closing in on his leg, desperately kicking out at it, but his bum moved away from the door, leaving him unable to stop the creatures from getting inside. He flinched when the door slowly opened to reveal dead fingers reaching around; the sight crushing his energy as the phone stopped ringing.

He couldn't stop looking at the door opening wider as the torn-apart zombie grabbed his right ankle. He knew he wasn't strong enough to stop the others from getting inside.

"What the hell are you doing with my leg?!" he yelled, shaking it to keep the creature at bay. "I'm no one's dinner."

He clenched a fist and punched the zombie on the head, almost smiling as it released the grip before slamming his size nine footwear into its face, cracking its jaw as it rolled across the room. He saw one of the freaks force away inside, hoping it didn't see him as he dived across the floor to hide under a table covered with a large white sheet hanging over the sides. He shivered as he watched the movement of the darkened shadows beneath the cloth, hearing the zombies whine as if communicating with each other to say something along the lines of – Where did he go? – But he gulped nervously after spotting a bloodline lead to his hiding place.

He closed his eyes for a second as another whine made his teeth hurt, but the shadows weren't closing in.

Hopefully, they haven't noticed, he thought, backing away to the other end of the table.

He puffed out his cheeks, eyeing the shadows as they moved further inside the room, eagerly waiting for them to leave enough space so he could escape.

"Just a little more," he whispered, smiling at the thought of finally getting away. "Just a few more steps."

He moved from underneath the table, but the sheet got caught around his head, leaving him guessing where the zombies were. He got lucky and freed himself before running past them like a sprinter during a race, nearing the door to almost touch it when the pain in the arse, chopped-up zombie gripped his foot again. Clive yelled at it as the grip remained strong, but this time he wasn't able to free himself. The zombie tugged hard and tripped him, leaving him falling back to crack his head on the floor. He was knocked out.

He woke again a minute later to his head throbbing like someone was drilling inside his brain, but, when he tried to move, he couldn't. He tried again, putting in extra effort, but his legs were stiff. He lifted his head to see two blurred figures sitting on either side of him eating some type of meat.

The canteen wasn't open until the morning so how did they get this food? he thought, feeling sick from the throbbing pain.

But, as his eyesight slowly returned, saw puddles of blood by his legs.

Clive stared at the zombies tearing and eating the flesh from his limbs; the pain not registering because of the shock. But, as it subsided, he bellowed out loud. He slammed his hands against the floor as more strips of flesh were yanked from his legs; opening his mouth to scream over and over again.

TWENTY-THREE

Wayne raced into the building, closely followed by a truncheon-wielding angry-faced Jason, whose mind was set on taking down something similar to the creature behind Nash's death. They heard a faint yell as they reached the reception desk but couldn't see anyone needing their help. But still, the sound spooked them enough to become alert.

They saw Hazel racing towards them from down the corridor before a tearful Julie rushed out of the waiting room; both closing in at the same time as another squeal was heard.

"Where's that coming from?" Wayne demanded, checking for the sound. "Seems far away."

"It's coming through the air vents," Hazel replied, pointing at one on the bottom of a nearby wall.

"How?" Wayne snapped. "I told Julie to make sure no one went down to the lower levels."

The young nurse raised a quivering hand as a teardrop slid down a cheek. "I'm Julie," she said, wiping her face. "I spoke to the staff and also placed a sign on the exits leading downstairs...No one should've gone down there."

"Well, it sure sounds like someone did," Jason said, staring at her.

Julie looked to the floor as a sense of guilt washed over her until finding the strength to fight back. She knew she may have been partly to blame, seeing as it took her a few minutes to go from watching over Gary to organising what Hazel told her, but this wasn't all down to her mistake. And she needed to let the officers know that.

"I did everything I was asked to do to prevent someone from going downstairs, but I can't keep an eye on all the exits. I'm not a superwoman you know."

Hazel hugged her before she lost it completely and ran out of the building, but another scream slipped through the vent to make them shudder.

"Someone must've ignored your signs!" snapped Wayne, glaring at the vent. "Who would be going down there tonight?"

"I don't know," Julie replied, sniffing as she struggled to cope. "Anyone who works in the morgue."

"There can't be many on duty at this hour, surely?" Wayne scratched his head. He tried to come up with a plan, but not knowing how many people were down near the morgue had him stumped. "Think...I need to know."

Hazel gripped Julie tight, becoming her protector to swipe away Wayne's aggressive approach to questioning her. She wasn't standing for it anymore. Julie didn't deserve it.

"That's enough," she said, holding out a hand. "She did her best...Now, haven't you got a job to do?"

Wayne scrunched his lips and nodded before glaring at the vent again, moving closer to it as Jason watched on.

"Are you okay?" he asked, seeing the concentration on Wayne's face.

"I don't hear anything now," Wayne replied, looking back at him. "I think that person is dead."

Julie gulped as she pushed her head into Hazel's breasts.

They shivered as the officers discussed a plan of action. They listened to them work out a way to enter the basement unnoticed before Wayne told them to do what was meant to have been done before. He and Jason would handle the rest. But, as the nurses followed them to the nearest exit, everyone's hearts beat faster.

"Was that the best sign you could put up?" Jason asked Julie, close to smirking after reading the sign again. "Beware! Keep out!"

Julie just huffed and shrugged her shoulders.

"Maybe you should change it to crazy people are in the morgue," Wayne said, grabbing his baton before smiling at her. "That'll work."

The nurses stood back as Wayne and Jason fought with feelings of dread; both breathing deeply as they neared the door. But Wayne froze as a flashback of him and Nash entering Vincent's living room crashed into him. He shuddered, fearing that a dead person like the mother who was buried in the garden was behind the door; his head fogging up to scare him into lowering his baton.

"You've got this," Jason said, gritting his teeth. "We need to do this for Nash..."

He was pumped up and ready to go but needed his superior to do the same. He knew the only way that would happen was if he opened the door, so he did but nothing was there.

"...Now are you ready?"

"I'm ready."

They slipped through the doorway to hear it being barricaded by the nurses before slowly walking along a corridor; both whacking batons against walls to listen out for any movement. But it was too quiet and it freaked them out.

"Right, let's get this done quickly and efficiently," Wayne said, smacking his baton against the wall again. "I don't want you racing around like a madman. There could be people still alive down there, so no over-the-top impulses...You got that?"

"So no guns then?"

"Keep it holstered until it's necessary...I don't want you shooting up the hospital and scaring everyone upstairs."

Jason nodded as they reached the lift, but, as he leaned over to press the button, Wayne grabbed his hand.

"No! Too much noise...We'll take the stairs."

"But we've just been banging on the walls," Jason said, acting surprised. "Now you don't want any noise?"

Wayne almost laughed. "We banged on the walls to see if any were up here, but now we know they aren't we need to surprise them."

They cautiously moved past the lift and aimed for the stairs, standing side-by-side until reaching them; keeping the truncheons out in front ready to swing at any intruders. But the silence scared them more than the thought of seeing one.

They followed the stairs, reaching the bottom to catch faint groans in the air; becoming louder by the second as they moved along another corridor.

"Stop..." Wayne softly said after spotting blood footprints on the floor. "We must be close."

"We sure are," Jason replied, pointing at a line of blood next to a bloody handprint on a wall. "Very close."

Suddenly, a phone rang, spooking them into falling back against a wall, its ringtone echoing all around them.

"Do you think one of them has a phone?"

"Not if they're dead," Wayne replied, sweating. "Must belong to the person who screamed."

Jason spotted Gary's I-phone lying on the ground so quickly picked it up and turned it off, eyeing up the area to see nothing approach as he pocketed it and carried on walking. Wayne kept close to him as they neared the corner where Clive had bumped into his killers before stopping abruptly after witnessing the tray and smashed glass on the ground.

"Shit!" Wayne said, holding Jason back. "Now we know someone was here."

"But what about others? Surely someone would've raised the alarm if they saw this?"

"True...So let's just assume that the person attacked was the only one."

Wayne cautiously peered around the corner but quickly jumped back after seeing a mutilated body laid out across the legs of a sitting zombie. It was trying to place the dead person's eyes into its eye sockets but one slipped from its bloodied fingers to fall to the floor. It groaned as it slammed a hand on the ground, moving it briskly as it sniffed the air. Wayne gulped as thoughts of the creature knowing he was there shook him up, but the sniffing stopped within seconds and the fallen eye was picked up again.

Jason closed in but Wayne placed a hand in the air to stop him. There was no need to speak, Jason knew he'd seen something.

He waited for Wayne to make a move but he was watching the zombie place the eyes into its sockets before seeing them fall out again to be picked up and placed in backwards.

"What are you doin'?" Jason whispered; slowly turning the corner to see the victim on the floor. "What the fucks happened to his brain?"

Wayne shook his head and stared at Clive's body, flinching to see the top of his skull missing.

"I have no idea," he whispered back, raising his baton to the sound of another groan. "But that thing is freakin' me out."

"You mean the thing that used to be the bank manager."

Wayne glared at the zombified version of Vincent as more groans rang out before striking it across the face with the baton. But it didn't fall. It just snarled and showed teeth. Wayne breathed fast, feeling scared as he slammed the baton against its face a few more times, seeing it topple over to slowly bounce back up again before looking at his shaking hand holding the weapon soaked in congealed blood.

"Why won't it die?" Jason questioned, cringing at the sight of the dark juice leaking down the zombie's face. "Hit it again..."

He touched his gun holster as Wayne struck the zombie again and again; each blow causing more damage than the one before as Vincent's jaw hung off. But the beast still wouldn't die. It got back to its feet, swinging hands like it was holding imaginary tennis rackets, growling as the officers avoided being touched.

"...Just put it down!" Jason worryingly shouted as the zombie aimed for him. "I can't deal with..."

But a blast from Wayne's gun sent sound waves crashing into Jason's ears, rocking him into falling against a wall to see Vincent collapse.

Wayne re-holstered it, cringing after seeing blood and brain matter dribble down the wall that the bullet ended up in.

"Are you happy now?" he said, close to vomiting. "It's down."

Jason nodded as he eyed the fallen creature that now had a large hole in its forehead before poking his ears to try to stop them from ringing.

"It's fuckin' freaky seeing one movin' about," he said, stepping over the body of Clive. "But what about Nash?"

"What about him?"

"He could be one."

Wayne stared at Jason. He knew he was right but it was taking a while to sink in. He shook his head and gulped before pointing towards the morgue room, feeling the hairs on his arms stick up from a sudden rush of nerves.

"Then let's find out," he said, moving past the bodies to follow the bloody footprints. "There's more of them...We just need to find 'em before they kill again."

They neared the door, but it flung open and knocked them over as the other naked corpses bundled out of the room. One was biting fingers off a torn-away hand whilst the other had a mouthful of Clive's brain. Jason panicked as he watched them closely before rolling along the floor to gain some distance. But the fingerless hand dropped next to him. He squirmed and got back to his feet, dodging the zombie's swinging arms before jostling it to the ground, but struggled to hit it with his baton. Wayne blinked fast as he rose off the floor to see Jason scuffle with the corpse of Frank. He wanted to help but couldn't stop shaking.

"Use your g...un," he rushed from his mouth before staggering backwards. "Shoot it in the head."

"You shoot it!" the angry reply came as Jason pinned Frank to the floor.

He was just about to crack the zombie's head in with the baton when the zombified version of Nash suddenly pounced on him, pulling him towards its mouth.

"Come on, Wayne, shoot them!" he bellowed, slamming the baton around Nash's face. "Snap out of it!"

But Wayne remained stunned.

Jason winced as Nash squeezed him tight; the strength stopping him from breathing as he lost the grip on the baton. He kicked out at the incoming Frank, sweating from fear as he smacked the back of his head against Nash's chin; happy to see the grip loosen to allow him to breathe again so he could reach for his gun. He pulled it from its holster and aimed it at Frank but Nash's cold hands wrapped around his stomach again, causing the gun to fire a bullet into a wall. Jason squirmed as he was lifted off the ground, but another bullet fired into Wayne's left arm to knock him over.

Wayne reeled around on the floor in a desperate effort to reach for his gun, but terror overcame him after seeing Frank crawl along the ground to reach him. He closed his eyes, expecting to be attacked, but the zombie just got back to its feet and snarled at him as it shuffled along the corridor.

Jason tried every self-defence move he'd learned at the police academy but none were working as the zombie kept the grip tight. It lashed out to bite him but a hand gripped the bottom of its jaw to force its mouth shut, but, as Jason tried to shoot it, it quickly threw him against a wall and wrestled him to the ground.

Wayne opened his eyes to hear Jason panting for breath before seeing Nash pin him to the floor like a mad cage fighter looking for a victory. But Wayne was still too shaken to reach for his gun.

"Hold on," he said, finding his courage. "I'm gonna shoot it."

But, as he lowered his hand towards his weapon, flinched from the pain in his arm. He saw blood slide down his hand, dripping off his fingers to splash onto the floor, the aroma exciting the zombie, causing it to lose focus. It almost let Jason go and he noticed.

Jason quickly slammed his head against the zombie's face again until able to point the gun at it, but it growled and gripped his gun hand, leaving him firing into the ceiling.

The beast was too strong for him.

He yelped as it squeezed his hand, breaking fingers before being punched with his other one. But it was no use, the zombie wouldn't let go.

"I need help!" he hollered, kicking out at it again. "NASH! STOP!"

The zombie let go and stared at him, acting like it recognised his voice. It moved its head from side to side as if remembering what it used to be, its eyes twitching as if absorbing the words until a smile was etched on its face.

Jason nervously crawled towards Wayne, avoiding the recent puddle of blood to grip Wayne's good hand, but the beast pounced on him again before he was lifted off the floor.

"Finish it!" Jason barked. "Before it bites me."

"Put your head down. I'm gonna blast its fuckin' head off."

Jason ducked as Wayne released his gun. He cringed as he shot the creature in the forehead, happy to see it roll off Jason to lay still.

"Is it dead?"

"I hope so," Wayne said smiling. "I hit the sucker in the head...So, as far as I'm concerned, in the head means it's dead."

"Good. Now get me up."

Wayne helped Jason back to his feet but closely observed him.

"How are you?" he asked, checking Jason's uniform for rips and bloodstains. "It didn't bite you did it?"

"Nah...I was lucky." Jason stared at Wayne's injury, feeling embarrassed by what he'd done. "You do know it was an accident?"

Wayne shook his head and winced. He knew Jason was a loose cannon but what happened wasn't his fault.

"Of course I do."

"Let's find the last one," Jason excitedly said, feeling a mad rush of adrenaline again. "Before it escapes..."

They raced away, but the corpse of Nash suddenly groaned, scaring them into stopping.

"...Are you sure you shot it in the head?" Jason asked, shaking as he faced the enemy. "Because it's getting up again."

Wayne gulped as the groans increased.

He stared at the zombie as blood poured from its head, its mouth snapping as it moved in his direction.

"It should be dead," he whispered, aiming his gun. "Well, dead again."

The zombie slobbered as the groans turned into roars; its eyes glowing pure evil as it closed in. But Jason hollered: "NASH!" again to confuse it. It stopped and stared at its arm before lifting the hand to its face, but another bullet fired, exploding the fingers before two more shots caved its head in.

"Now it's dead," Wayne said, lowering his gun.

TWENTY-FOUR

The snarling corpse of Frank had made some distance as it navigated its way towards the stairs. It sniffed the air, taking in the still lingering aroma given off by the officers before following the smell to the first step, but it struggled to walk onto it. It grimaced as it snapped its teeth before showing signs of someone thinking; awkwardly raising a leg before planting the foot onto the step; doing the same with the other one as memories flooded back. It picked up speed as the other steps became easy, reaching the top to follow the corridor leading to the exit door, but it stopped and looked confused. It bumped into the door a few times but it didn't budge so turned its attention to the handle, gripping it to smile as it was turned. But still, the door wouldn't open because a 2-seater sofa was forced against it on the other side.

The zombie snarled as it leaned a shoulder into the door.

It gritted its teeth as it pushed against it, moving the sofa with ease before walking onto the hospital's ground floor, but it seemed undecided on which direction to take. It glared from left to right, grunting as it moved away from the area, seeing no one because of Hazel's order to keep it clear. But a sudden whiff in the air excited it. It licked its lips and followed the smell, twitching its nose after staring at an EXIT sign hanging from the ceiling; its head shaking as it neared the reception desk. But even that area was empty of people.

It snapped its teeth again as it neared a room where the aroma seemed strong, standing by the door to glare through its small window before gripping the handle to turn it.

———

Wayne and Jason raced up the stairs leading back to the main floor but stopped after seeing the door open.

"Fuck!" Jason snapped, feeling worried after spotting tiny traces of blood on the floor. "It's already here."

"But how?" Wayne questioned. "Those things don't move that fast...We weren't that far behind so should've caught it up."

They exited to see the sofa before splitting up to go left and right; both scanning the floor tiles for more of the red stuff. But none was seen.

Wayne gripped his baton as he slowly closed in on the reception desk; focusing firmly on the floor as a stunned receptionist stopped talking to Hazel.

"What's he doing?" she asked, staring at Wayne and pointing to get Hazel's attention. "Did he lose some money?"

Hazel turned to watch Wayne peering through the windows of a few doors, his heart racing as the pressure to find the creature increased.

"Are you okay, officer?" she asked, slowly walking towards him. "Is there anything we need to worry about?"

Wayne wiped the sweat from his brow as his breathing slowed before placing the baton behind his back. But Hazel had already seen it.

"Hiding that thing from me won't make me feel less worried," she said, glancing over Wayne's shoulder to see Jason appear from a room. "What's going on?"

"You need to keep this to yourself," he whispered; awkwardly checking to see where the receptionist was. He was glad to see she was still at her desk. "You remember Frank, the truck driver?"

"Of course I do," Hazel replied, feeling saddened by the mention of his name. "I was there when he died."

"About that..." Wayne gripped her shoulder before drawing her closer. "He's not dead anymore..."

Hazel almost fainted.

"...He's escaped from the morgue and is up here somewhere."

Of all the theories as to why Wayne was on edge, Hazel hadn't thought of this. She stood open-mouthed, trying her best to let it sink in; secretly hoping he was winding her up, but his expression wasn't changing. He was still sweating and was still nervous.

"Bu-t how?" she asked, feeling the hairs stand up on her arms. "I couldn't restart his heart."

Wayne never had time to explain because he needed to find the thing. But, after Hazel became teary-eyed, he quickly told her about what happened on the roadside.

"I knew it was a human who bit him," she said, putting the pieces together. "But I wasn't expecting this...That the person was already dead."

"It's hard to believe, I know. But it's the reason why I'm

armed now." Wayne shook before dropping to one knee, seeing the blood still seeping from his arm.

"Jeez!" Hazel said, kicking herself for not noticing before. "Are you okay? How did that happen?"

"I'm fine," the reply came as Wayne got back to his feet. "My partner shot me." He looked into her eyes, sensing she was nervous. "But don't worry. It was an accident...He's not who you need to worry about."

Hazel pressed her hands over the wound as Wayne flinched.

"Stop being a baby," she said, smiling. "I need to fix it."

"I'm all yours after I find Frank," Wayne said, gritting his teeth before glancing over at the receptionist. "Do you think she saw it?"

Hazel let out a nervous giggle. "Do you think she'd be at her desk if she did?"

"Good point."

"She's just come back from her break. We walked down together."

Wayne nodded before sighing at the thought of still not knowing where the creature was, his vision now switching from Jason to the receptionist as he tried to figure out its location. He knew it had to be nearby. *But where?*

"So, Gary wasn't lying about the walking dead," Hazel muttered after remembering his weird outburst. "Everything he said was real." She quivered before adding, "Who was it that screamed down there?"

"I don't know, but he was one of your staff," Wayne replied, taking in what she said. "Where's Gary now? I need to speak to him."

"He's in the waiting room...He's badly shaken up."

"Lead the way."

Hazel smiled at the receptionist as she walked Wayne towards the room, but a deafening squeal rocked her, causing her to stop in her tracks.

Wayne gripped her tight as Jason appeared, nervously holding his baton as he sluggishly neared the door.

Hazel squirmed after spotting the broken fingers on his free hand, shocked that he wasn't flinching. She saw him avoid contact with his injury, knowing it was his way to keep the pain at bay.

Jason looked through the small window in the door but instantly wished he hadn't after seeing the zombie with Gary's tongue in its mouth.

"What?!" Wayne shouted as Jason coughed up spit. "Is it in there?"

"Yes."

"Then we need to finish it. NOW!"

Wayne let go of Hazel to race towards the door, barging his way into the room to see the zombie bite into Gary's face. But it didn't seem bothered that it was being watched. It just wanted to taste more of the man who was still lying on the floor.

It attacked again, ripping away part of Gary's left cheek to leave the officers shaken up, as Hazel closed in to hear another scream.

"What's happening to Gary?" she rushed from her mouth, moving between the men to witness the sickening sight. "AAARRGGGHH!"

"Get her back!" Wayne ordered, pushing Jason towards her. "She doesn't need to see this."

Jason did; holding Hazel to guide her away from the door.

"Do you want me to shoot it?" he asked, excited to hear a yes.

"No! The noise will attract more witnesses...We need to use our truncheons to make that thing extinct."

Hazel shook her head towards the receptionist after seeing just how distraught she was, holding out a hand to stop her from using the phone. She knew the woman was about to call someone, and that someone could easily end up bringing people to the hospital to catch whatever it was that brought Frank back to life. Hazel wasn't prepared for that to happen, especially seeing as the officers were about to eliminate the last of the infected.

Wayne and Jason cautiously entered the room, hearing Gary's last breath as the zombie sat next to his body chewing on his flesh. It didn't even move when Jason hit it with his baton. It just kept on chewing.

"It didn't even make a dent," he nervously said, raising the baton again. "But this time it'll go down."

He swung at the zombie again but it gripped the baton to scare him, rising off the floor to pull it from his grasp.

"Do something," he said, close to wetting himself. "This one is frightening..."

Wayne stared at the creature, feeling sick as it slobbered red liquid onto the baton before seeing it glare at Jason as he backed up against a wall. It pointed at him, revealing blood-stained teeth before walking in his direction.

"...Wayne!" he bellowed, almost in tears after the creature raised the weapon. "Do somethi---"

But blood splashed over his face before he could finish the word.

He wiped it off to see the zombie stagger before seeing Wayne angrily swing a fire extinguisher at its head again, caving its skull in as it dropped the baton. But it took two more strikes before the beast fell.

"Maybe we should carry these around instead of truncheons?" he said, shuddering at the sight of the dead again Frank with brain matter spilling from the top of its cranium.

Jason gulped as Wayne put the extinguisher down.

They stared at the creature before hearing Hazel's voice, turning to face her as she entered the room.

"Is it over?" she asked, squirming at the thought of the thing getting up again. "I hope it is."

"No, it isn't!" Wayne snapped at her. "Gary's been infected...He'll become the same unless we fuck up his brain."

"I don't want to see you do that to him."

Hazel choked from thoughts of Wayne smashing the extinguisher down on Gary's head but he wasn't attempting to pick it up. Instead, he seemed lost with what to do.

"Don't worry, I'm not some sadistic monster like that thing over there...I don't have the stomach to crush his head in while he's still human."

"But I will," Jason happily said, reaching for the extinguisher.

"What's wrong with you?!" Wayne blasted at him, standing in front of the recent weapon. "Were you dropped on your head as a child or somethin'?... He's still one of us, goddamn it."

Jason sighed before apologising for his sudden urge to impress Wayne, as Hazel stared at the body.

"Hey, guys," she said, tapping a finger against her lips. "What about taking him to the incinerator room?"

In the space of a few seconds she'd gone from being a caring nurse to a sick-minded killer, but, once this was over, she would feel sick to the stomach for even mentioning it.

"You mean to burn his body?" Jason asked, not sure if she meant it.

"Yes...Unless you can think of another way?"

Jason nodded. "But won't people see us?"

"Not if we hide his body under some sheets."

Wayne stepped in before negative thoughts entered his mind. He knew it was risky to try but Hazel's idea was a better solution than caving in an innocent, dead man's head. He told her to keep the receptionist busy whilst Jason looked for a mobile bed and some sheets, but, as they left the room, Wayne suddenly felt uneasy. He watched Gary's body to see if it moved, sweating again from thoughts of not knowing when the virus would take effect before checking his watch for the time.

The seconds seemed like minutes.

He heard the sound of wheels turning, getting closer and closer before seeing Jason outside the room with both items. He was glad he was quick.

"Help me lift him onto the bed," Wayne said, reaching for Gary's legs. "I've left you the best end."

Jason shuddered as he neared the patch of blood surrounding Gary's head; wincing and coughing as he gripped the shoulders.

"Thanks," he sarcastically replied, as the body was lifted.

Hazel returned to grab the sheets, swiftly throwing them over the corpse as it was laid down on the bed, but Wayne looked at her oddly.

"What!" she barked, feeling exhausted. "I'm helping."

"We still need to add the other body."

"Sorry." She removed the sheets and waited; desperately wanting it to be over as the body of Frank was piled on top.

"Happy now?" she asked, blinking fast as the sheets came down again. "I'm not in the mood for this."

Wayne smiled at her. "None of us is in the mood but we need to do it." He gripped the bed before saying, "What happened to the receptionist?"

"I gave her another break." Hazel pulled bandages from her pocket. "But we're not going anywhere until I've wrapped you guys up."

"Okay...But make it quick," Wayne replied, sighing.

———

They reached the incinerator room with ease after only seeing a few nosey nurses, as Hazel's authoritative glare kept them at bay. She may have been struggling with the chaos surrounding her but she was still in charge and her staff needed to know it.

She pointed at the large furnace, knowing it was about to roar like a raging, hungry dragon before standing next to a control panel; checking the temperature device as she waited for the men to slide the bodies onto a conveyor belt. She watched them push the bed next to it before the mangled corpse of Frank was dragged on top; being pushed further down to allow room for Gary's body to be added before Wayne pressed a button to set the rollers in motion. She saw the bodies move towards the incinerator's large, glass door before glancing at the men, watching them puff out their cheeks and wipe their brows as if exhausted. But they quickly jumped back after seeing Gary's corpse attempt to sit up.

"Open the incinerator door!" Hazel shouted, reaching for the control panel. "I'm gonna start it up."

Wayne cranked up the speed of the belt as Jason raced for

the door; making sure to avoid being touched by the now violently shaking zombie as he opened it. He was pleased to see Frank's corpse enter the incinerator, hearing it fall off the belt to roll into it, but Gary's hands gripped the metal machine to freak him out.

"Do something!" Hazel worryingly shouted as she watched from beneath her fingers. "Fuck it up!"

Wayne looked at her with his jaw dropped as Jason quickly smacked the hands with his baton, smiling as they let go before waving at Gary's corpse falling next to the other one. He slammed the door shut to see flames suddenly appear, watching the colours glow as the fire attacked the intruders. But the zombified version of Gary got up to bang its face against the glass.

Jason shuddered as hot bubbles formed on Gary's face before deathly eyes popped against the glass; the fire slicing through the corpses to leave just bones and ash.

Hazel turned the incinerator off before slowly walking away; her head down to hide tears as Wayne caught her up.

"Now it's over," he said, placing an arm around her.

TWENTY-FIVE

THURSDAY

The ringing of the phone caused Mike to startle as he recovered from the night before. He looked over at Chris as thoughts of – *How did he get into my house?* and *Why have I got a hangover?* – raced inside his mind; feeling angry after remembering what happened.

"Hello," he murmured, answering the phone and wanting to puke. "Is everything okay?"

"Mike, where have you been all night?" Susan worryingly said. "There's been a crisis at the hospital...George was constantly trying to get hold of you."

"Sorry about that...I was very busy."

"There's no need to apologise to me. I know you had a stressful day yesterday but you need to go there."

Mike closed his eyes as he swallowed rising sick, cringing at how bad he felt as Susan mentioned his name again to wake him up.

"I'm on my way."

He ended the call and checked his messages, shocked to find fifteen missed calls and ten texts all relating to something bad happening at the hospital to make him feel embarrassed and guilty.

"Hey, Mike, what's up?" Chris happily asked, trying to read Mike's facial expression. "You don't look good."

Mike glared at him.

He wanted to punish Chris for last night, but, after taking a second to think about it knew he was as much to blame.

"I'm not good. I feel sick from the booze." Mike choked and shook his head. "Why are you not feeling the same? You were out of it."

Chris laughed, loving the moment. To see Mike, the big bad cop suffer from a hangover while he, the small reporter had nothing, not even a mild headache was hilarious for him.

"Don't worry about me," Chris replied, grabbing his coat. "You need to drink plenty of water."

"I need to get to the hospital."

"Right...Then I'm coming with you..."

Mike glared at him again whilst rubbing his temples.

"...There's no need to give me a look. You agreed."

"Agreed on what exactly?"

"Chris placed on his coat. "That I'm now working with you."

Mike sighed as he left the room, muttering to himself as Chris followed. He knew he'd made a huge mistake. But, he was a man of his word, so, as he opened the front door to almost puke after the fresh air hit him, smiled and let Chris pass.

"Just don't piss me off," Mike snapped, closing the door before wiping a hand across his face. "If you're gonna follow me around then you do it on my terms."

"You got it, chief."

They then walked towards Mike's car.

———

It was extremely hectic in and around the hospital grounds when they arrived as busy *reporters* scrutinized the area whilst grabbing hospital staff for an interview. Mike knew something bad had happened. He didn't need to go inside to find out.

"Shit! This doesn't look good," Chris said, opening the car door. "Do you need me to do anything?"

"Yeah...You can see what's going on with your chums over there while I see where I'm needed inside..."

Mike exited the car and shook his head before pushing Chris towards the reporters; hoping he wouldn't act like a fool when distracting information from them.

"...Come find me when you're finished."

Mike entered the building, rushing his vision from left to right before moving forward, but he couldn't see any of his officers, so just followed a group of doctors and nurses down a corridor. He waited for one of them to speak, to say something involving the incident, but neither said anything.

"Excuse me," he softly said. "Do you know what happened here?"

He saw their faces turn pale before a tall, deep-voiced *doctor* said, "You need to go to the morgue."

He then turned and walked away, followed by the others.

Mike felt like catching him up and shaking him for more information but had a feeling the man was traumatised, so just left it before heading back to the main reception. He saw

Chris race into the building, looking flustered as he nodded his head.

"There's news spreading about more of those creatures being inside here," Chris said, fighting his way through a crowd of people. "They attacked some hospital workers."

"I guessed as much." Mike swallowed hard as he walked towards the exit leading to the morgue. "I've been told to go down there...So get your notebook out. You're gonna need it."

They aimed for the stairs, moving down to the lower levels, but a *doctor* stopped them.

"I'm sorry, but he won't be able to go past this point," he said, staring at Chris. "He's not authorised."

Mike scrunched his face and nibbled his lip.

"He's with me."

"But I've been told not to let any press enter the morgue to snoop around."

"Really?!" Mike snapped, feeling his head pound again. He didn't need this right now. "This particular member of the press is helping the police."

"But still," the doctor replied, feeling extreme pressure. "I have my orders."

Mike waved an index finger in his face. "You can take your orders and---"

"Calm down," Chris interrupted, smirking. "He's only doing his job."

Mike did.

He apologised to the doctor before looking over his shoulder to see more people in white coats walk down a corridor.

"I'm not going to tell you again," Mike said, facing the man. "He's needed, so he stays."

The doctor nodded shyly and moved away, allowing them to carry on walking.

"Bloody hell, man, you sure told him," Chris said, grinning.

But Mike wasn't finding the situation as funny.

He still wasn't sure he was doing the right thing by letting Chris hang around him, but they were too close to the morgue entrance for him to have doubts now.

"I want to see everything that you write," Mike ordered, closing in on the room. "And keep your mouth shut."

"But what about asking questions?"

"I'll do that...Your job is to take notes only."

Chris frowned as they caught up with the doctors, but three, chalked outlines of people on the floor stopped him in his tracks.

"Wow!" he shouted, taking notes. "This has just got real for me."

"Now keep it real because it is," Mike said, seeing the doctors enter the morgue room. "Time to get serious."

He looked at the door again to see Wayne leave the room, noticing his shirt sleeve missing and his arm wrapped in a bandage.

"All right, chief, we've had a busy night," Wayne said, glaring at Chris. "What's he doin' here?"

"Never mind him. What the fuck's happened to your arm?"

"Jason shot me by accident, but I'm fine. I've had the bullet removed."

Mike's face burned red with anger.

He was still tired, but after hearing that one of his officers shot another was close to running off to find the culprit. Jason wasn't one of his favourite recruits. He'd been in trouble more times than any other constable, so hearing this was the final straw. Mike had now the ammunition to rid the force of the unreliable man.

"Where is the little shit?!" he blasted towards Wayne, shaking with rage. "I should never have given him a weapon... He's a fuckin' lunatic."

Wayne gawped at Mike chewing on his lip like he was about to rip it off.

"Calm down," Wayne softly said, holding out a hand. "It wasn't his fault...Serious."

"Then who's fault was it?"

Wayne filled Mike in on most of the recent events from the past few hours, including how he'd been shot; happy to see him calm down.

"You see, it was an accident...He was scared for his life."

"Is he okay?" Mike asked as all thoughts of sacking Jason were erased. "I can't lose more of my officers."

"Yeah, he's fine. Well, apart from a few broken fingers he is...I've sent him home to rest."

Chris kept out of the way but listened intently as he jotted down more notes. He was still lost with some of the information but it still sounded interesting to him. He smiled to himself after reading over the notes, loving the feedback on how Wayne and Jason fought with the naked corpses; knowing that news would be a hit with readers. But he stopped when Wayne glared at him again.

"Mike," Wayne said. "Are you going to tell me why this sleaze bag is here writing stuff down?"

Wayne pushed Chris after the reporter smirked at him, so Mike stepped between them before fists were thrown.

I knew this would happen, he thought, pulling Wayne away. *But I don't blame him for wanting to punch Chris.*

"I'm helping," Chris happily said, smirking again. "I'm one of you now."

"You're not and never will be one of us!" Wayne screamed at him. "You're a vile man who almost cost the chief his job."

Mike gripped onto him as he tried to reach Chris, but the reporter wasn't fazed. It was like he was getting off on it, enjoying every second.

"Hey! Hey! Hey!" Mike yelled, freezing the men with his words. "We don't have time for this...So shut up and do your jobs."

"But, chief..."

"No, Wayne, we need him." Mike let him go before shaking his head at Chris. "We need to put aside the hatred between us and use our energy for what we need to face." He tapped Wayne on the shoulder before adding, "We need someone on the inside...Someone who can sneak around unnoticed."

"He's a sneak alright," Wayne said with a sigh. "But I'm still not sure about this."

"It's okay to be worried. I'm worried also." Mike turned to face the door again. "At least we know where he is if he's helping us."

"But I thought we were keeping the public out of it for now?"

"Too many people know something isn't right, especially those who work here, so it's a bit late to remain quiet."

"Yeah, I suppose you're right," replied Wayne as he moved towards the door to be followed by a still smirking Chris.

———

They entered the room to find it full of important people from the hospital's career ladder plus over-qualified healthcare workers from outside of town, all gathered around a table. Mike couldn't see why? But he could hear them discussing amongst themselves about what to do with something lying on the oblong, sturdy shape.

He led the way, pushing through the crowd to get closer until his eyes widened at what he saw. It was one of those things, but its appearance was so deformed that he couldn't identify it. It had parts of its anatomy missing; its right cheek had a massive hole in it and its stomach had been removed. It was snapping teeth at anyone who neared, but the sight of them through the hole in its face freaked everyone out.

"What's going on?" Mike questioned, knowing full well what was going on. "Who is this?"

"Who was this you mean," replied an upset nurse before coughing into her hand. "It used to be Colin."

Mike closed in, feeling sick to his stomach by what was on the table; shocked that it was indeed Colin.

"But I was only speaking to him yesterday," he nervously said, trying to get his head around how Colin was attacked. "Who found him?"

"I did," Wayne softly replied. "After I sent Jason home I came back down to find that thing writhing around on the floor, groaning like it was hungry."

"And you risked your life to pick it up?!" Mike snapped, thankful Wayne was okay. "It could've bitten you."

"But it didn't...I got some hospital staff to help me strap it to the table."

Mike grunted under his breath as an elderly, thin *man* dressed in doctor's attire stepped out of the crowd, smiling towards him.

Now he looks important...Maybe he's here to explain why the dead are rising? Mike thought, watching the man near.

"Maybe I can assist you?" the man said, holding out a hand to be shaken. "My name is *Victor Swanson*. A qualified surgeon from the city hospital...I've been asked to attend and comment on the creature that's in front of us."

Mike wasn't impressed to find out that a snotty man from the city had known about this.

"I don't know why you're here?" he questioned, grunting in anger. "I've got the situation covered..."

Victor looked at his outstretched hand, impatiently waiting for Mike to shake it, but was soon feeling a sense of hostility towards him. He tried again to get a positive reaction, making sure Mike knew about it, but still, nothing happened, so he slowly lowered his hand.

"...I seriously don't need you people coming into my town sticking your nose in and telling me how to do my job..."

Mike slowed his breathing and stared into space; counting back from ten inside his mind to quench his anger. He was extremely worried. He feared the truth had probably travelled across towns and cities, leading to a replacement heading in to take his job, but until then he was still the chief and everyone needed to know.

"...My men and I are dealing with this."

Victor backed off to let Mike release his tension. He wasn't a fool; he knew the chief was struggling. Had been since his world was turned upside down yesterday.

"Before you bite my head off," Victor calmly said, backing off some more. "I think you've misunderstood me...I'm here only as an advisor." Victor talked like a teacher who was educating a class of students; his hands moving in synchronicity to gain Mike's attention. "If you're worried that others like me are coming in from the city then don't be. This is all confidential."

Mike lowered his guard.

He listened to Victor explain how he came about the news, sighing when Hazel's name was mentioned. In a way, he was glad it was her and not someone else. Victor said she'd phoned him to ask for his help, and because she sounded scared and confused he couldn't say 'no'.

"When Hazel told me about what happened here and that she thought there was a deadly virus being spread, I had to come quickly to help find a cure."

"But I thought you were a surgeon?"

"I am," Victor replied with a faint giggle. "But I'm also a scientist who deals in viruses."

Mike nodded.

He turned to see Chris busily writing in the background before extending his search to seek out Wayne, pleased to see him just as engrossed as he was.

"I hope you've found out why this is happening?" Mike asked Victor, flinching at the sound of the monster's teeth snapping again. "Because this can't spread to the outside."

Victor rubbed his chin. "Not yet, but I'm working on it."

He explained more about what he thought the virus was and how it was passed on, but Mike got the feeling he was just trying to impress him. It was fast turning into a battle of who knew more, with Mike having a different theory entirely. He wasn't convinced that Victor had the answer in the bag, especially after seeing him frown, but knew this wasn't the time to see who had the biggest set of balls. He needed to trust that the man would do something useful.

He saw Victor smile at the corpse like it was a gift for Christmas, his hand lowering towards its mouth playfully as if he had no respect for who it used to be. It annoyed Mike, making him want to slap the man for his lack of empathy.

"Watch, as the creature concentrates solely on my hand," Victor sadistically said, lowering and rising it. "It has no inners and is very much dead, but somehow it still needs to eat."

"We know that already…We just need to know why?" Mike asked in a huff, mesmerised by what was unfolding. "It's not norm—"

But the teeth snapping at thin air spooked him again.

The crowd flinched and moved back, with most close to spewing from the thought of Victor losing his fingers. But he was quick to concede with his crazy action and placed his arm by his side.

"A brain is a wonderful tool," he said, smiling towards the crowd. "And without it, we'll all be dead." He moved away from the table as the zombie's vision followed him, its eyeballs rolling from left to right to scare the closest watchers. "The brain is giving this monster the order to feed…Maybe that's all it's giving? Just a signal to hunt and kill." Victor pointed at the chattering monstrosity. "I need to find out why it needs to feed and control its hunger."

"Control its hunger? To not eat?" Mike questioned, becoming as lost as he was when he first spoke to the man.

"No, no, no…I don't think it will ever stop eating but maybe I can change what it eats?" Victor grinned like a madman obsessed over a person. "I have to say, I'm seriously fascinated by this find."

Mike's blood boiled again and Wayne noticed.

He knew his chief was on the verge of losing it with the pompous, non-caring fool, so closed in to calm him down. He feared Mike would shoot the zombie just to annoy Victor, but he couldn't let that happen. The surgeon may have been acting like a spoilt prick but the thing on the table was important. It was the only one left as far as he knew to find answers from.

He saw Mike send out eye-stabbing glares towards Victor until the other man looked away. And Wayne smiled because of it. He knew Mike would now feel superior enough to go back to the task at hand and become one step closer to leaving the hospital.

"What will happen to it?" Mike quickly asked Victor. "After you've extracted all the information."

"What do you think will happen to it? ...It will be destroyed..."

Victor murmured to himself as he suddenly walked around the room, waving his fingers in the air like he was drawing invisible shapes.

"...The walking dead or whatever you want to call them have been invading this town since yesterday, so something must've occurred recently to account for it?"

Wayne and Mike nodded but didn't attempt to speak. They just wanted Victor to get everything off his chest so they could get back to work.

"...We've had numerous murders that were linked with the same symptoms. All leaving people to be reborn again," he said, rubbing his head. "There could be a virus that I've never heard of being spread through this town."

"But it's over now," Wayne popped up to say, pointing at the zombie thrashing about again. "That's the only one left... I'm sure of it."

Victor licked his lips. "But you're not a hundred per cent are you." He shook his head at everyone inside the room. "If I don't find out what the virus is soon then we could all die..."

Everyone skipped a beat after the dreadful words echoed around the room, but they knew he was right.

"...Have you guys given a blood sample yet?" Victor asked the officers.

"I gave mine to Hazel last night," replied Wayne.

Victor raised his eyebrows at Mike.

"I'll give one before I leave here."

"Make sure you do...And please advise everyone else who has been in close contact with one of the infected to do the same."

Mike nodded towards Victor before turning to leave the room; closely followed by Wayne and a still jotting down notes, Chris.

TWENTY-SIX

Chris arrived at the news station gripping his notepad tight. He was nervous. He knew he needed to deliver on air and to deliver well enough to convince the townsfolk, but also knew he couldn't stray away from what was said before. He rushed past a few employees, not looking at them when they spoke; his heart smashing against his chest as he reached a room. He opened the door and sat down, grabbing a tissue from a box on a table to wipe his brow as he opened the pad.

"You're on in five!" shouted someone from behind the door. "Do you need any assistance?"

"I'm fine," Chris replied, shaking. "I'll be there."

He breathed in deeply as he flicked through the pages, desperately searching for something he could use. But shook his head in anger at knowing he couldn't.

I can't mention any of this. It'll spook everyone out.

He closed his eyes until finding his inner strength before allowing the confidence to flow back through his veins; happy to be the reporter that most people loathed again.

He moved towards a sink and filled it with water, splashing it over his face to feel reinvigorated before drying himself and smiling at the mirror. "You've got this."

"Are you ready?" the person asked from behind the door. "It's showtime."

"I'm on my way," Chris replied, grabbing the notepad and slipping it inside his trouser pocket. "I'm right behind you."

———

He slowly sat at a newsdesk before smiling at a cameraman; nodding to say he was ready as the countdown for the news report began. He looked down at his notes then lifted his chin, smiling again as the introduction music played.

"Hi, I'm Chris Maudlin and this is the news."

———

Blake was back at home, watching the report with anticipation as Karen sat beside him; both eagerly waiting for new information to arrive. They noticed Chris was stalling like a blanket had been thrown over the words he was meant to say, but, after a few more seconds his focus was back.

"It's thought that a strange virus was to blame for several mysterious deaths that happened in Clifton Falls recently... Those deaths are now being investigated by the health authorities...There is no reason to believe that the virus is still spreading but, to be on the safe side, you should be vigilant while the matter is being investigated." Chris stared at the camera. "If you have been in close contact with any of the deceased then get a blood test, just to be sure."

Blake became emotional and Karen noticed.

"Are you okay, love?" she asked, watching him turn away from the TV to frown at her.

"I'm fine."

"No, you're not. I can tell...What's wrong?"

Blake glanced at Chris as more news was read.

"There's something odd about the reporter's newsfeed."

"What do you mean?"

"Vincent and Mary were the first to be caught up in this mystery virus so why did the police tell us something different the first time we asked?"

"I thought that officer spoke to you about it at the station?"

"He did." Blake paused. "But the story changed from an electrical failure to them both collapsing after a game of twister."

It was now Karen's turn to frown. "I'm not sure what you're saying."

"I know their deaths are connected to this virus, but I'm not sure how?"

"Let's not think about it now; it's too upsetting."

Karen couldn't hold back the tears.

"Sorry, babe," Blake said, hugging her. "But something isn't right." He let go and stood up before reaching for the TV remote, turning the TV off to say, "Remember the fertiliser that I received the other day?"

"Of course I do."

"I sold one to Vincent."

"I know you did. So."

"Now he's dead."

Karen shot up from her seat to grip Blake tight, cradling the back of his head as he sunk his chin into her shoulder.

"Don't you dare think it, accusing yourself...This had nothing to do with you."

"But I don't know what's in the stuff." Blake pushed himself away and kicked a bin. "It has experimental ingredients in it...I was in charge of the fertiliser and I let him try one."

"But wouldn't your staff succumb to the same fate if it was the bags?"

Blake hadn't thought of that.

"This is why I love you," he said, feeling a bit better. "You always know what to say."

"I hope you love me for more than my words," Karen replied, smiling cheekily. "If you know what I mean. Wink, wink."

"Yeah, of course, I do...Your cooking skills are also way better than mine."

Blake smiled, but a sudden pain burned in the depths of his stomach, making him feel agitated. He couldn't let what the reporter said drop. Not while he felt like this.

"I'm sorry, Karen, but I need to speak to the police again, if only for my peace of mind." Blake picked up his mobile phone and dialled the number. "Hey! If they think it to be not important then I'll drop it...You have my word."

Karen nodded.

She sat back down as the phone was answered, but Blake *panicked* as he spoke, making his speech about the fertiliser sound comical.

"I'm sorry, sir," Susan politely said. "But I have no idea what you're referring to."

Karen watched on as Blake struggled to speak; his chest tightening like he was about to collapse. She knew he was on the verge of a stress attack. It was something that happened to him a lot, especially when things didn't go to plan. And right now, everything he wanted to get off his chest concerning the fertiliser was being thrown back at him and he couldn't cope.

"Do you need me to…" Karen softly said, holding out a hand.

But Blake smiled at her when the words – "Hold on, I'll put you through to someone who may be able to help…" entered his ears.

His breathing slowed down as he waited for someone else to speak, but his anger returned when the person said, "Good afternoon, this is the chief inspector speaking. What seems to be the problem?"

Blake knew it was the guy who spoke the lies at the hospital, but instead of letting out his frustrations just bit his tongue to hear Mike repeat what he'd just said.

"I've got some information which might be of use to you," Blake replied, sneering into space. "It's about the deaths of Mr and Mrs Smythe."

"What about the deaths?"

Mike recognised Blake's voice also.

He knew Blake had been looking for him at the station last night so remained calm, not wanting to scare him away.

"I've got a good idea what the source behind the deaths might've been."

Mike rubbed his chin and checked his watch, feeling disinterested in Blake's words. He needed more and he needed it quickly. He wanted to know why the people were coming back to life but Blake just waffled on about his fertiliser and Mike couldn't see the connection. He listened to Blake explain how Vincent took one of the sacks and that he wasn't sure about the safety of the ingredients, but his words just went in one ear and out the other.

"Let me stop you there, Blake. Are you saying that you think the fertiliser killed him?"

"I don't know." Blake became nervous again as thoughts of Mike laughing at him made him sweat. "I know it sounds too farfetched but the truth is, he had the fertiliser - and now he's dead."

Mike wasn't impressed to hear the outcome. Of all the theories that could've been said, the fertiliser one just didn't wash with him.

"Okay, Blake. Thank you for that useful information." Mike placed a hand over the phone and choked on a laugh. He then shook his head to say, "If I need anything else then I'll be in touch...Bye."

The phone went silent before Blake had time to respond.

The poor man has lost the plot if he thinks there's a fertiliser monster out there, Mike thought, returning to a whiteboard on a wall inside the room.

Blake stood with the phone in his hand, looking baffled as Karen slowly neared. She knew the outcome of the conversation without him saying anything but wanted to hear it anyway.

"What's up? What did he say to you?"

"I have a feeling he didn't believe me." Blake sighed and lowered his phone.

"Are you surprised? It's a bit hard to swallow, the fact that you think the fertiliser is the killer..."

Blake felt more depressed as each word sunk in, leaving his mind scrambled as he bowed his head and sat down.

"...But anyway, at least you tried telling him what you

thought...Best to just forget about it now and let him do his job."

"Yeah, you're right, love."

"I'll just go and put the kettle on, make you a nice brew to cheer you up."

———

Mike stared at the whiteboard as Blake's words crept back inside his mind; his head shaking as if fighting with his decision to dismiss the compost for being the reason why the town was in chaos.

It couldn't be? he thought, writing the word – fertiliser – on the board before adding a question mark.

He thought back to who was on call when the Smythes were murdered, remembering it was Wayne after seeing him pass his office window. So, he rushed over to bang on it to gain Wayne's attention.

"What's up?" Wayne said, opening the door. "You look troubled."

"Take a seat." Mike walked over to the whiteboard, pointing at the recent word, but Wayne just shrugged at him. "I thought this was hilarious a few minutes ago but now I'm not so sure."

"Sure about what?"

"About this," Mike said, pointing at the word again. "The fertiliser that arrived in town recently."

"Excuse me. I think I'm a bit lost," Wayne replied, smirking. "Do you want to buy some of it?"

"No...Let me explain...I've just had that Blake guy on the phone telling me some weird shit about the stuff."

"Go on."

"He claims it may be behind the murders. Says he sold a bag to the bank manager." Mike knew Wayne was thinking what he was thinking. He could tell because he was trying to hide a laugh. "I know, sounds like a hoax, right, but it's doin' my head in."

Wayne tried to focus but he couldn't. He was gone, laughing into his hand. Mike knew he should've stopped him but the more outrageous Wayne's laughing got, the more tempting it was for him to do the same. And seconds later he was at it, giggling like a child.

"Stop it, man, my sides are splittin'," Wayne said, roaring with tears of laughter. "The fertiliser you say...How scary is that?"

"I'm being serious," Mike replied, wiping his eyes. "Did you notice anything unusual about the garden at the Smythes property?"

"Apart from an open grave, you mean?"

"Yeah."

"No, not really."

"So, you didn't see a nine-foot-tall, angry fertiliser bag with a serious attitude coming towards you?" Mike spluttered, as more tears of joy dripped from his eyes.

Their laughter was so intense that everyone in the building could hear their juvenile squeals.

Mike slapped a hand against Wayne's shoulder before almost falling over; sucking in the air as he wiped his eyes again.

"...Did you see anything that we can go on?"

"I only glanced at the garden...I was too busy inside with that creature," Wayne replied, shuddering. "Do you want me to go back?"

"No..." Mike said, knowing Wayne needed to rest. "Doug and Craig can go...Let's hope they find something."

"Sure...I'll go look for em'."

———————

Wayne knew where they were. It was obvious. He found them in their most-used room inside the police station, eating in the canteen.

"All right chaps. I see you're busy," he said, sneaking up on them to freak them out.

"Man, don't do that," Doug replied, choking on his food. "Now you've interrupted our serious discussion."

"About what?"

"About which dessert to have after our meal."

Wayne shook his head.

He was in two minds about going to the Smythes house himself after seeing the pair act like squabbling teenagers, pulling on either side of the menu to annoy him.

"For God's sake, guys, get a grip."

"What's got into you?" Craig popped up to say, snatching the menu. "This is our downtime...We need it."

"I know you do, but don't switch off completely. I don't want anything happening to you both." Wayne smiled at them before adding, "Oh, yeah, the chief's got a job for you."

TWENTY-SEVEN

It didn't take long before Doug and Craig arrived on the newly named '*death street*', both staring at the Gilberts' house as they exited the car. They walked with caution, not knowing what was in the garden belonging to the Smythes, gripping their batons as if expecting to be pounced on. But it was very quiet on the street.

They slowly walked down the side of the house, moving police tape out of the way before stepping into the garden, but nothing had changed since yesterday. They stopped and looked at the gravesite, seeing muddy piles of dirt to make their knees shake; feeling thankful for not being caught up in the turmoil.

"That must've been where it came from," Craig said, thinking of Nash. "That fuckin' twisted freak."

"I feel ill just looking at it," Doug said, turning to see the hole in the fence. "Now we know why the dog went mental... It must've come through there and got infected."

Craig shook his head, feeling sick to his stomach. He

hoped that the other households were safe, that the virus hadn't reached them. He couldn't handle another outbreak.

He moved away from Doug and aimed for the shed, peering through the window to see a half bag of fertiliser resting on the wheelbarrow; smiling at the thought of this visit being over quickly. He checked the door, seeing it was padlocked with an old rusty lock.

"Are you okay over there?" Doug asked after seeing Craig stall. "Can't you get in?"

"Oh, I can get in alright," Craig happily replied, stepping back to kick the lock open. "I was just getting into my Bruce Lee mode."

Doug laughed as Craig opened the door. "Bruce Lee, my ass...More like Rusty Lee to me."

He watched Craig disappear into the shed, feeling nervous as the seconds ticked by, but he smiled when the wheelbarrow was seen. He nodded as Craig pushed it out, pleased to see the bag.

"Right, I think I've found the stuff that we came here for," Craig said as thoughts of where he wanted to be next brought on another smile. "Let's get this back to the station so we can select that dessert before someone else nabs it."

Doug was in full agreement as he walked over to grab the bag, picking it up before heading back to the car.

"Let's get out of here. I need some food."

Craig caught him up and burst out laughing. "You aren't hungry for food, mate, you just fancy that new canteen lady." Craig pushed him. "I know you do so don't even think about denying it."

Doug shook his head and kept on walking.

"No...I don't fancy her," he said, acting annoyed. "My fuckin' stomach's rumblin'. It means I'm famished."

"I'll let you off this time."

"And anyway," Doug said, puffing out his cheeks as he placed the bag down by the car. "Why are you always trying to set me up with someone? I'm fine on my own..."

But Craig stared at him, making him feel uneasy.

"...What?!"

"You've got it all over you," Craig worryingly said, pointing at compost stains on Doug's clothing. "What if it's infectious?"

Doug slowly looked at his chest. "Infectious, my arse," he cried out, wiping the stains away. "I'll infect you if you don't get me back to the station..."

Craig raised a hand and laughed as Doug picked the bag up again.

"...Are you gonna' open the boot or just gawp at me?"

"Yeah, sorry."

———

They arrived back at the station, leaving the bag inside the car as they headed for the chief's office; hearing him laughing with Wayne as they entered the room. But they shushed as soon as Doug closed the door.

"Alright chaps. Did you find anything?" Mike asked, controlling himself. "At the house."

"The job is done, chief," Craig happily said. "We found half a bag of the stuff inside the shed."

Mike wasn't expecting those words, especially since he and Wayne had just been laughing again about the tall fertiliser bag with the attitude problem, but he was now taking Blake's story seriously.

"Nice one...I need one of you to send it off to the lab. Tell the technicians to search for anything out of the ordinary."

"Will do, chief," Craig softly replied, turning to walk away.

"I want to know everything about it. Every slightest detail must be accounted for."

Craig waved as he left the room.

Doug rubbed a hand over his face and sighed before sitting down to attract Mike's attention. He wanted to get a few things off his chest but was now feeling stupid for even thinking about it.

"Make yourself comfortable," Mike said, watching him closely.

"Sorry, chief," Doug replied, sweating. "But I need to talk to you about the house."

"Go on...Don't keep me in suspense." Mike leaned against his desk, noticing Doug was fidgeting. "Spit it out, Doug," he said, turning to Wayne. "I don't have all day."

Doug explained his theory about what happened in the garden, making sure to mention the hole in the fence being the possible link as to why the dog attacked the vet.

"Shit!" Wayne hollered, shuddering after a reminder of the deaths from both houses hit him. "So, you think the mother from the grave infected the dog?"

"Must've...Right?"

"It's the only obvious reason as to why it went crazy," Mike butted in to say. "But what I want to know is how does the fertiliser fit into all this?"

"Didn't Blake say there were some weird ingredients inside it?"

"Yeah, Doug, he did, but his fertiliser isn't linked to the women found on the country lane or the rotting corpse splattered by the lorry."

"You're right," Wayne interrupted, feeling drained more than ever. "I was so close to believing Blake's theory but now I'm not so sure." He walked around the room, cursing under his breath. "Shit, we're back at square one again."

"Okay, let's reel it in," Mike quickly said, waving his hands around. "As far as we know, the deadly infection is passed on when someone has been attacked by one of those freaks."

"That's correct," Wayne replied, feeling Mike was aiming the words at him. "But it's all over now...The last of the infected was burned to a crisp."

"But Jason was caught up in a battle with those things."

"Yes, but I told you. He only had his fingers crushed. He's fine."

"But are you sure he is?"

"Don't scare me, Mike," Wayne said, gulping. "I was with him. He never mentioned he was bitten."

"Maybe he didn't know?" Doug awkwardly questioned, squirming at the thought. "He may have been scratched."

"Scratched?" Wayne nervously laughed. "You've seen what happens. The fuckers rip chunks out of you...He had no chucks taken from him..."

Wayne was close to losing it as his mind raced back to the zombies from the morgue. But he couldn't pinpoint when one could've bitten Jason. Then he remembered something.

"...Damn! He did have one all over him, climbing on him when he was on the floor."

"And did it scratch him?"

"Mike, I don't know...It all happened so fast."

"Okay, just stay calm and go visit him...He needs to supply a blood sample anyway."

"Will do."

TWENTY-EIGHT

Jason lay on his bed sweating onto the sheets, as a fever ripped through his body. He had taken a few painkillers since leaving the hospital last night but none had made any difference.

He winced after a sharp pain smacked against his lower back before rolling onto his side to place a hand against it, feeling his skin burn against his fingers to bring tears to his eyes. He slowly lifted off the bed and walked to a standup mirror, raising his shirt to see the skin around the area had changed colour, his pale cream complexion an irritating mass of red. He noticed faint lines spreading around a blood patch near his spine, feeling confused and stunned that the blood belonged to him before collapsing back onto the bed. He had no idea what was happening.

Dawn, his mother, shouted up to him from the foot of the stairs, holding a bowl of chicken soup, but Jason was in too much pain to respond.

"Jason, love!" she shouted again, slowly walking up the

stairs. "I've made you some warm soup...It should help bring your fever down..."

She walked up to his bedroom door, listening out for a reply, feeling heartbroken that he was poorly.

"...Are you asleep?"

But the words – "Fuck off you bitch and shove the soup up your arse," – almost made her cry.

She couldn't believe what she'd heard. Jason had never spoken to her like this before.

She opened the door, almost dropping the bowl after seeing him squirm around on the bed, his face cringing from the discomfort.

"Are you alright?" she asked, knowing he wasn't.

"Didn't you hear me before, I said *fuck* off!" Jason screamed at her, rolling into a fetal position to grab his stomach.

Dawn raced over to a set of drawers to place the bowl on top before sitting next to him, stroking his hair as he groaned.

"What's happening to you?" she asked, watching him pant for air. "You were fine yesterday."

"Help me," Jason whispered, contorting his face. "It hurts."

Dawn wiped a tear from her eye and shook, feeling useless for not being able to fix him.

"*Donald!*" she hollered towards the door. "Get up here... Jason's getting worse."

She tried to smile after the sound of footsteps was heard racing up the stairs, but she couldn't do it, so, just remained stroking Jason's hair as her husband appeared in the doorway. But he froze once spotting his son squirming in pain.

"I think we'd better find you some help," he said, snapping out of it. "I'll start the car."

But Jason raised his head and glared at him. "You're not taking me anywhere, you old fart...Just piss off and leave me alone."

Donald and Dawn just looked at each other, not knowing how to respond to Jason's vile words. They knew this wasn't their son shouting out spiteful nonsense. It was as if a demon had entered his body, taking a swear book with it.

Jason flipped out without any prior warning.

He leapt from the bed to push his father against the wall, but his falling tears distracted Donald, preventing him from retaliating. He saw the extreme pain in Jason's eyes as more sweat dripped from him, but he still didn't resist. He just let his son unleash his anger, knowing he was now like a wounded animal.

Jason yelled as he aimed for the doorway.

He staggered as he reached the stairs, almost falling to the bottom as he tried to escape while his parents sadly watched on. They couldn't find the words to say to him as he opened the front door, but Jason stopped in his tracks before entering the outside. He seemed to be looking at something, but it wasn't clear what until Wayne was heard closing in on the house.

"Hey!" he shouted towards Jason. "I've been phoning you. Left you loads of messages...Why didn't you pick up?..."

Jason glared at Wayne as he approached before collapsing into his arms, shaking like he was having a seizure to scare Wayne.

"...Hey, calm down buddy," he nervously said, watching Jason groan in his arms. "What's wrong with you?"

"Get out of my...fucking way...twat," Jason stuttered, as

the shaking died down. "And take your greasy...hands off me."

Wayne turned to see Doug close in.

He shrugged at him as Jason belted out more hurtful words, but Wayne shook his head towards Jason, feeling lost as to why he was doing it. He held him tight and stared into his eyes, hoping to see beyond the mask of mystery. He knew Jason was frightened.

But of what?

He nodded at Doug to help him pick Jason up, feeling he was too tired to do it on his own. But Jason SCREAMED as soon as Doug touched his lower back.

"What's wrong?" Wayne asked, feeling emotional. "We're trying to help you."

"It's too late...for that." Jason wept as the pain increased. "I've been infected."

Doug let him go and backed away, panicking as he wiped his hands down his trousers; gulping as he stared at Jason sobbing on the ground.

"I can't do this," he said, backing away some more. "He's got it...That thing."

"Doug!" Wayne yelled. "He's one of us...Now help me get him to the hospital."

Dawn stood on the doorstep, snivelling into Donald's chest as Doug arrived to help lift Jason; her heart crushing more and more by the second.

"You need to be checked over," she said, smiling at her son. "Please, do it for me."

Jason winced again but he did listen to her.

He smiled weakly at his parents as he was escorted inside the police car before collapsing in the backseat to writhe in pain again as the sharpness twisted his insides.

Wayne and Doug were left gobsmacked as they entered the car.

"It's okay, we'll get the help you need," Wayne said, holding back a tear. "Just you wait...You'll be good as new in no time."

Then the car drove off.

TWENTY-NINE

Wayne parked the car outside the hospital and exited before rushing to open the backdoor to help Jason out, but Doug was keeping his distance. He was itching from the thought of the virus being spread to him so didn't want to get any closer.

"Hey!" Wayne screamed at him, grabbing onto Jason. "Get a wheelchair...NOW!"

But it took him another attempt at shouting before Doug focused again.

"Sorry," he nervously said, racing for the main entrance. "I'm on it."

Wayne grimaced at him as he helped Jason out of the seat; holding him against the car to see the blood drain from his face.

"Stay with me, Jace...Just stay with me."

Doug raced out of the main doors with a wheelchair, positioning it next to Jason before helping Wayne sit him inside. Then Jason was wheeled towards the hospital.

Wayne glanced at the clock on the wall to see it was now

2:15 pm, but he couldn't see Hazel anywhere. He'd asked Susan to give the hospital a heads up so was expecting to be greeted by a barrage of hospital staff, but the only person walking up to him was a pretty blonde nurse with amazing curves. Her name was *Katrina* and her presence had Doug hooked. He wasn't thinking about his health anymore because he was too busy staring at her breasts.

"Where's Hazel?" Wayne quickly asked, pushing Doug. "I thought she would be here."

Katrina smiled. "I'm sorry, but Hazel's resting right now. However, she has filled me in on what's been happening recently."

"And you are?" Wayne grunted at her. "She has seen what's been happening here so knows first hand...You know nothing, so why am I talking to you?"

Katrina awkwardly glanced at the floor.

"Come on, Wayne," Doug interrupted, touching his arm. "She's only doin' her job...You can't take it out on her."

Wayne looked at Katrina, seeing just how upset she was before holding up a hand as an apology. He knew Doug was right.

"Look," she said, feeling confident again. "A few of us have been drafted in from the city hospital to help with the crisis, so you need to get used to it."

"That's not the problem," Wayne replied, looking over her shoulder to see another new *nurse* arrive. "I'm just worried that too many people know now...We can't have any more chaos...Not today."

The second nurse placed on a face mask before gripping the handles of the wheelchair, but Jason had no energy to look at her. He just felt sick and wanted to hide.

"I'm taking you to a quiet room," she softly said to him, turning the chair around.

"How quiet?" Wayne asked, not sure of the plan. "And is the mask necessary?"

"Yes, it is," the nurse politely said. "His infection can spread so he's being quarantined."

"Hell no!" Wayne gripped the chair. "Quarantine, my arse...You can't do that to him."

"Look, he needs to be isolated so everyone can feel safe... Please, it's for the best."

Jason glanced at them fighting over who was going to hold the chair; his face turning red with embarrassment for being some kind of freak show act. He wasn't having this. People shouldn't be fighting over him.

"Wayne," he said hoarsely. "It's alright...I need to be put out of the way."

"But..." Wayne was about to let go of the chair but Jason gripped his arm. "It's okay, I'll make sure you're safe."

"I...need to have...a...quiet word."

The nurse nodded before walking over to stand next to a troubled Doug and a concerned Katrina. They watched the other men as Wayne wheeled Jason down the corridor.

"What is it?" Wayne asked, shivering because he knew what was going to happen. "I'm here for you."

"I'm sorry...for being infected," Jason said sobbing. "I didn't know."

"How did it happen?"

"The fuck...er scratch...ed my back."

Wayne sighed, feeling sad that he wasn't able to shoot the creature before it happened. He knew that moment will haunt him forever.

"Now we know about the virus, we will be able to cure you."

Jason stared at him and shook his head. "If I die and return as one---of---those---things." He gripped Wayne's arm with all his strength, which wasn't much before whispering, "I...want you...to kill me." Then he wiped his eyes dry.

His words were brutal but expected, leaving Wayne wanting to break down. But he knew he couldn't. He needed to be strong for Jason so wasn't going to lower his guard.

"You won't die, mate," he whispered back."

The others knew this was a sad moment between the pair so kept their distance for as long as was needed; all trying hard to catch what was being said as Wayne leaned in closer to Jason.

"I don't want to be a murderer...like the rest of 'em," Jason croaked. "So, will you kill me...if I cha-nge?"

This time his words were overheard by the others.

"I'll do it," Wayne whispered, as the grip on his arm was released.

Katrina placed on a face covering before following the other nurse over to the men, as Wayne nodded and moved out of the way. He let them take over before apologising again for his bad attitude. But they understood.

"We'll take Jason down to the isolation unit," Katrina said, as the other nurse gripped the chair again. "You can wait here if you'd like...We can get you once he's been tested."

Wayne smiled at her before glancing at Jason, but he just stared bleakly ahead, now ignoring Wayne as more tears dripped from his eyes.

"I'm here for you, buddy!" Wayne hollered, as the nurse pushed Jason down the corridor. "I'm right here."

Doug closed in and patted Wayne on the arm.

"What happens now?" he asked, feeling a lump in his throat. "Are we staying?"

"You need to get a blood test," Wayne said, pointing down the corridor. "Then report back to Mike."

"You're kidding me?" Doug awkwardly asked, feeling sweaty. "I don't need a blood test, right?"

"What's up?" Wayne noticed Doug become as nervous as he did when talking about the rising dead. "You're not scared of a little needle?"

"No, of course not...Why'd you say that?"

"No reason. I was just wondering..."

Blood samples are becoming more popular than a cheeseburger, Wayne thought, as he waited for Doug to make his move. But he wasn't budging.

"...Do you want me to go with you?"

"Yes," Doug spat out. "Just for moral support...That's all."

"Whatever," Wayne replied, smiling. "Whatever you say."

———

They sat in a room that reminded Doug of a time when he was ten years old, the first experience he'd had at fainting after feeling sick from the sight of his blood in a tube. And now, as a *nurse* slowly appeared, his face was turning pale again.

"What's up with you?" Wayne said, holding back a laugh. "I thought you liked pricks in you."

"Fuck off!" Doug leaned back and panted. "This isn't funny, man. I just don't like needles...There, I said it. Are you happy now?"

"You'll be okay," Wayne replied with a wink. "As long as the needle isn't a long one."

Doug shot out of his seat, ready to run away, but the nurse smiled at him, leaving him weak in the knees. Wayne watched him closely as he eagerly waited for the nurse to do her job, but, as she took a few more steps towards Doug, he fainted. Wayne didn't know whether to laugh or cry because Doug had hit the floor very hard, but he smiled, feeling relieved after seeing the man get back to his feet.

"Sorry for mocking you," Wayne said, holding Doug as he sat down again. "But I needed a distraction for a while to help me stop thinking about Jason."

"It's okay," Doug woozily replied, gulping after seeing the needle. "I need to man up...Jason's problem is much worse than mine."

"Hey, It's cool," the nurse politely said, smiling at Doug. "You're not the only person who faints at the sight of a needle."

———

Twenty minutes passed before Doug was ready to leave the building. He walked to the main entrance with Wayne, feeling pleased with himself for overcoming one of his fears, his mind back on his job as he entered the outside. Wayne nodded as he walked away, feeling sad at the thought of having to let Jason's parents know what was going on. He moved into a quiet corner and pulled out his phone, shaking as he dialled Donald's number; knowing he needed to be firm with the news about his son.

"Hi, Don," Wayne said, checking the area to see if he was the only person there. "I have an update for you."

Donald listened to what Wayne told him, but the news about Jason being put in quarantine left him mystified to the point of wanting to scream.

"He is an officer of the law," he croakily said, breathing heavily. "How dare they treat him like an experiment."

Wayne heard Dawn in the background trying to calm Donald down, but he was fuming.

"Don! Don!" Wayne shouted, hoping the man would cool down. "He needed to be put in there...To stop the spread of the virus."

But the word '*virus*' rocked Donald.

He shook as Dawn held him tight, holding back tears to hopefully prevent her from also crying.

"But is he comfortable?" Donald softly asked Wayne as he held back the urge to go over there to see his son. "I need to know if he's okay?"

"As far as I know, yes," Wayne replied. "But no one is allowed to see him until he's had tests done."

"Tests!"

But the sound of Dawn calming Donald down interrupted Wayne's reply.

"I'll be in touch soon to let you know when you can visit," he finally said after waiting for the parents to go quiet. "Okay?"

"That's fine," Dawn replied. "It's just a lot to take in...I will let Don know."

Then the phones went silent.

Wayne walked away and entered the waiting room, noticing someone had been there to clean up the mess. He placed coins into the drinks machine, choosing to have a coffee to help him stay awake; waiting for the cup to fill before grabbing it and sitting down.

He picked up a magazine from a table; taking a sip of the drink before giggling at the front headline – An alien sighting at a shopping centre – He looked at the photo as more laughter escaped his mouth before skimming through the other pages to find more pathetic headlines – One about a 'six-legged animal' and another about a 'woman who gave birth to thirty children.' But he was pleased to not see a story about the dead rising to kill people in a small farming town.

———

He checked his watch to see that two hours had drifted by before shaking his head in disbelief as thoughts of where the time went messed with his mind. He smirked at how easily he'd gotten wrapped up by the fake news, pleased to have briefly forgotten about everything else so his brain could recharge.

He yawned and stretched but a knock on the door spooked him.

"So, you're still here," Katrina said opening it. "That's good to see."

"I'm staying for my friend." Wayne rose from his seat. "How's he doing?"

"He's comfortable...We've cleaned the wound and taken tests, so just waiting on the results."

"And how long's that goin' to take?"

"I don't know." Katrina smiled sadly, feeling Wayne was struggling with it all. "But the good news is, he's been asking to see you."

"Cool...Lead the way."

"But I must warn you, he's been freaking out and cursing at everyone he sees."

"Yeah, I've already witnessed it."

"But he was fine when I saw him with you earlier."

"Let's hope he's still fine this time."

———

Katrina led Wayne towards the room, filling him in on what she knew had happened since he last saw Jason, in the hope the news would help. But Wayne was nervous and on edge.

"Almost there," she calmly said, tapping his arm. "Don't be worried. He needs you not to be."

Wayne smiled but didn't speak. He just wanted to see his friend.

Katrina stopped outside the room and said farewell, leaving Wayne panicking as she walked away, but his hand stalled on touching the door.

"Just go in," Katrina said, turning around. "He won't bite you."

She giggled as she carried on walking, but her words made Wayne gulp. All he could do was nod as she disappeared around a corner.

He entered the isolation room to see Jason behind a piece of glass, sitting upright in a bed. But his skin was now a mustard-yellow. Wayne struggled to cope as he nervously sat in a chair. He saw Jason point at the wall, so followed the direction until spotting an intercom system attached to it.

"How are you feeling?" Wayne said after pressing a button on it. "You don't look good, mate."

Jason raised a portable version of the intercom device to his mouth, pressing the button to say, "Thanks," before gritting his teeth.

"Are you still in pain?"

"It comes and goes," Jason replied, trying to smile. "But it's not as bad as it was."

"You must be on the stronger meds."

"Must be."

Wayne felt sad after noticing Jason looked thinner. He wanted to kick himself over and over again for letting Jason get infected, knowing whatever the virus was could well be eating him from the inside. But, as he took another look at Jason's complexion figured he'd guessed what he was thinking.

"Don't blame your...self," Jason spat out, coughing over the sheets. "I made...the er-ror."

But Wayne would always blame himself for this.

He looked around the area Jason was in to see just a bed and some hospital equipment before seeing a tube lead into Jason's arm.

"Do you want me to do anything for you?" he asked, feeling queasy.

"Could you tell... my... pa...rents... to... come and... see... me; bring me some clo...thes?"

"Clothes? ...Why do you need clothes?"

"I'll...need...to...get...chan...ged be...fore leaving...here."

Wayne wanted to hug him.

"Will do," he replied, leaving his seat. "I'll tell your folks."

Then he slowly exited the room.

THIRTY

Mike sat in his office staring at Wayne, Craig and Doug. He'd just replaced his phone after speaking to someone from the lab, but just from the short conversation, the others knew it sounded important. They waited impatiently for Mike to speak, to let them in on what had happened, but he just kept staring.

"Is everything okay?" Wayne popped up to ask, hoping for some good news to tell Jason. "Please tell me they found something useful."

"Chief!" Doug quickly snapped. "Are you alright?"

Mike slowly looked away before breathing in deeply; sighing as he breathed out to say, "No...Not really..."

He explained what the person on the phone told him about the fertiliser sample, saying it was still going through the testing process but early signs suggested there were abnormalities not recognised by anyone from the lab. The news had suffocated all positive thoughts that the men had hoped for.

"...I should get the final results soon," Mike sadly said,

leaving his seat. "But, in the meantime, I need you two to go to the factory owner's house."

Doug and Craig looked at each other.

"What are we going there for?" they asked in unison, frowning at Mike.

"To get him to give you any remaining fertiliser sacks left at the factory." Mike walked around the room, hoping the distraction would help him to remain calm. But it wasn't working. "Bring him and the sacks back here...He has some explaining to do..."

Mike reached for a pack of pain relief pills and took two out, popping them into his mouth as Doug and Craig left his office. He swallowed them and rubbed his head.

"...Bloody headache," he said to Wayne, rubbing his head again. "It's all I need right now."

"Are you talking about those two?" Wayne asked, laughing. "Because they sure do give me a headache."

Mike smiled even though it hurt his head.

"How's Jason doing?" he asked, wincing. "I'm sorry I don't have better news to tell him."

"He's stable, for now...His parents are visiting him." Wayne noticed Mike seemed preoccupied with something. "What else was mentioned that's got you all flustered?"

"While we were laughing over how dangerous the fertiliser was, the boys at the lab were finding some strange shit inside it."

"You said they found abnormalities."

"But I never said what type..."

Wayne froze.

"...If what was said is anything like the truth then this town could well be in danger...Let's hope that Blake guy can help solve this before more of what you fought comes back from the dead."

"Don't leave me in suspense, chief, we've eliminated the last one and Jason's in quarantine."

Wayne listened to Mike's rant about the bank manager using the fertiliser on his garden and that his dead mother woke up because of it, plus, how the farming fields at the factory had been sprayed with the stuff.

"Yes, I know all that," Wayne said, still feeling confused about where the conversation was going.

"What happened on the same day that came out of the blue?"

"That crazy rain shower."

"Exactly!" Mike rubbed his temples again and sat back down. "That strange shower must have washed the fertiliser onto the grave and also away from the fields."

"Damn, you're good," Wayne said, springing to life again. "Do you think the John Doe run down by the truck was infected with the fertiliser that washed away from the field?"

"I'm not sure but it's a good observation." Mike clicked on his computer mouse before looking over the incident reports, but his expression changed by the second. "If the shower washed the fertiliser away then it may have ended up at the cemetery?"

Wayne hadn't thought of that and didn't want to think about it, but, if what Mike said was true then it was a possibility. The cemetery wasn't that far from the fields.

"Do you honestly think something inside the compost is waking the dead?" Wayne nervously asked, fearing it to be true. "But, surely it couldn't spread that far."

"I don't know for sure, but I'm not taking any chances...If

the results come in to confirm our fears then I want everyone from the holiday village evacuated until further notice."

"Let's not be so hasty." Wayne closed in on Mike to see frown lines appear on his face. "That village is busy this time of year...We don't want to spook people if we can avoid it."

It wasn't long ago that Wayne wanted to tell the world but now he was trying to stop his chief from thinking the same thing.

"Hopefully, the results will be in our favour."

THIRTY-ONE

Karen almost jumped out of her skin after her front door was knocked on, her heart skipping a beat after opening it to find two officers standing on her doorstep.

"Hello, officers," she nervously said, thinking they were there to tell her to return to the hospital to identify the Smythes. "Can I help you?"

"Yeah...Is your husband in?" Doug replied.

Karen frowned. She didn't expect that.

"Yes, he is...Why?" she asked, feeling upset about not being considered as an option to talk to about her boss. "What has he done now?"

"Can we come in?" Craig politely asked, smiling. "It's important."

Karen opened the door wider and let them inside before closing it to lead them into the living room, but their presence spooked Blake.

"Alright, officers," he said, trying to remain calm. "What appears to be the problem? ...Have I upset the chief?"

Blake panicked when they stared at him, thinking he was about to be arrested for disturbing the peace.

"Everyone upsets the chief," Doug said, smirking to make Blake feel relaxed. "We're here because we need to confiscate the fertiliser you've stored."

Blake's eyes lit up.

"Hold on," he quickly rushed from his mouth. "Are you telling me that my fertiliser's infected?"

"We don't know the full details...The chief just gave us the order to see you." Craig smiled again at Karen before turning back to Blake. "He needs a word with you after we've retrieved the bags."

Blake placed a hand over his mouth, feeling shocked that his theory about the compost was even given a second thought by Mike. He trembled from more fears of being arrested as he nervously kissed Karen on the cheek.

"Stay by the phone," he said, kissing her again. "I won't be gone too long."

Blake walked into the hallway and grabbed his coat from a wall hook, placing it on before slowly moving towards the front door, seeing the officers close behind as he opened it. But Karen raced out of the other room to hug him.

"Now make them believe you were right about the fertiliser," she whispered, letting go to watch him leave the house.

————

The police car pulled up outside the factory gates at *5:30 pm* as staff members clocked off for the evening. Most either stared at the car or checked to see who was inside, but not Todd. He was still finishing off the daily paperwork.

The officers escorted Blake from the vehicle as people remained eagerly watching on, but their nosiness slowed everything down. They swamped Blake with questions about – Why he was with the police? And If he knew what had been going on in town? – but he just smiled at them as Craig rushed him to keep moving.

"Go home!" Doug shouted at them as he blocked their view of Blake. "He's helping us with our enquiries."

"Enquiries about what?" one of the workers asked, as his concern for Blake escalated. "Are you okay, boss?"

Blake looked up and waved. "I'm fine...Now please go home. Your shift has ended."

He then followed the officers towards the main doors.

————

Todd saw them on the CCTV as they entered the building; his face scrunching from many thoughts of what was going on as they walked towards Blake's office. But he didn't move until hearing them close in.

"Hey, Blake, what are you doing here?" he asked, leaving his small office to reach the others. "I thought you were spending some quality time with your wife?"

Blake glanced around the area to worry Todd before whispering, "Is anyone else here?" Happy to receive a 'No' as he reached his office.

But Todd seemed curious.

"What's goin' on?" he quickly said, following Blake inside to see him search for something. "Should I be worried?"

"Maybe!" Blake snapped, flinching after seeing Todd become emotional.

He wanted to tell his foreman everything but knew he couldn't.

"...Look," Blake calmly said as Todd stood by the door. "I can't go into too much detail but I need to find the key for the storage barn."

"Why?"

"Because these officers are here to take the fertiliser away."

"In that car outside?" Todd almost laughed at the officers. "Do you know how many sacks we have?"

"We're waiting on a van to arrive," Doug said, checking his watch. "It should be here soon."

Blake searched his desk to find the key under some papers, smiling as he picked it up. He then headed for the door but Todd stood in his way.

"What's wrong with the fertiliser?" he nervously questioned, moving to one side. "Is there something wrong with it? I hope not because we've used some of it."

"Todd, I honestly don't know, but the police want it just in case."

"Just in case of what? Come on Blake, you're scaring me now."

"I wish I could tell you more. I honestly do...But you just have to trust me." Blake stared at Todd until he made eye contact. "Do you?"

Todd nodded.

He found no other reason to question Blake. The officers were enough proof that something wasn't quite right.

"I'll give you a hand shifting the stuff," he said, hoping his offer could be used as a way of an apology. "It's the least I can do."

Blake tapped him on the arm and smiled.

———

The men entered the storage barn as a van closed in.

Craig waved at the *driver* before moving a hand back and forth, guiding the reversing van inside the barn to smile as it came to a halt. But his smile fast turned to a grimace once he remembered seeing the contaminated fertiliser all over Doug.

"Best to put on gloves," he said, cringing. "We don't want to catch anything."

Doug agreed to it, but Blake and Todd felt lost. They looked at each other and gulped as thoughts of touching the compost scared them; both looking at their hands and wanting to disinfect them before going anywhere near it.

"Is it that dangerous?" Blake worryingly asked, putting on gloves. "My hands won't fall off if I touch it, will they?"

"Do you want to take that chance?" Doug quickly snapped, walking towards a pallet filled with the bags. "I wouldn't...Not now, so best to keep those gloves on."

The driver got out and joined the others, grabbing a bag before carrying it towards the van. Then, he put it down and opened the back door.

"I'll get inside," he said, entering. "And stack 'em up."

"You do that," Craig happily replied, closing in to hand over the bag he was carrying. "And now for the one you've dropped down here."

He picked up the other bag as Doug, Blake and Todd arrived; each sliding the compost sacks towards the other man as he raced around trying to stack them. No one was letting up. They moved at speed and got the job done.

"Thanks for that, Todd," Blake said, taking off a glove to shake the man's hand. "But you need to keep this to yourself."

"He's right!" Craig and Doug yelled; almost laughing because of the insane timing.

"I hear ya'." Todd backed away and nodded. "You have my word."

THIRTY-TWO

They arrived back at the station to deposit the sacks inside the police storage warehouse before escorting a nervous Blake towards Mike's office. But every step brought with it a faster heartbeat as he closed in on the door.

"Come in!" Mike shouted as the door was opened to reveal the three men. "We meet again, Blake...Take a seat."

Blake tried to smile as he sat down but struggled to do it whilst Mike's expression remained firm. He couldn't work out what emotion the chief was showing, so, until he saw a glimmer of a smile, wasn't going to relax. He waited for Mike to speak again but the silent seconds caused him to sweat.

"Why don't you two go home, and get some rest while it's quiet," Mike said to Doug and Craig, nodding as they walked back to the door. "I'll keep you informed if anything happens."

"But what about you? You need to rest as well, chief," Doug said, glancing at Blake.

Mike shrugged his shoulders. "I'll grab a nap in here when I can."

Doug waved before walking away with Craig.

Mike turned to Blake to see him fidget nervously. He knew the man was worried.

"Do you know why you're here?" Mike asked, now smiling to ease Blake's tension.

"You think something's wrong with the fertiliser."

"Yes, that's right." Mike walked up and down the room before stopping to say, "I want to know where you got it from. I need to speak to your contact..."

Blake leaned forward after finding his courage again; smiling because Mike's thought pattern had swayed towards what he'd suggested about the strange delivery.

"...But don't get too excited," Mike quickly added, walking a little more. "I'm not overly convinced that the fertiliser is extremely dangerous to the public but I've opened an investigation based on what you told me and because of a weird ingredient found inside it."

Blake's curiosity was knocked for six after hearing that the fertiliser did consist of something strange, but he knew the evidence wasn't enough to accuse his stock of the murders.

"My supplier lives in the city...I will phone them, and see if I can get the scientist's number who helped create the stuff."

Mike nearly fell over after a sudden intake of shock swept over him.

"Hold it right there!" he bellowed, pointing at Blake. "A scientist helped create it? ...You never mentioned this before."

"Because I didn't know that what was added could be harmful before."

Blake explained again why he phoned about the fertiliser, and it wasn't because it smelt a bit funny. He mentioned why a scientist got involved in helping to create the compost and how the ingredients inside it could change the future of the farming industry by making it more profitable, but none of what he said sounded convincing enough to suggest that the stuff could harm anyone.

"Do you know what ingredients are inside it?" Mike asked, staying calm.

"No, but I'm sure I can find out for you..."

Blake dialled his supplier.

Mike watched closely as Blake rushed over to the whiteboard, writing a phone number onto it before smiling and ending the call.

"...This is the number for where the stuff was made," Blake said, drawing a line underneath it. "The scientist's name is *Doctor West*."

"Okay," Mike blurted out, becoming excited. "What are you waiting for? Get dialling."

But Blake wasn't budging.

"I've done my bit," he said, replacing his mobile back inside his trouser pocket. "This is down to the police now."

Mike wasn't expecting to be snubbed.

He waited for Blake to change his mind, thinking he would come to his senses and make the call, but Blake just looked to the floor. He seemed nervous like he was about to experience another panic attack; his hand gripping his chest to worry Mike into reaching for his phone.

"Okay!" he hollered, hoping Blake was alright. "I will do it."

He stared at the board and dialled the number before

turning to see Blake sit back in his seat, close to laughing as the call was answered.

"Good evening, this is Doctor Shane West speaking. How may I help you?"

"This is Chief Inspector Mike O'Sullivan...I'm phoning from Clifton Falls Police Department...We have a very serious problem down here and I think you can help sort it."

"I'm sorry Inspector, but how am I going to help you?" Shane asked, scratching his head.

"I have Blake Taylor with me...Do you know him?"

"I've never heard of the man," Shane quickly said. "What's this about?"

Mike glared at Blake, thinking he was being played by the man, but Blake whispered, "He doesn't know me directly but he'll know my supplier."

Mike nodded and returned to the call.

"We may have our wires crossed...He said he received a delivery of fertiliser the other day that was tested at your lab."

Shane scratched his head again. "Blake, did you say?"

"Yes."

"If my memory serves me right I think his factory was down as a guinea pig for the first batch, but I've not received confirmation of its progress."

"That's because he's had problems with it."

Blake gave Mike a weird look like he was waiting for him to let Shane have both barrels from an imaginary shotgun, thinking he would surely give the man a hard time over what the fertiliser had done to the town. But Mike was calm.

"What sort of problems?" Shane asked, opening a folder on his laptop labelled – PRIVATE – "It should've worked fine."

Mike nibbled his bottom lip and glanced at Blake;

covering a hand over the phone to whisper, "He's a bit of an arrogant prick."

Blake just nodded.

"I need to know what you mixed it with?" Mike asked Shane. "And I need to know now…"

But the "*now*" bit annoyed Shane.

Mike didn't wait for a reply, he just dived straight in, demanding a full list of the ingredients inside the compost as Shane grunted and coughed. Mike knew he had him rattled.

"…Oh, and I need you to hand-deliver it."

"Is this some sort of a joke? A windup? …You're miles away…"

Mike wanted to punish the man for the downfall of the town but knew he couldn't just arrest him; especially since it hadn't been confirmed that his stuff was the culprit. But Mike had a strong feeling the results would confirm it. So, for now, he would make Shane travel with the results.

"…I'll tell you what I'll do!" Shane barked. "I'll deliver the list when my schedule isn't so hectic…Maybe sometime tomorrow."

Mike sensed a challenge emerging, knowing he needed to be more demanding to receive the other guy's attention.

I will knock that smarmy look off his face.

"Listen up buddy," Mike snapped down the phone. "I don't know you, but right now you're pissing me off to the point where I don't fuckin' like you…"

Blake was left gobsmacked as Mike went ballistic on the other man.

"…If you don't get your arse down here tonight then I'll go to you with my truncheon and stick it where the sun doesn't shine…Are you hearing me now?" Mike's face turned blue after he'd held his breath for too long. "We've got a major situation developing here," he said, breathing again. "And we need your assistance."

Blake waited for Mike to completely blow his top, but it didn't get that far. Shane had been put in his place.

"I'll sort it," he cowardly croaked. "See you soon."

————

The clock hanging on the wall in Mike's office had just ticked to *7:45 pm* when Shane entered the building; his nerves now shot as he approached George at reception.

"You must be the reason why the chief keeps shouting," George said smiling, teasing Shane into almost running away. "Follow me."

Shane walked with him until reaching Mike's office, feeling pleased not to hear any shouting as he entered the room. He saw Mike nod towards George before the latter walked away, his ears pricking as Shane waited for another violent outburst of words. But Mike just smiled at him.

"Take a seat..."

Mike sensed Shane was a bit unsure of what was expected of him, even though he'd already been told to bring the list, so reassured him all was going to be okay. Then Shane nervously smiled and sat down.

"...This is Blake," Mike said pointing at him.

Shane nodded towards Blake whilst gripping the list tight.

"Why am I here?" he asked Mike, holding the list in the air. "It can't be just because of this."

Mike sighed. "I need you to remain calm."

"Remain calm? Why?"

"Is that the list?" Mike asked, wanting to see it so badly.

"It could be important to an investigation about the stuff inside the fertiliser."

Shane handed it over to Blake but he didn't recognise half of the ingredients.

"I'm no use to you with this," he said, handing the list to Mike. "Most of the names on it are unpronounceable."

"Unpronuncible is also hard to say," Mike said, releasing a much-needed giggle.

Shane stared at the whiteboard, seeing the crime scene photos attached, but none of them made any sense to him.

"...I've sent some of your experimental compost to the police lab for tests, but I'm still waiting for the final result." Mike stared at Shane until he turned and looked at him. "I know there's something strange in it. And something probably illegal."

Shane flinched before almost bursting into a fit of laughter. It wasn't because he found it amusing, it was because he was annoyed.

"Have I driven all the way here just to explain the ingredients inside the fertiliser? ...I could've done that over the phone."

"You're right, you could've, but you wouldn't have been able to witness the damage that your wonder stuff has caused this town."

Shane felt guilty about something now, *but what was Mike going on about?* He thought fast for a few seconds until recent memories printed pictures inside his mind.

"Hold on a minute, does my fertiliser have anything to do with what was on the news earlier?"

"Now you get it!" Mike snapped at him. "I think there's some form of chemical inside the stuff that's caused ultimate chaos, but I don't know how yet?"

"I'm sorry...I had no idea." Shane stared at the whiteboard again, shivering from the thought that he was accountable; his head shaking as he retraced his steps back to when he made the bug killer. "We tested it inside the lab on a small number of crops."

"How?" Mike questioned, spooking Shane.

"We placed the bugs that cause infections and those that eat the plants amongst the crops before sprinkling the new fertiliser over the top...Then, after a few days, we checked on progress."

"Come on, man!" Mike bellowed. "Get to the point...What the fuck happened?"

"What we expected would happen...The bugs died, but the crops had grown a few more centimetres..."

Mike and Blake stood open-mouthed as Shane's explanation about what the fertiliser did came to an end. It was no different from what Blake had said when he described its uses. Mike felt more confused now.

If everything he is saying is true then why are the dead in my town coming back to life?

"...So I ask you again, why am I here when my creation worked?"

Mike gulped.

"It may have worked but something still stinks about it... The quicker I can get the ingredients on your list sent off to our lab, the quicker I can eliminate your stuff as a line in our enquiry..."

Mike didn't want to tell Shane about the zombie breed and he didn't want anyone else telling him either, so, whatever the man heard from the news was enough for now.

"...What's this Moltovenium?" Mike asked, checking out the list. "I've never heard of it."

"It's new." Shane rose from his seat to stand next to Mike's desk. "It's a poison to get rid of those bugs."

Mike rubbed his chin before jotting down the magic word, hoping it was a breakthrough.

"I'd best notify our guys," he said, looking over at Blake. "Do me a favour...Open the door and shout out to George. He should be at the reception desk."

Blake nodded and did what was told, shouting out to get George's attention. He was glad he didn't have to shout twice.

Mike heard the man rush towards the office; his heavy breathing bouncing off the walls as he closed in.

Mike shook his head. He knew George was overweight and it worried him. He'd told the man several times to lose weight but every order sounded like a punishment to George, so he did nothing about it. But now, as his breathing slowed down, Mike could only think of how lucky George was that his main job wasn't strenuous.

"You need me, chief," he said, holding his stomach before taking a final pant. "I need to cut back on the chocolate."

"I think you need to cut back on more than chocolate," Mike replied, shaking his head again. "Before you end up unable to work."

"It won't come to that," George said smiling. "I'm fitter than I look."

Blake and Shane had to look away because they were on the verge of laughing. George noticed, but, like the happy-go-lucky type of guy he was, he just ignored them.

"Phone the lab and give them this." Mike passed the piece of paper over to George. "And don't rush back to your desk. I don't want you getting an injury."

George pulled a face and left.

Mike stared at Shane, grabbing his car keys before ushering him out of his office.

"It's time I showed you some of the horrors that have been going on around here."

"But I need to get back to work."

"Not yet you're not."

Mike followed Shane out of the room, leaving Blake feeling ignored and unwanted. But he was pleased that his time there was over.

He left the room, catching them up as they entered the outside to see Mike escort Shane towards his car, but Shane didn't seem to be enjoying being ordered about.

"Where are we going?" he asked, feeling a little fearful.

"You'll see soon enough," Mike coldly replied. "We're going for a little drive."

THIRTY-THREE

Mike never spoke to Shane during their journey to the hospital and his silence left Shane worried. He watched Mike park the car as thoughts of feeling unsure of what the plan for him was scared him; his heart racing as the chief grunted for him to get out. But he waited for Mike to open his door first.

They entered the main doors as the clock in reception ticked to *8:30 pm,* but Mike still never spoke. All he did was pick up the pace like he was in a hurry to get somewhere.

"Why are we here?" Shane asked, catching him up. "I really need to get back to my job."

But Mike didn't reply. He just kept on walking.

They turned a corner, heading for a room with a makeshift sign saying – **PRIVATE** – attached to the door, but the closer Shane got to it, the more he panicked.

"We're here," Mike said, staring at him. "I need you to be quiet when we go inside."

"You mean as quiet as you've been since we left the station?"

Mike cringed.

He wanted so badly to lash out at the man, but he sucked in a deep breath and opened the door.

They entered the room to see *four* people suddenly stare at Shane, but he was still in the dark about why and who they were. But the more they stared at him, the more he wanted to leave.

He wasn't stupid, he knew something bad was going on.

Why else would there be an officer, a nurse and what looked like a married couple here?

He saw Mike walk over to the nurse with a sense of sadness on his face, touching her arm before smiling.

"How's he doing?" Mike asked her.

"He's stable at the moment, but that could change at any time," Hazel softly replied, smiling back. "He's very weak now...I don't think he'll make it to tomorrow."

Mike couldn't bear to think that he was about to lose another officer. It was all too much.

He turned to see Jason's parents close in with their heads bowed as if saying a silent prayer. But he just watched them. He had no words.

"Let's hope a cure can be found soon," Dawn spluttered, lifting her head to reveal tears rolling down her cheeks. "I can't lose my boy."

Shane stood in the background feeling invisible as the others huddled together, with the other officer also getting involved, their actions making him sense this was why he was here, to see what his wonder growth had done.

He stared beyond the others at a large curtain before guessing who was behind it, knowing deep down it had to be a relative of the distressed couple. He remained silent and out of the way as Hazel slowly moved towards a cord. She gripped it and pulled back the curtains, revealing a lifeless-looking man behind a piece of glass lying in a bed.

"It sickens me to see him like this," Mike said, tearing up. "And he only had a tiny scratch."

Hazel placed an arm around his shoulders. "But it was very infectious and spread extremely fast...Once it reaches his heart it'll be the end for him..."

"But you'll find a cure before then?" Donald interrupted; eyes wide, hoping she'd say "YES."

Hazel shook her head to leave him crumbling into a seat, breaking into pieces as he sobbed into his hands. And Dawn closely followed, sitting beside him to do the same.

"...I'm so sorry," Hazel said, feeling her throat quiver like she was about to puke. "I wish I had more positive news."

Now Shane became emotional.

He stared hard at Jason as he tried thinking of an ingredient that he'd missed from his list, his heart melting to find an answer to save the man before it was too late.

But there wasn't one.

He backed up against a wall, punching it after hearing many woeful cries, wanting to kick himself for not being able to prevent everyone's hearts from being ripped from their chests once the poor man in the bed faded off into the blackness of no man's land.

Mike swallowed hard as he turned to him to say, "Follow me."

But Shane took one last look at Jason before moving away from the wall. He followed Mike out of the room, feeling rotten, as thoughts of the fertiliser sending him from hero status to villain crashed inside his mind. He knew he would have to destroy it if it ended up being to blame.

"I'm confused," he nervously said, fearing Mike was about

to unleash hell on him. "First you said I am to blame for all the tragedy and then you say maybe I'm to blame...Which is it?"

"Whenever there's a victim, your stuff ends up being top of our most-wanted list," Mike replied, nudging him. "So you tell me...Are you to blame?"

Shane shrugged his shoulders. "I don't know, but I'm here to help if you need me."

"I know you are..."

Mike smiled sadistically to worry Shane into backing away.

"...Don't worry, I'm not going to hit you," Mike said, reaching for his phone to scroll down the numbers. "But I need you to take Blake's number."

"Why?"

"So you two can team up and find an answer..."

Shane gulped.

"...Right, let's get out of here," Mike finished; looking back at the door before walking away.

THIRTY-FOUR

Wayne watched Hazel escort Jason's parents out of the room, feeling sad after an image of them crying entered his mind. He knew he had a job to do but he couldn't leave Jason, not right now, so, just sat and stared at him through the protective glass shield.

He leaned back in his seat, glancing at his watch to see it was *9:00 pm*; feeling drained of energy as he tried to stay awake. But he nodded off a few minutes later as Jason stirred in his bed.

He turned to look at Wayne before silently crying, as the virus clogged up the arteries in his heart; releasing his last breath to collapse and close his eyes. But they turned a cloudy white within seconds from within the lifeless lids.

Jason had changed from human to monster at a quicker rate.

———

Chris entered the hospital again looking more like his usual self, but Hazel stopped him before he reached reception. She knew he was a fraud when he visited before to see the Smythes but somehow he'd managed to manipulate her into thinking he was a relative. But not this time. This time she was ready for him.

"No flowers today?" she questioned, close to sniggering at how awful they smelt. "I hope you're not here snooping around for more info on the recently deceased?"

"That all depends on if the officer in quarantine is still alive..."

Hazel froze for a split second, feeling shocked at how abrupt and cruel the reporter's words came across. She hoped he was joking but somehow knew he wasn't.

"...I'm messin' with ya'," Chris said, winking. "I'm here looking for Officer Strong...He's not at the station, so I thought maybe he was here?"

"Yeah, he's here."

"Cool...Where is he?"

Hazel held off from telling him. She sensed he may be scheming again, his words making her think he was trying it on like the last time.

"No disguise today?" she asked quickly, trying to fluster Chris. But he was too calm and it worried her. "The staff here have nicknamed you Mr Benn."

"Why?"

"Didn't you watch the TV show? He wore many costumes."

Chris just shrugged his shoulders and tapped his watch.

"Listen, love," he said, itching to get away from her. "I've not got all day...I've just seen the chief and he told me about the awful incident with the copper...So, is Officer Strong here or not?"

"Okay! Okay! Keep your hair on...Follow me."

Hazel led Chris down the corridor of gloom, keeping close to him in case he snuck off. She still wasn't sure he was being honest, but it was too late now to change her mind because the door leading to where Wayne was had now been noticed by him. And he was closing in on it.

"Slow down!" she hollered out to him. "You can't just walk in."

"Watch me," Chris replied, opening the door.

Hazel swore under her breath.

She tutted and left him to it, walking away feeling angry for being so easily put in her place.

––––––––

Chris entered the room to see Wayne fast asleep, close to falling off his seat without even realising it. Chris knew the man was out of it, whacked from doing too much in such a short amount of time, so left him alone to concentrate on the body in the bed. But he was left shocked after seeing a sheet covering Jason's face.

Damn! Looks like he's already gone.

He stumbled back, nudging into Wayne's outstretched leg to jolt him awake before seeing him rub his eyes frantically. He knew Wayne wasn't pleased to see him.

"What the *fuck* are you doing here?!" Wayne screamed at him, rising from his seat. "I'm only tolerating you because Mike ordered me to. Otherwise, I would be punching you right now."

Chris soaked up the angry words but remained calm.

"When did he die?" he asked, pointing at Jason.

"What the fuck is wrong with you?! Are you deliberately trying to annoy me?"

"Just look!"

Wayne slowly glanced at Jason.

He almost collapsed after seeing Jason's face covered before scratching his head in disbelief for not hearing a nurse enter the room.

"But, he can't be." Wayne closed in on the glass chamber and touched it. "No one's been here but me...He must have done it himself..."

But those words weren't convincing Chris.

"...See," Wayne continued smiling. "It's how he likes to sleep, with the covers over his head...He's fine. Just fine."

"Why don't you go in there and find out?"

Wayne shook from the words as he glanced at Jason again; his heart pumping fast after thinking that Chris may be right.

"I can't...It's out of bounds until a cure is found for him."

"Just look at him!" Chris shouted, banging on the glass. "He's dead...I know he is."

Wayne grabbed Chris around the throat, pushing him against a wall as tears rolled down his face. But he still wouldn't admit that Jason may well be gone.

"Just leave it," he said, cursing under his breath. "He'll be okay."

But Chris shook his head.

He was angry that Wayne attacked him, but after seeing more tears fall, knew this wasn't the time to retaliate.

"You got a girlfriend?" he calmly asked, putting Wayne on the spot.

"Why you askin'?"

"I just figured, if I'm goin' to stay with you for a while, I may as well get to know you."

"But you don't need to stay...You can go."

Chris held up his hands. "Hey! I'm not here as a reporter or as your enemy. I'm here because Mike is worried about you....He's so busy trying to find an answer, so I volunteered to come here." He then put his hands down to say, "So, is that okay with you?"

Wayne just mumbled at him as he sat back down before glancing at Jason, hoping he would move. But he didn't.

"Okay. I will play along."

"Cool," Chris replied, sitting next to him. "So, do you?"

"Yeah, but it's early days...Not many people know."

Chris smiled.

They chatted for a few minutes until Wayne felt less agitated. He was pleased that Chris was trying to distract him.

"Thanks," Wayne said, shaking the man's hand.

"For what?"

"For making me smile...For being here at this moment in time...For not being a complete twat." Wayne almost laughed. "Why don't you pick one."

"Can I pick all three?..."

Now Wayne was laughing.

"...So, can we bury the hatchet and become friends now?"

"I'd rather bury the hatchet in your back than become friends with you," Wayne replied, looking away. But a second later he was smiling again.

Chris knew he was joking and so the tension wall between them tumbled down.

"Would you like a cup of coffee? I need to stretch my legs," Wayne said, lifting from his seat again.

"Yeah. That would be great." Chris watched Wayne walk towards the door before shouting out, "Two sugars please!"

Then Wayne left the room.

Chris stared at Jason again, noticing his head move from beneath the sheet. He felt spooked as it continued before Jason gurgled to send his mind spiralling out of control.

He must be still alive if he's gurgling – right?

I bet he can't breathe under there.

Chris panicked; not sure of what to do next.

He knew he should go and find Wayne but Jason was moving frantically to soak up all his attention.

"I need to help him."

He scratched his head and neared the glass door, but held back after remembering what Wayne said – 'The room was out of bounds' – Chris knew it was a forbidden zone and that no one was allowed to enter but the more Jason moved, the more anxious he got. He needed to get in there.

He heard more gurgling sounds from beneath the sheet; the noise sounding like a starter pistol to get him to move as the door was finally opened. He sweated as he slowly neared the bed, shivering as the body writhed more aggressively before reaching out a hand to pull the sheet from Jason's face. But, as he slid it down past the nose, the dead man's eyelids shot open like a roller-blind to reveal bloodshot, milky eyes.

Chris jumped back, grabbing his chest from the sudden fright. But he wasn't anticipating Jason to be one of the living dead. He just thought that the sick man had woken up.

"Wow, man, you scared me," he nervously said, calming down again. "How are you doing? ...I bet you're hungry?"

But the risen corpse just glared at him, sitting upright to reveal gnashing teeth.

Chris cringed as the sheet lowered past Jason's arms; the colour now a pale grey to worry him into backing away.

"Hey, buddy. Are you alright?" he anxiously asked, thinking the drugs being pumped into Jason were to blame. "Do you need a doctor?"

But it was taking longer than it should for Chris to believe that Jason was one of those things. He'd not seen one before, but, as he eyeballed this latest one, his nerves exploded.

If this is what one of the walking dead look like then it's fuckin' scary.

His mind went blank and he couldn't move.

He stared at the door before swiftly watching the creature, hearing it snarl as it slowly lowered its legs onto the floor to aim in his direction. Chris gulped as it closed in but he still couldn't move. He squinted as the zombie's eyes lit up, its mouth dribbling as its toxic breath almost knocked him to his knees. But he was now able to move.

He backed away, close to reaching the door, but the creature swiped hands at him; opening and snapping its mouth as if already tasting its first meal. But it didn't frighten Chris anymore and he didn't want to leave.

He smiled at the monster, enjoying the life-threatening moment; his adrenaline flowing just from the excitement of being caged with something that wanted to rip him to pieces. He knew that one false move could end up with him being bitten but the sick and twisted side to him was relishing the chance to live on the edge.

"Come on you piece of shit," he said, taunting the zombie. "Do you think you can kill me?"

He wagged his tongue, showing no fear as he laughed in the creature's face, but, even though it kept gaining on him, he still wouldn't leave the room. He just moved in circles, allowing the thing to follow; its nose twitching after smelling his fresh meat.

It moved at a quicker pace, startling Chris into losing his footing. But he quickly rolled under the bed before the beast could strike. It whined like someone had taken its food away before angrily smashing its hands onto the bed, but the sound of Chris chuckling as he rose from the other side reignited its passion to attack.

————

Wayne moved closer to the door, carrying two cups of coffee, but he heard shouts coming from the room, the sound making him nervous as he rushed to get inside.

What is that prick up to? he thought, barging into the door to spill coffee over the floor as he entered.

But, as soon as he saw Chris inside the forbidden room, the cups dropped to the floor.

"What the hell are you doing?!" he shouted; not noticing the reborn Jason until a growl spooked him. "It's dangerous."

"I'm just havin' a laugh with it," Chris replied, dodging the zombie's attempts to grab him. "That thing won't catch me...It's too slow."

Wayne's hatred for the other man brewed up again. And it wasn't just because he was up to his old tricks of pissing people off. The man was a fool, but to see him disrespect Jason, alive or dead version, was too much to take.

"Are you fuckin' crazy? That thing will kill you."

The zombie stopped and looked at Wayne, drooling as it tried to speak. It moved closer to the glass, placing hands on it; its face sad to bring tears to Wayne's eyes, as he too placed a hand against the pane.

"I will do it," he whispered, reaching for his gun.

But he stalled after tears dripped down the creature's face.

He followed the movement of its mouth to guess what it was trying to say, but, what he thought it said confused him.

"...You want me to kill the reporter instead of you?"

Chris overheard him and panicked.

"Hey! Don't listen to that thing...It's dead, remember?"

But the zombie snarled.

It turned and faced Chris before picking up the pace again; its teeth showing to scare him.

"I'm outta here," he blurted out, leaving the room quickly. "It's all yours."

Wayne watched him race out of the door like a sprinter in a race as the sound of his shoes crashing against floor tiles faded in the distance. But the zombie smacked a fist against the glass to grab Wayne's attention. It growled at him as if wanting him to make it dead again, but he was struggling to enter the room to kill it. He sighed as he whispered the word - 'sorry,' but the word made the beast angrier. It lifted the bed and threw it against a wall, snarling like a hungry lion as Chris returned with Julie, but her nerves poured out emotions she couldn't control and she shivered on the spot.

"Why'd you bring her here!" Wayne screamed at Chris, keeping one eye on the creature. "She needs to get out."

"She wanted to come...Honest."

"Why?"

"I don't know...You ask her."

Wayne shook his head at Chris before cringing at how trembly Julie was. "Just stay with her...I've got this."

He slowly raised his gun and walked towards the glass

room, watching to see if the zombie would strike. But it just let him enter.

"Be careful," Chris popped up to say, disturbing Wayne's focus. "Just don't make it mad..."

Wayne cursed under his breath as he aimed the gun, but his hand shook to worry the others. They knew he wasn't able to shoot the ex-officer just by the look in his eyes.

"...Just do it!" Chris blasted, comforting Julie. "Before it sees you as food."

But Wayne couldn't put the beast down.

Chris moved closer to the glass, banging on it to receive the zombie's attention, but its glare startled him to almost back away. He breathed in deeply as it whined at him; its head tilting before showing teeth. But Chris just copied the noises like he was rehearsing for some kind of double-act.

Wayne watched Chris closely, wishing he was the zombie; knowing he would easily put him down without having a second thought.

"Stop messing about," Wayne said, aiming the gun at Jason again. "I've got this."

But the zombie suddenly lunged at him, gripping his arm. It threw him through the glass, shattering it to pieces as he landed on top of Chris, both unconscious as the creature walked barefoot over the sharp particles to reach Julie. But she just let it attack her, her bravery to escape was long gone as the beast extracted its first morsel of flesh.

She stood dazed as blood poured from her face, not screaming as the zombie tore out her eyeball; staggering and gritting teeth as it tore flesh from her neck.

Chris staggered to his feet; his head throbbing as he saw the beast bite into Julie again. He showed no fear as he dived at it, but it quickly swung a hand, hitting him across the mouth to knock him back to the floor. Chris glared at it, feeling frightened at how quickly its strength and speed increased after eating its first meal.

Julie fell next to him, freaking him out to want to scream, her face now a bloody mess that made her unrecognisable.

The zombie chewed on her eye as Chris kicked out to keep it at bay. He had never been as scared as this in his life.

He rose off the floor and grabbed a chair, smacking it against the beast's back. But it took the hit and snarled to leave Chris holding the chair like a lion tamer. He looked pale as he moved it towards the creature, seeing it back away to give him room to attempt another strike, but this time the chair broke against its head.

"Wait!" Wayne shouted, spooking Chris into lowering what was left of the chair. "I made a promise to Jason that I would finish him if he returned like that, so move aside..."

Wayne slowly climbed to his feet but winced after seeing glass stuck in his leg; nervously aiming his gun at the zombie's head as Chris rose a chair leg.

"...I said WAIT! ...If you don't get the hell out of this room now then I'll kill you instead and give the zombie your job. I'm sure nobody would tell the difference between the pair of you..."

Chris was lost for words as Wayne turned the gun on him.

"...I don't want to hurt you but that thing over there used to be my partner, so, I think I should deal with this on my own."

Chris finally took the hint, knowing now that this meant a hell of a lot to Wayne. He backed away towards the door but Julie's zombified corpse gripped his leg, scaring him into almost falling into Jason.

"Get it off me!" he bellowed, pushing Jason away from

him. "I thought it took longer than this before they transformed?"

"It does – or it did," Wayne replied, feeling puzzled to see Julie looking menacing so fast. "Just shake it off..."

Chris stamped on her head until she let go before a sudden blast from Wayne's gun splattered her brain. It frightened Chris into backing against a wall.

"..Now leave me to finish this."

Chris was close to fainting as he left the room, his ears ringing as another gunshot was fired. Then, seconds later, Wayne limped out to join him.

To be continued...

ACKNOWLEDGMENTS

To all who kept faith in me during the hard-fought years. You know who you are.

To all my friends and family who allowed me to use them as characters. You're all stars in the making.

––––––––

Andy Barker for narrating *Clifton Falls Part 1* & my alien, man-eating insect story – *Bedbugs (can you see them?)*

http://mybook.to/cliftonfalls
http://mybook.to/Bedbugs

Brian James Twiddy for narrating *Clifton Falls Part 2*

http://mybook.to/cliftonfalls2

Dave Neal for narrating my killer rats novel – *The S.T.A.R.S Project*

http://mybook.to/thestarsproject

Thank you all from the heart. It's been a roller-coaster ride.

ABOUT THE AUTHOR

Lee lives in Bedworth, Warwickshire, England.

He writes novels that read like movies playing out on paper, taking the reader into an imaginary world that he created. He adds comedy moments in his stories to break up the horror, with silly characters who will make you laugh.

Lee wants readers to see inside their minds the stories he writes, and to live with the characters as they battle the enemy.

Lee's stories are not written to confuse, but to entertain the reader, and to make the reader smile.

———

His novel - *Clifton Falls* - was originally released as *Zombies (Morgue of the Dead)* around 2011, but he changed the name to the movie script version. He has rewritten the novel as a 2 part story, releasing Part 2 in the summer of 2022.

mybook./cliftonfalls2

Part 3 is scheduled for release in 2023.

———

Lee has also written a novel based on the old saying – "Night, night, sleep tight, and don't let the bedbugs bite." It's titled – *BEDBUGS (Can you see them?)*...It's a sci-fi-style, alien, horror/comedy story about flesh-eating insects. It was released in 2021 and is available for sale from Amazon Worldwide.

mybook.to/Bedbugs

———

Lee's other released novel is a story about "Killer Rats." Titled - *The S.T.A.R.S. PROJECT* – (Scientific testing aimed at a rat's survival)

It was released in 2018 and is also available from Amazon Worldwide.

mybook.to/thestarsproject

———

Lee also writes movie scripts, with 11 written to date. And he's also written a Sci-fi, horror TV pilot for a British Production Company.

———

To keep tabs on Lee's progress please LIKE his Facebook author page –

facebook.com/mrwritermanauthor

or check out his website –

taylorlee544.wixsite.com

Ingram Content Group UK Ltd.
Milton Keynes UK
UKHW010857060623
422954UK00001B/14